BLIND
reality

BLIND
reality

HEIDI MCLAUGHLIN

ISBN: 978-0-9906788-7-8
COVER DESIGN: Sarah Hansen at Okay Creations.
EDITING: There For You Editing
COPYEDITING: CAE SERVICES
INTERIOR DESIGN: Tianne Samson with

emtippettsbookdesigns.com

If you're a reality fan – this is for you

prologue

Thirteen bulbs shine brightly, adding a certain glow that I can't define. The unlucky number is supposed to create a romantic ambience or give the person looking back in the mirror the confidence they need to push through what's coming next. They do neither for me.

This is not how I pictured my wedding day to be. The strapless gown I'm wearing is gorgeous and something I never saw myself in. The smooth satin gathers at my waist and is held there with a diamond-encrusted pin provided by none other than Neil Lane. My blonde hair is side swept and cascading down my shoulder, and my make-up is flawless. I look like the bride I've always envisioned I would be, but I would've never been able to achieve this vision, until now.

As I look around the small dressing room it becomes harder to breathe and I close my eyes, wanting to cry. I want to run. I want to strangle my mother and ask her what the hell she was thinking. But I've come this far, and it would be foolish to back out now. There was a time in my life when I used to believe in true love. *Used* to.

Imaginary lint is brushed off my shoulder and my curls are flipped forward one more time. I want to tell my mom to stop touching me, but there's a look of pride in her eyes and I don't want to ruin this moment for her.

"Smile, Joey."

"I have nothing to smile about."

My mom stands tall behind me, creating a picture perfect moment. If this were any other day, any other wedding, I'd want to capture us like this with maybe my hand on top of hers as she rests it on my shoulder. Even with my fake wedding looming, she seems happy and probably thankful that her daughter is finally getting married.

"You've been moping for a year. It's time to put that behind you and take a chance on something new."

"I'll get a cat."

She moves to my side, sitting on a sliver of the bench that I'm currently using. She doesn't ask me to move, nor do I slide a little to the side to give her more room.

"Joey—"

"Don't you get it, Mom? Every time I see a man, I'm going to wonder if he's looking for the next me to come into his life. My new husband will be walking on eggshells, fighting a battle that he probably doesn't deserve because I walked into my ex-future husband's apartment to find him in a situation that should've never come about. Tell me, how is that fair to that man standing out there?"

"Your father and I think this will do you some good. You can take the time away to reflect, grow, and work on your communication skills."

I sigh with defeat, accepting the fact that once my mom's mind is set, there's no changing it regardless of how much I try and convince her otherwise.

"I know, Mom," I sigh, taking a deep breath to fight off the tears. I'm probably not in the place my parents expected me to be, especially after we spent so much time planning my wedding earlier. I can't imagine what my parents went through when I called everything off.

My thoughts are interrupted by a soft knock on the door signaling that my new maid of honor is ready for me, except she won't be standing by my side and holding my bouquet. That job will be left up to some model being paid to stand on stage and look pretty for the television audience. With one last look in the mirror, I say good-bye to any sanity I may have left. The next moments in my life are going to be shrouded in darkness.

A production assistant greets me with a smile, though I can't seem to match her enthusiasm. She has on a headset and has a clipboard in her hand. She hands me the blindfold and tells me to put it on. I do and think about how the hairdresser just spent an hour on my hair for it to be messed up by a stupid piece of cloth. What will my new husband think?

Husband.

I can't even begin to comprehend I'm about to get married to a complete stranger, sight unseen. I should've run when my mother burst through my bedroom door and told me she had submitted my profile for the show *Married Blind* and I'd been chosen. I'm twenty-six; this isn't how my future is supposed to be. It should be filled with family and friends. I should be devoting my life to someone I'm in love with, not someone who is trying to win his share of one million dollars. I want to marry a man who rocks my world, who makes my palms sweat and can look at me with smoldering eyes, knowing that the moment he touches me I'm his.

I've read the rules in the contract I had to sign. We'll be allowed an annulment at the end of the show if we haven't consummated our relationship, which won't be a problem. As husband and wife, we'll compete for 'household' prizes against other couples who are also getting married today.

The last couple standing at the end of three months and voted on by TV viewers will win the money.

How can you have a dream home with someone you don't know?

I run my fingers over the black silk. It's shiny, smooth. In all my fantasies where I'm blindfolded, I never thought it would be for something like this. I sigh and slip the fabric over my eyes, tying it tightly in the back. The production assistant takes my hand and pulls gently, making my feet move forward. Faintly, over the clack of my heels, I can hear the announcer talking. The audience laughs and while the laughter should ease my tension, it doesn't.

With each step closer, my heart races faster. I get that I'm the bride that found her fiancé cheating with her best friend and that I've been moping around my parents' house for the past year, but this isn't right. A mother should never want her daughter to experience her wedding this way. It'd be one thing if I signed up for the show; I'd be prepared mentally. Right now, the only thing I'm prepared for is to lose my bladder from nerves.

"And here comes our bride."

I fumble over my own feet when I hear the announcer say those words. My hand tightens around the assistant's as she walks me on stage. The bright lights burn my skin, making me sweat.

Attractive.

I'm handed off to another arm, one that's clad in a coat of some kind. In my mind, it's my dad, and he's in a tuxedo walking me toward the man of my dreams.

"You look lovely, sweetheart."

My throat swells, and I try to fight off the tears. The last thing I want is for the groom to see me with mascara dripping down my face because my dad just spoke to me.

"Dad, what are you doing here?"

"I couldn't let you get married without walking my baby

4

girl down the aisle, or in this case on the stage."

I shake my head. "Daddy, this is so stupid. I don't think I can do this."

He leans in and whispers, "You have a microphone pinned to your dress, and everyone can hear you. It's only three months. Think of it as an adventure."

All my life, my dad has supported every harebrained idea my mom has come up with. From the time I was going to be a figure skater to pageant queen, from soccer star to head cheerleader, my dad's support has never wavered.

"Don't leave my side, okay?"

"Never," he says before placing a kiss on my cheek.

The Wedding March starts, and the crowd hushes. I'm curious to know if there are illuminated signs telling the audience when to laugh or to be quiet. Will they be prompted to say ooh and *ahh* when we say our vows? Are there hecklers out there? So many unknowns face me right now, but the biggest one on my mind, the one that I'm trying not to think about, is my groom good-looking? I know it's vain, but damn it, if I have to spend three months with this guy I at least want some man candy. Someone who looks like Joshua Wilson would be nice.

Joshua Wilson is an actor with the most perfect shade of brown eyes I've ever seen. I've tried to replicate that color with my coffee and cream, but I can never get it just right. His hair is brown and red, and simply the most attractive color on a man. When I first met Tony, they matched in that sense. I spent most of my relationship with Tony comparing him to Joshua. Where Joshua is tall with nicely defined muscles and arms—I can't even begin to describe how I feel about his arms—Tony is thinner and less muscular, but still cute. I think that may have been some of my downfall with my ex. I used to prattle on and on about how hot Joshua is, how sexy and how I'd give anything to have his muscular arms wrapped around me. Tony would roll his eyes and complain, but that didn't stop me from watching every movie, TV spot, reading every interview, and buying every magazine that he's in. I'm slightly obsessed. It's easy to admit when you're never going to meet your celebrity crush.

I hear a few gasps and can only assume that I'm approaching where I need to be. My father hasn't let go yet, and for that I'm thankful. He's keeping me steady on my feet and somewhat calm, even though thoughts of hanging my mother by her pedicured toenails are filtering through my mind. If she thinks I'm going to share my winnings with her, she's off her rocker.

Winnings? How can I even think about winning? I'm not going to be able to pretend to be okay with this for three months. And what if he likes me? What if he finds me attractive and tries to kiss me? Then what? Ninety days of purgatory that's what. I'm so not ready to live in a house with five people I don't know all while trying to compete for *Best Betty Crocker*.

The announcer clears his throat and gets the audience cheering. Behind my blindfold, I'm rolling my eyes and glaring simultaneously at my groom. I know he's standing in front of me; I can smell him. If anything, his cologne smells good, but it's probably something his production assistant told him to wear.

Is he nervous like I am? Is he sweating from standing under these heat lamps? Are his parents here, too? What made him so desperate that he had to come on national television to find a bride? That's the answer I want to know, but will never ask for fear of what he might say.

Neither of us should be doing this and yet here we are. I could run. I could slip off my blindfold and run without looking back. But what if he's my soul mate and I don't know it?

What damage could three months do?
Everything!

My father places my hands into those of my groom and while I should cringe, I don't. My fingertips, hands, wrists, arms and everywhere else tingle. I feel warm, but not from the lights. It's a different kind of heat. My tummy flutters. My heart pounds furiously in my chest, drowning out the audience, the music blaring overhead, and the crackle of the microphone. It's all too soon when the music stops and I'm quickly reminded that this is just a show. I shouldn't be excited.

"Do you take this man to be your lawfully wedded husband, to have and to hold, to compete with in good faith, from this day forward for better, for worse, for richer, for poorer, in sickness and in health, or until three months has expired?"

Um … what? What's his name? Don't I get to know his name at least?

"What do you say?" the announcer's voice bellows through the microphone. I can hear mumbling from the crowd as they wait with bated breath on what I'm going to say. Do people actually come on this show and say no?

"We need your answer."

I bite my lower lip and nod. If he can make me feel the way he did when he held my hand, maybe three months won't be so bad. "Yes," I squeak out, my voice barely audible.

"She said yes," the announcer roars, and the applause is deafening. I can't help but smile even though I'm dying on the inside.

My groom's voice is almost as quiet as mine, making me feel somewhat better that he's just as nervous. I sigh in relief when he says yes. The crowd cheers again and the announcer pronounces us man and wife.

Here it comes. I sense my groom moving closer, and I hold my head high. His hand fumbles on my neck until he rests it gently on my cheek. The crowd is hushed and everyone is waiting for the moment that seals us. His lips brush softly against mine, and he pulls back before I feel his wet lips press against mine again, this time fully. If not for his hand, I'd be crumbling to the ground. My knees start to buckle. My palms, already damp from earlier, are sweating profusely. My heart has stopped beating, but I can hear his. This is a first kiss for the records, and the only thing missing is his face.

The announcer clears his throat and my groom steps back, much to the delight of the viewers. "This is the moment we've all been waiting for," the announcer says. I read from the rules that the groom's blindfold comes off first. There's a collective gasp, followed by a series of 'oh my God's' and 'that lucky bitch'. *Gee thanks, audience members.* I can safely assume my groom is cute. Great, perfect. I have a cute husband who can turn my insides to goo when he holds my hand. Hopefully he's not planning on winning many competitions that require physical touching because I don't think I'll be able to handle it.

Someone comes up from behind me and starts to untie my blindfold. I keep my eyes closed. I want to see him fully when I open my eyes. I open them slowly, but keep them focused on the ground. Slowly, I take in what he's wearing— black patent leather shoes, with black tuxedo pants. His hand rests at his side, and I see the glint of a wedding band and quickly look down at my own hand. Was I so lost in my rambling thoughts that I don't remember him slipping a ring on my finger, or me giving him one?

I remind myself that this marriage is not real.

"I'll get you a bigger one," a familiar voice says.

My head moves up quickly, and I'm caught in the dark, smoldering eyes that I've studied for hours on end. I swallow hard and say, "Holy shit," before the darkness takes over, and I crumble to the ground in a heap.

CHAPTER
one

Joshua

"I can't believe you're doing this."

My best friend and roommate, Rob, follows me into my bedroom. My pile of clean laundry sits on my bed, waiting to be packed. It's hard to pack for three months knowing that I can't just run to the mall to pick up something new. When I'm on location, it's no big deal, but this time tomorrow I'll be married and confined to a house with no outside contact.

"I don't have a choice," I remind him.

"You were drunk. We both were. What we say and sign under the influence should not count."

Except it does and it's binding. Most producers run to the hills, waving their newly inked contracts around when something like this happens. As an actor, you shut up and do your job.

"What's done is done. Matt already tried to get me out of the show, and short of claiming that I have some disease, which will ruin my career, there's no reason I can't fulfill my obligation."

"We were set up!"

I wave him off. Yes, we were drunk. Yes, I feel as if I were duped. After trying desperately to get out of the contract, only to be told repeatedly that it's binding, I gave in. Once I let the idea settle in, it stuck with me. I have nothing to lose by going on *Married Blind*—quite the opposite really. I can use my fame and fans to deliver a public good message. If we win, it's one million in our pockets, my wife's and mine. We'll split it and go our separate ways. My lawyer still thinks it's a risk and encouraged me to file an injunction against the producer because he fears that I'm going to get stuck with some clinger who'll want some of my fortune. That won't happen because there will be no sex involved. It'll be the two of us and some simple game playing. We'll woo the TV viewers with my charm and hopefully her good looks. My female fans are going to hate that I've done this, but I'll be sure to give them a lot of shirtless screen time to make up for it. They just have to remember it's only for three months.

"Some brilliant ideas happen when people are drunk," I say as I watch Rob's face morph into something indescribable. Before he moved to Los Angeles, he was a character actor and most of the time can make me laugh. This is not one of those times. If it weren't for him, I wouldn't be in this position right now.

"You know you could leave, catch a flight somewhere."

Ignoring Rob, I continue to pack. It's a chore that I hate, but this time I'm taking my time to fold my shirts nicely, making sure my jeans aren't rolled into a disastrous ball, and even separating my underwear and socks. I don't want my new wife to think I'm a slob, even though the state of my apartment confirms that I am.

"What about a non-disclosure agreement?"

I shake my head, causing Rob to throw his hands up in the air in frustration. Matt and Jason are going to their graves prematurely.

"I see your acting lessons are paying off." Rob is what Hollywood considers a B-list actor. He gets minor parts here and there, but hasn't been considered for anything major. That's all me. After one small part that turned into an Oscar nomination for Best Supporting Actor, my career has skyrocketed. Matt Stokes is my agent. He's older, sophisticated, and works amazing deals for me. Jason MacNicholl is my lawyer. He's young, resilient, and a workhorse. He's currently having a mild heart attack because I refuse to have my future bride sign a non-disclosure agreement. I can't have one signed. We can't do it before the ceremony because that will give away my identity and once we're married, it'll be too late. I've assured them both that we won't be consummating the relationship, so there shouldn't be anything to worry about.

"I'm trying to look out for you," he says with a shake of his head. "I just don't get why you're doing this."

I set down my shirt and sit on the edge of my bed. This all started late last fall. Rob and I had met for a few drinks and ran into Barry Barnett, one of the producers from the reality show. The more the drinks flowed, the more Rob started joking about me submitting my name for the next season. I laughed him off until Barry insinuated I didn't have what it takes to compete. I didn't take too kindly to that and Barry told me to prove it. I let it go, but the drinks continued to flow and then my on again/mostly off again girlfriend, Jules, showed up and started acting like we were together, which we hadn't been for a while. She laughed when I told her I was going on the show to find real love, but stormed out of the restaurant once I took the pen from Barry. She never saw me sign on the dotted line.

I never thought in a million years Barry would hold me to it, but he has. I have a feeling that with my celebrity status they'd enjoy the rating increase, but having me on is a liability. Yes, they're viewership could double or triple, but unless they follow me up with another celeb in the next season, they will lose that market.

I'm doing this for one reason … well, two actually. Aside from my contractual obligation, I'm going to use my time on television to talk about my charity. When I got my first big break, I helped revamp the community center where I grew up. Yes, I grew up in a community center. I had three meals a day, someone to help me with my homework, and people to listen to me when I needed them. I have parents, but until they divorced they did nothing but fight. What kid wants to listen to their parents fight every single day? Not me, that's for sure. So each day before and after school, I biked over to Valley Hill Community Center. I thought after my parents split, things would get better. They didn't. They both remarried and found new hobbies to occupy their time. They've both since divorced and remarried multiple times. It's all I know. That's why I can take this so lightly. Marriages, especially in Hollywood, are a dime a dozen.

"I'm doing this because being married for three months without any outside interference is going to be easy. This girl and I are going to walk away with five hundred thousand each and Valley Hill will be front and center on everyone's mind. I'll have ample airtime to talk about it, and maybe people in the community will see what a gem it is and help fix it up. Jason only lets me donate so much to them a year, so after I win, the Center will have enough for some major renovations."

"You're going to have a wife."

"It's a showmance at best."

"She'll develop feelings for you."

Not gonna happen. "There's no way. I'll tell her the moment we're off camera that this is nothing but a business transaction. Hell, for her it's a chance to say she was married to an actor for three months and she made some money out of the deal."

Rob turns to leave, lingering in my doorway. "Jules is flipping out. And you're making your future wife sound like a gold-digging whore."

"Jules has no say in what I do." It's been all too convenient that she's been away filming and we haven't been able to talk face-to-face about me leaving.

"Does she know that?"

I shrug, not caring how Jules feels. "She left me for someone else, and when he wasn't good enough, she came back thinking I'm a revolving door. We're toxic together, you know that."

Rob stares at me for a minute before shaking his head. "Everything about this is bad for you. Take my advice and talk to Jules before you leave, get your head straight, and treat this new wife of yours with respect while you're living in that house. Remember, your legion of fans will be watching and they probably have this crazy idea that you're a stand-up guy."

"I am a stand-up guy."

Rob taps his knuckles on the doorjamb. "Anyway, I have an audition. I guess I'll see ya in three months." He leaves me sitting in my room with a lot to think about. I know a lot of gold diggers, most of them being my numerous stepmothers. My dad has no qualms about using my name to get a wife, and it only takes them a few months to realize that I'm the one with the money. He's not. They fight, he borrows money for a lavish vacation, and they stay together only to break up months later. Boom, another divorce. My mom, on the other hand, marries rich and is happy until her husband leaves her for a younger version.

I pull out my cell phone, pressing the green phone button. Jules' name is at the top for my most recent missed calls. Her name is actually in red all the way down my screen. I'll have to scroll to see who else I have a missed call from. I contemplate calling her, but that ship has sailed for me. I'm only waiting for her to catch my drift and move on. Jules Maxwell is every guy's dream girl, except for mine. She's gorgeous, Italian-American, and has a rocking body. Her curves go on for miles. At first, I couldn't get enough of her. That all changed when I missed two callbacks because she wasn't answering her phone one day. I found out she was with Bronx Taylor, helping him prepare for a role that I was auditioning for. I was so consumed by her that I was messing up my life. We broke up only to sort of get back together. It's complicated and messy.

I'm not nervous. I thought I'd be pacing the floor, counting the reasons why I need to bail, but I'm not. There's no sweat dripping down the back of my neck, and I'm not pulling on my bowtie so I can breathe easier. I'm actually looking forward to this. I met the other two guys getting married today and one was sweating so bad his shirt was soaked. I made a mental note in the back of my head that he won't fare well in competitions. I have to live with these guys, and from experience I know guys are slobs.

Listening to Cole Brooks—the non-sweaty bachelor— prattle on about how he's here to find his soul mate, his destiny, makes me want to shake him. He needs a healthy dose of reality poured over his head. Soul mates don't exist. My mom has found five of them in my twenty-seven years. My mom averages a new *destiny* every three and a half years. Good luck, Cole.

Gary Williams—the sweaty bachelor—is called first. The production assistant hands him a blindfold and before he can put it on, he's retching in the trashcan. I make eyes with the PA, making sure he knows to get rid of it. Gary and Cole don't know who I am. Not that I blame them. I can't imagine they watch many chick flicks. I have a feeling once we're in the house though, the women will know. I just hope my new wife at least likes my movies.

My name is called next. I stand and adjust my tux. The blindfold is handed to me, and I slip it over my eyes and tie it behind my head.

"Hold onto my arm, Mr. Wilson," the PA says, placing his arm under my hand. When we came down the hall, I did notice that it was free of obstacles so I'm not worried about tripping on anything.

Loud cheers erupt when I walk on stage. The audience has no idea that it's me under this blindfold, but I can tell by some of the murmurs they're guessing. I suppose if they knew, then the women in the audience would be fighting my bride for her spot. Truth be told, I sort of like how I'm about to get married.

The bridal march plays overhead and my nerves start to get the better of me until her hand is slipped into mine and a peaceful calm takes over. The announcer, who is also an ordained minister sanctioned by the state of California—it was in the contract—starts yammering on about the show and how everything works. He tells the audience that *Married Blind* will air twice a week and that viewers will be able to tweet us questions as well as vote on some of our competitions. This seems to please them, but they're just following the prompters when it tells them to laugh.

I should be paying attention to him, but I can't. These small hands in mine are shaking, and I find myself thinking of ways to calm her down. I want to assure her that we'll have fun and win this thing. I'm not going to let us fail. I run my thumb over her wrist and find her pulse, pressing down slightly. She calms down some, but not entirely.

We say our vows, but names are conveniently left out. That is something I asked for specifically. I don't want anyone, including my new wife, to know my identity until after we've sealed the deal. My fear is that she could either rip her blindfold off and run, or marry me simply because of who I am. I like it this way better. It also didn't escape my notice that the announcer had to ask her for her answer. I have a feeling this might not bode well for me. I could be the first groom in the show's history to be left at the house, alone. With no wife, I'd have no chance at the money.

When I slip on her ring, she seems lost, and as much as I like the concept of not seeing her until after, I'm not sure she's even paying attention. Shouldn't she be eager and listening to what's going on? Once the ring is on, which feels entirely too foreign, I hold her hands again. We're pronounced husband and wife, and I do what seems natural in this moment. I let my hand travel up her arm, over her shoulder, to her neck until I'm finally cupping her cheek. Her skin pebbles under my touch, a reaction I haven't felt from another female in a very long time.

Leaning down, I brush my lips softly against hers. I flinch back and bring my fingers to my lips, feeling the burn that was left behind. It doesn't take long for my brain to register that I like that feeling, and I go back for another kiss. This time I trace the outside of her lips and my tongue rejoices while my lips balk when I pull away.

Kissing might be on the list, but no sex. That's where I have to draw the line.

My blindfold is removed, and the crowd lets out a collective gasp. I wave and smile, turning on the charm, and bring my attention back to my now wife. She's blonde and skinny. Not my type. She's definitely athletic and only a few inches shorter than I am.

Her blindfold is removed, but her eyes stay focused on the ground. She's probably not used to the lights like I am. I look at the ring I just placed on her finger and feel nothing but embarrassment and disgust. It's just a simple solitaire, maybe an eighth of a cut.

"I'll get you a bigger one," I blurt out before I know what

I'm saying. Did I really just commit to buying her a bigger diamond? *Yes, yes I did.*

Her head moves so fast, it almost gives me whiplash. I smile at her and throw in a wink. Her face turns beet red, and it's not from the studio lights overhead. She's embarrassed. I know that look. She knows who I am.

I try to break eye contact with her, but I can't because we're still filming. The producers are eating this shit up when all I want to do is walk off the stage. I'm not mad she knows who I am, I'm upset that she's wearing a cheap ass ring when I would've gotten something better for her.

"Holy shit," she says before her eyes roll back. I catch her before her head hits the ground, saving her from a concussion.

"Well, will you look at that, Joey Mitchell ... I mean Joey Wilson is so taken by her husband's charm that she's passed out."

I roll my eyes, scoop her up, and follow one of the assistants off stage. They direct me to her dressing room, opening the door for us. After I set her down on the sofa, I make sure her legs are covered, but that her dress isn't getting ruined.

"Can you get me some juice for her?"

I don't look to see if they've followed my directions as I try to make her comfortable. I'm sort of happy that she's out cold so I can stare at her without being considered a stalker. Her skin is tan, definitely sun-kissed and in perfect contrast to her blonde hair. If I were to see her on the street, I probably wouldn't give her a second glance because I normally don't go for blondes, but something tells me that she's my match. It's too bad we'll only know each other for a few months.

Her eyes flutter open, and I find myself quickly mesmerized by the light blue, almost gray color. I've heard of this color, but have yet to see it until now.

"Hi, Joey."

She squints her eyes and recoils farther into the couch. "How do you know my name?"

"Dick VanPeriwinkle said it after you passed out."

"Is that his name?" she asks, trying to stifle her laughter.

"I don't know actually, but it sounds funny."

Joey tries to sit up, and I'm just eager enough to help her. I like the way I feel when I'm touching her. It's like serenity. She makes me feel like I belong.

"Are you real?" she asks just as she pokes me in the forehead.

"I'm not going to pop, if that's what you think."

Sighing, she glances at the door before she looks at me. "I don't know what to think. This seems all too surreal."

I run my hand through my hair and decide to sit down next to her. "Yeah, I guess getting married to a stranger can be surreal."

Her head starts shaking back and forth very slowly. "The surreal part is that I'm married to *you*."

CHAPTER
two

Joey

Someone pinch me. No, that's not good enough. Someone needs to slap me across the face, repeatedly, so I can wake the hell up. This can't be happening. I've dreamt of meeting him, of shaking his hand and having a photo taken with him. Those are my daydreams. At night, this is the man that I've fantasized about, the one I have wet dreams about, the one I play The SiMS with on the computer and have wild monkey sex with over and over again. He's sitting next to my sprawled out body, running his hands through his hair and telling me its surreal being married to a stranger?

Um, I'm married to Joshua freaking Wilson. It doesn't get any more surreal than that!

I try to sit up by myself, but no, he has to touch me. Why is this happening to me? I know this has to be some sort of joke, right? Am I on some sort of *I feel sorry for you, so I'm going to marry you* game show? Joshua Wilson does not need to come on *Married Blind* to find a wife! He has a girlfriend. I always see her in the tabloids and I hate her. She's pretty and perfect and everything I'm not.

I'm trying to focus, but I can't. My eyes are moving from his eyes, to his hands, his jaw, smile, fingers, chest, oh God, his arms ... he's going to think I'm a freak. Closing my eyes, I count to ten twice. Nothing is working.

"We have to leave in a few minutes for the house. Are you going to be okay?"

I nod then shake my head. He laughs. *Great, now he's laughing at me.*

"How did you end up on this show?" I ask the question that is plaguing my mind.

Joshua sits back, but not far enough away that he's out of my personal space. I know I like him in my personal space, but I also know this isn't real.

"Yeah, about that," he says, pushing his hand through his locks. "I suppose you get the shit end of the stick by being married to me, but I got drunk, lost a bet, and signed the contract." He shrugs as if it's no big deal. It probably isn't to him, but to me it's everything. "I never expected Barry to call me out on it and make me hold up my end of the deal."

"Barry?"

"One of the producers."

My head moves up and down as I bite my lip. I won't cry and admit that my dream guy just crushed my already broken heart into a million tiny pieces and lit them on fire. No, that would be admitting defeat in the man department, and I'm not there yet. Give me three months when life and reality come crashing down on me.

"Anyway, I figured we'd win and we'll split it down the middle, except I'll pay your portion of the taxes."

I'm going to need some extensive therapy after this is all said and done.

"Right, so at the end we go our separate ways. Makes sense," I say through a broken voice. I know I shouldn't have the emotions that I do, but it does sting a little knowing he's not committed. I mean, we just got married, and he's already put an expiration date on it. It's Hollywood, right?

"I want to win, Joey, and I think we can. I saw those other guys and am pretty confident I can beat them in most of the competitions. I studied how the game has been played the previous two years. I think we can do it."

"Okay," I agree because what else am I going to say? He should've just paid the producers to make sure he married his girlfriend. At least then, he'd be able to win this game and actually act like a husband to someone. But nah, I'm weak, heartbroken, and madly in love with the man sitting in front of me ... in the fantasy sort of way.

"Great. This went easier than I thought."

Of course it did. You're Joshua Wilson, the most sought after twenty-something actor. I'm putty when it comes to you. You could tell me to jump off a cliff, and I'd be like "okay!"... duh. I know I'm being childish, but I can't help it. I have a feeling there's going to be a lot of eye-rolling coming from me in the next few months. I hope America is ready for it.

The loud knock on the door followed by a shout of 'five minutes' is our sign that we have to go. I'm not allowed to change out of my dress even though I so desperately want to. Joshua takes my hand in his and leads us out of the room, down the hall to the exit where a limo is waiting for us. Another assistant hands me a bouquet of flowers, and I realize that this is our "leaving the church" moment. As soon as we step outside, viewers have the opportunity to throw birdseed at us, as if we're a normal couple.

Joshua doesn't ask if I'm ready; he just barrels through the open door to the massive cheers and a few jeers from the crowd, dragging me half running behind him. He's pulled on by grabby hands, but hangs firmly onto my hand. The door to the limo is open, and he steps aside, picks up the train of my dress, and helps me in the car. Once inside, he pops open a bottle of champagne as if we have something to celebrate.

Of course, I take the flute that he offers and guzzle down the fizzy liquid. I'm going to need a lot of liquid courage to get through these next few months. I've seen the show before, but I'm not a fan. I know that we have to compete for luxury dinners, household prizes, and the master suite each week. In the past, the "master suite" was the only room where the video cameras were turned off at night to afford the winning couple some privacy. You'd think that with the video cameras always rolling, it would actually deter people from having sexy time in the house. Not so much. Granted, viewers can't watch what goes on unless they purchase a subscription to *After Midnight*. Then it's a free for all, per our contract.

I won't be getting any action, so I have nothing to worry about.

The limo drive is relatively short since we haven't left the studio lot, but it's enough time for us to polish off the bottle of champagne. Liquid courage is great and all, but we'll have to take part in a competition in about an hour or so.

Joshua doesn't talk, and for that I'm thankful. I'm not sure how much more of his voice I can take. It's not a bad thing. I love his voice, I always have, but hearing him in person takes my obsession with him to a whole new level. It's even better when a microphone doesn't muffle it. This level of crazy is going to buy me a one-way ticket to the psych ward. I'm happy he's not talking because I don't know if I'd be able to contain myself. I have visions of mounting him in this limo and begging him to talk dirty to me. His voice is smooth and calming. I'm like a dog in heat when he comes on TV. I can hear him a mile away. Yeah, it's a good thing he's not speaking because if he asked me a question I might start squealing like a tween girl at a Justin Bieber concert. No one needs to hear or bear witness to that. The fact that he's sitting right next to me is causing me to clench my thighs in a wedding dress. It's not an easy task, but one I'm gladly participating in.

The limo pulls up and more nerves start to set in. I have to pretend to play house with my celebrity crush for the next three months. We have to make viewers fall in love with us so they'll vote for us for the finale.

I need to learn how to protect my heart. This is my dream come true. This is what every girl, who has a crush, dreams about, but reality is never taken into consideration. I'm not an actor, but I'm going to have to learn how to be one fast.

"Ready?"

Joshua doesn't wait for my answer before pulling me out of the limo by my hand. Again, the viewers are there, lining both sides of the carpeted path leading into the sound stage where I'm assuming our house is. Everyone is yelling and screaming his name, plus a few things that I don't want to repeat. I heard the jeers earlier when I was on stage and didn't understand then, but I do now. They're jealous. I would be, too. Just as we get to the door, Joshua scoops me up bridal style and turns in front of the crowd. They go crazy and even more so when I lift my bouquet up high and fling it into the masses.

When we get inside, the door closes, and he drops me almost immediately. I fall to the side when my heel doesn't land flat on the ground, and it's some man walking by who catches me, not Joshua. I have to get it through my mind, and fast, that he's only here to win. I have to dig deep for my game face, shut off my heart, and only use my brain. And my brain is telling me that someone like Joshua Wilson, who has women throwing themselves at him—not to mention a beautiful girlfriend—would never fall for someone as plain and ordinary like me.

"Follow me," a small pixie of a woman says to us, and we do. When she stops abruptly, I peer around her to see the set where the host is talking to the crowd.

"It's now my pleasure to introduce for the first time, since he made his bride pass out, Joshua and Joey Wilson." The audience erupts in cheers as Joshua grabs my hand and pulls us out onto the stage. The lights are bright again, and I feel myself getting dizzy. Of course, the embarrassment I feel has nothing to do with my overheated body or my spinning head.

This is the first time I'm getting to see the other couples. Joshua mentioned earlier that he saw the other grooms, but the brides weren't together. We sit in the two empty chairs, forming a triangle. All eyes are on Joshua, but for different reasons. The men are staring because they're pissed off that he's here, or at least that's what I assume. The women stare because he's hot, and he's famous. They're about to walk around in their bikini-clad bodies in front of him, and they're probably thinking the same thing I am: did I bring my cellulite cream?

"Now that we're all here, let's go over the rules."

The host of this segment of the show is Patrick Jonas, a former boy band musician who turned his career into a television gig. He also hosts a few other shows on daytime TV.

"You will compete as a couple against each other weekly. The prizes and competitions will vary. At the beginning of each week, you'll vie for the master suite."

The crowd *aahs*.

Gross.

"Each week there are two, sometimes three, competitions. Remember, you're competing for not only prizes, but for votes from nationwide viewers. Don't worry, newlyweds, you'll have plenty of alone time to get to know your new spouse." Patrick laughs and so does the audience.

Gag.

I refrain from rolling my eyes because while the other

couples can get their freak on, there will be a nice divider between my spouse and me. I'll just have to continue to play out the wet dreams in my head or the shower where he's not likely to catch me.

"Newlyweds, the time has come for you to enter your home. The first competition starts in one hour."

I don't move, allowing the others to rush to the front door. We have an hour to prepare; it's not like the house is going anywhere. Joshua senses my hesitation and uses this moment to talk to me. The moment he leans down, the crowd quiets so they can hear what he says.

Rude.

"I think we should let the others win first since we won't be consummating our nuptials," he whispers in my ear, but is completely unaware that he's just caused a major eruption of goose bumps. Not to mention he's effectively ruined what little self-esteem I had left. I mean, why would someone like him want to be with someone like me? Why would anyone want to be with someone like me? I'm the woman whose mother signed her up for a show in order to marry her off.

Married Blind

"I'm Patrick Jonas, welcome to the third season of *Married Blind*. This season promises to be explosive as we watch three couples battle it out for a million dollars all while trying to muddle their way through being newlyweds as America watches. Not to mention this year's twist-one of our grooms is none other than Joshua Wilson, star of *Finding Mister Right*. Will Cole and Millie Brooks or Gary and Amanda Williams be able to obtain enough fan votes to beat the Wilsons? Find out on this season of *Married Blind*!"

CHAPTER
three

Joshua

There's a knot in my stomach. It appeared as soon as the door shut, and we were sealed in for the next three months. Joey separated from me the moment we walked in, which I know is for the best. I know we'll have to be allies, but anything more will just complicate things for her. My emotions are shut off, the wall is up and nothing can bring it down. I have one focus: the end. I have to win this game for my foundation, to help give them a fresh start and to save face after my drunken ass landed myself here.

I press my fist into my gut, hoping to alleviate some of the pressure. I can't be sick. It won't be good for either my game, or Joey's. Being sick would sideline me and delay our opportunity to woo the viewers. They need to believe that Joey and I are … well, not in love because my fans would be pissed, but that we're fighting for the same cause.

Joey needs to be on board with fighting for my foundation. She needs to tell the viewers that she supports me one hundred percent in donating our winnings because technically we don't need the money. Except she probably does or she wouldn't have signed up for the show. I already promised that she'd get her half, regardless of what she says on national television. We'll get the sympathy vote as well, but we need to convince the viewers that we're sincere and falling for each other. I mean that's the idea behind the show—to actually fall in love.

Joey is nowhere to be seen when I realize our next step in my game plan. I'm standing in the middle of the room with my fingers pulling at my lip. I'm too deep in thought and that's not good. The other houseguests will know I'm plotting. I should be by Joey's side as she tours the house, but instead I'm showing the viewers that I don't care about her.

My change of plan starts now. I have to show them that I'm sensitive and interested in her. The interested part shouldn't be hard because she's a beautiful woman and will make her next husband very happy, I'm sure. I'm just not him. The annulment will be easy, though. It'll be as if our marriage never existed and since we're not having sex, there will be no lasting repercussions. It hasn't escaped my notice that I have to remind myself that Joey and I aren't having sex. It's slowly becoming my mantra.

Wandering through the house, I find Joey in one of the bedrooms. The walls are painted dark red with black furniture. The producers know what they're doing with this room. Red is for passion, courage, and romance. This room screams sex. They're trying to ignite the couple that stays in this room.

It's working, and I don't want it to. I need to keep my focus on the prize and not worry about a romp in the hay, especially when this one could cost me a fortune in the end. Watching Joey walk around the room, oblivious to the fact that I'm standing in the doorway taking her in, stirs something inside of me. She doesn't fit my normal mold. She exceeds it, and that scares me. I can already tell that she has the right attitude for Hollywood. I have no doubt she'd fit in if we had met under different circumstances. Sadly, that's not the hand we've been dealt.

"I like this room," she says, catching me off guard.

I clear my throat. "It's nice. How'd you know I was standing here?"

Joey shakes her head and continues her exploration of the room. Before I can ask her again, Gary and Amanda come running into the room. The somber mood that Joey is in quickly turns and she smiles before coming over and standing next to me.

"Oh, I love this room," Amanda gushes as Gary chases her around with his eyes. I feel sorry for him. I think Amanda is out of his league and it'll definitely be interesting to see how they get along. Cole and Millie, the third couple, seem close. I suppose you have to have an open mind when you're doing something like this. I stealthily slide my hand into Joey's. She tenses, but doesn't pull away. Like I said, she'd be perfect for Hollywood.

"You're so lucky." Amanda's smile fades when she speaks to Joey. Gary's shoulders slump, and I instantly feel sorry for him. He probably came on the show to find a wife to love him and that might've been possible if I weren't here. I have to make it clear that I'm only interested in Joey. That means no staring or acknowledging the passes the wives might make. It also means I have to talk a good talk when it comes to Joey and me with the guys.

"We're both lucky," I say while staring at Joey, who's trying not to blush. She smiles, but it doesn't reach her eyes. I lightly tug her hand and motion for her to follow me; she does so without hesitation. We walk down the hall to the next bedroom and go in. There are three bedrooms; two on the main floor separated by a communal bathroom, and the master suite, which we'll compete to move into weekly, is upstairs. That's where every couple wants to be as it has the most privacy and the video camera is off at night so you can get your business done if you so wish. It's going to be hard to stay celibate for the next few months, especially when I'm pretending for the viewers, but I'll get it done.

This room is accented in all white, which gives off the feelings of freshness, innocence, and newness. They're trying to convey a new start. It's a nice room, but I like the red one better.

"It's too clean," she says as her hand runs over the white comforter. Her fingers dance against the fabric and for a brief second I wonder what they'd feel like against my skin.

"We should talk, Joey."

She shakes her head and looks over my shoulder, pointing at the camera. I nod, understanding her meaning. Joey steps closer and places her hands on my hips. I like that she's nearly my height.

"We can't speak freely, at least not the way you want unless we're in that room," she whispers in my ear before resting her head on my shoulder. I know what she's doing, and I follow her lead by wrapping my arms around her.

"You're smart and I love it, but I don't want to win this first competition. We already have my fans behind us. We don't want to come off as greedy."

Joey nods and starts swaying. I hold her a little tighter and pretend that I'm on the set of a movie; soon the scene will cut and we'll move onto something else. Except the only thing we're moving toward is somehow sleeping in the same bed without touching.

"Newlyweds, in twenty minutes please move into the backyard for your first competition."

Rubbing Joey's shoulders, I kiss the top of her head. I don't know what possessed me to do that, but I enjoyed it.

"We should probably change." I step back and look at our clothes. We're still in our wedding attire, this being our reception. Maybe that's why she was swaying earlier, giving us the wedding dance that we'll never share. Last year's couples didn't make it. Two of them called it quits before the show was over and the last, shortly thereafter. Joey and I will be that statistic. We'll be headline news for the next three months and the fairytale romance that we'll build here will all come crashing down. My image will take a hit, but I can bounce back.

Joey and I opt to change in the bathroom, unaware of where the other couples are. Our bags were all lined up in the hall so it's easy. When she steps out, she's dressed in running shorts and a tank top. We look at each other and laugh. I should've known that the show would add to our wardrobes so that the couples matched. Now that Joey is out of her dress, I get a good look at her. I already knew her arms were toned, but so are her legs. *My wife works out.* I shouldn't call her that. I need to be careful and refer to her, especially in my head, as Joey. When I'm talking out loud for game purposes, it'll be okay to slip, but keeping myself separated from her in that way is what's best.

"Do you like to workout?"

"Yes," she answers without looking up from tying her shoes. "It helps me focus." She stands, almost chest-to-chest with me. Stepping back, I put space between us. We should be able to win any endurance challenges we face as well. The more I think about our chances, the better I like them.

"We need to go outside," she says, walking away from me. I groan as I watch her sashay out of the bathroom. The temptation is there and if she makes a move, I'll be hard-pressed to deny her. I have to remind her—and myself—that this is a game, and we can't cross that line because we aren't going to be married once this show ends. All I can think of right now is, *Why couldn't we have met outside this show?*

I follow her outside and start taking in everything around me. There are three stations set up, each with our names. Joey steps behind *Joshua and Joey Wilson* and my heart stops beating for a moment. Seeing my name like that, tied with hers, makes me anxious, in a good way. It also makes me nervous that I like seeing our names together. Marriage isn't for me, at least it shouldn't be. I don't have any good examples to follow.

Joey slips an apron over my neck, and I stop her from tying it behind my back. I'm barely holding on to the resolve I have now. I don't need an excuse to touch her. I'll be making plenty of those later.

I step in behind Joey and she slightly steps back, erasing the gap between us. Her neck is at the right height, allowing me to get a good dose of her perfume. It's stronger than I remember.

"When did you put on more perfume?"

"In the bathroom when I changed. I wanted to smell good."

"Jesus Christ," I mutter.

"What?"

I shake my head even though she can't see me. "You smell nice, Joey."

"Newlyweds, it's time to play 'Name That Pie'. I'm going to show you a series of ingredients for a certain pie and the first one to chime in with the correct answer scores a point. The first team to seven wins the master suite for the week. Are you ready to see how domesticated you are?"

"Yes, Patrick," we say in unison.

"Remember, let someone win," I remind Joey. She doesn't acknowledge me, giving me the impression that she's as stubborn as I am.

The first ingredient appears: Celery.

I cringe. "Who puts celery in pie?"

"Potpie, haven't you ever had one?" she chides me.

"No, can't say I have."

"I'll make you one."

No, you won't, I want to say, but my stomach growls, and

32

now I'm really looking forward to having a potpie with Joey.

The next ingredient appears: Carrots

"I know this," she says.

I set my hand on her hip and apply a little pressure. "Let them win."

She nods and writes something on the board and chimes in.

"What's your answer, Joey?" Patrick calls out over the loud speaker.

"Mushroom Pot Pie."

"That is incorrect. You and Joshua are out of this round."

"That was brilliant," I whisper into her skin. She reacts, unwillingly I'm sure, as her skin pebbles under my touch. She nods and tries to step away from me, but I hang on, not allowing her to move.

I'm lost on all things Joey right now, and it's only when I see Cole and Millie being congratulated do I realize we've lost and the game is over. Cole looks excited and Millie looks nervous. I don't blame either of them. Millie is a pretty woman, but she doesn't hold a candle to Joey.

Holy shit, what the hell is wrong with me? I need to stop thinking like that. She's a friend … just a friend.

CHAPTER
four

Joey

I have never felt so much anger toward anyone that I can imagine his or her head exploding until now. Visions of my mother's head popping off and bursting like a watermelon appear each time I close my eyes. Not even when I found Tony and my former best friend slash maid of honor playing doctor, did I feel this much anger. How can a mother do this to her daughter? I know she had no idea that I'd be paired with my celebrity crush—the man I have imagined doing wicked things to—that *Joshua Wilson* would end up being my husband. I'm sure she's sitting at home just waiting for the scenes to play out where Joshua Freaking Wilson and I fall madly in love and have wild and crazy monkey sex.

Sorry, Mom, it's never going to happen, and why? Because my "husband" doesn't want to have anything to do with me, that's why. Yet, he continues to touch me and each touch sends the most glorious chills down my spine. Each touch is longer than the last, giving me false hope, only for him to open his mouth and have some stupid comment spew out—like how he likes my perfume.

He's my fantasy. He's my dream come true. Millions of women wish they were me right now, and all I want to be is them, at home with my pint of *Ben and Jerry's* watching this show and hoping that the people on here are finding true love and some sort of happiness in this crazy, messed-up world where we have to resort to reality television to find a lover.

For one brief moment, when I opened my eyes and saw that Joshua was standing in front of me with his hand on my cheek and possibly dizzy from kissing me, I thought I was getting my fairytale. Passing out, of course, wasn't part of said fairytale, but being romanced by him was. I thought I was going to find my own piece of happiness, to prove that I am worthy enough to be loved by someone like Joshua. Clearly, Tony couldn't love me the way I deserved. Weeks before our wedding, he was caught cheating. His confession was one that I didn't want to hear, but listened to anyway as tears clouded my vision. He had been cheating since before he proposed and thought that once he did, he could stop, but he couldn't. He didn't know if it was the thrill or the fact that he had been able to keep a drunken night turned torrid affair a secret for so long. Tony said he didn't love her and that she was a mistake, but I find that hard to believe. If she didn't mean anything, how could he have been sleeping with her for so long? She was my best friend, and she knew how I felt about Tony, yet she crossed the line. I'll never forgive them. They have forever branded me with a stigma, and have put me in that awkward position where every time I look my family members in the eyes, the sympathy in them is clear as they ask how I'm doing.

Today I want to tell them I'm doing fan-flipping-tastic, but I'm not. This is going to end up being yet another failure to add to my list. Maybe it's me. Maybe I don't love them enough or can't show it in a way that binds them to me. I'm probably broken and unfixable.

As soon as the competition is over, I'm back in the house heading toward the bathroom. From past episodes, I know it's the only place where one can find peace and quiet without a microphone hanging overhead or a video camera capturing our most embarrassing moments, although our body mics are on and subtitles are added for your viewing pleasure.

Joshua is hot on my tail, and I get that he's trying to stay close to me. For what, I don't know. Everything with him is awkward and fake. He doesn't need to pretend to be happy to be here. He has a mission. He's here to win for his foundation. I just don't think he realizes the ramifications of spending three months with someone that you have to grow close to. I don't care if you try to turn off your feelings, it doesn't work. At some point your brain and heart stop communicating and your heart takes over, especially when only one of us is an actor. I'm not trained for this.

Needing a few minutes to gather myself, I shut the door before he can follow me in. I'm going to have to figure out my game plan with him fairly quickly. I need to find a way to hate the guy who is standing outside this door right now and play like him. As much as I've fantasized about marrying him, it was just that, a fantasy, and now that it's really happened, I don't know how to deal with it.

"Joey?" His voice is muffled, and I can only guess that he's trying to be quiet. I want to tell him to go away, but that will be caught on camera, and I want to win as badly as he does. When I crack open the door, he slips in. The last place I want to talk to him is in here, but I'm not ready to face the other couples. They both look like they've gotten to know each other, and I'm slightly jealous.

"What's going on?"

I roll my eyes, telling myself that he's acting. He's a great actor, so this comes easily for him. I shake my head, only for him to step closer. There are so many things I've dreamt of doing to him. I should just do it, right? I mean, this is *my* opportunity to be bold and make a statement. Technically, he's my husband. He at least owes me one toe-curling kiss. I can't leave this house without some memory of what his lips taste like against mine.

He's either going to catch me or push me away. Fear be damned. I launch myself into him, and my arms lock behind his head as my legs step in between his. There's no hesitation in my actions, and I don't give him any time to react. The velvety touch of his lips is enough to keep me going. He's going to be an addiction I won't be able to beat. My hands loosen and slide to his shoulders, my fingers kneading his muscles as his tongue traces my lips. My mouth opens, allowing him in, and I welcome the fact that he's pursuing this kiss, not me. He's taking charge.

Joshua's fingers glide over my cheek until he's cupping my face. Heat spreads where his fingers had just been. His arm holds me close, his hand cupping my ass. I moan into his mouth when our tongues touch. This kiss is everything I thought it would be and more. I plunge my fingers into his hair, pulling lightly. His lips leave mine as he hisses, showing me so much more of himself than anyone else in the house will ever get to see. Joshua brings me closer; grinding my hips against his as our heads move back and forth in the most epic make-out session I've ever been a part of.

Voices outside the door force us apart. I rest my head against his shoulder as our chests move together from our laborious breathing. I wasn't expecting a kiss like that, but I'm so ecstatic that I have it burned into my memory. I'll need it when I'm home alone, reading over my divorce papers.

Joshua taps my side before kissing the top of my head. "We need to talk about that kiss," he whispers into my hair.

Shaking my head, I disengage from his hold. "There's nothing to talk about. That is something I've wanted to do for a very long time, and I just did it."

"What do you mean?"

Closing my eyes, I cover my face. I shouldn't have said anything and only agreed with him. Joshua tugs on my arms, pulling my hands away from my face. I keep my head down, mentally counting the tiles on the floor. The last thing I wanted to do was embarrass myself, but I've done it. He places his finger under my chin and pushes lightly until we're eye to eye.

"Joey, please tell me."

I feel like I want to cry, but I refuse to show him any weakness. I take a deep, shuddering breath and look him square in the eyes. "You're on my list, my hall pass if you will. You're my number one celebrity crush. Two days ago I was watching an interview you gave about falling in love, and I kept rewinding it because I felt sorry for myself and thought 'wow, he just needs to fall in love with me' because I believed I could be the one for you in my messed up fantasy world. And now look at us. Here I am and we're married, which I find so bizarre, but there will be no taming you. You're here for one reason only, and it's not to find a wife."

His hand drops, and he steps back. I look down at the ground again, afraid to see his expression morph into something horrid. He's probably trying to remember the contract and what situations allow us out of the marriage and the house early. Sadly for him, I don't think having a wife as your stalker counts since he's the first celebrity to come on the show.

Joshua slides his hands into his pockets, and I don't know if it's a relief for me that he won't be touching me any time soon or more heartache because he doesn't want me touching him.

"I never thought it'd be a possibility that I'd marry a fan."

I laugh out loud, which sounds more like a bark. *Great. I can't even laugh like a normal person around him.* "Yeah, well, if I knew you were a possibility, I probably wouldn't have gone up there."

"Why did you?"

"Technically, I didn't," I say, looking at him. I have to tread lightly here. I can tell him my story, or I can sugarcoat it as an overbearing mother who thought I'd find the man of my dreams on this show. "I was engaged, and he cheated. I found out right before the wedding and had to move back home. My mom ... I love her, but she's nuts. She submitted everything and didn't tell me until I got the call. Well, she got the call and packed my bags. My dad was there, though, to walk me down the aisle. My mom thought I'd find my soul mate or the man of my dreams. She's probably on the phone to her bridge friends telling them all about my sordid infatuation with you."

Joshua grows quiet, and the voices that we heard earlier are no longer lingering outside the door. Who knows what they're thinking, but I'm tempted to mess up my hair just to get them talking. I lean against the sink, crossing my ankles. I could leave and go join the others, but being in this confined space, even though its torture is worth it.

"That was a really good kiss we shared."

"Yeah, definitely one for the memory book," I reply, bringing my fingers to my lips.

"We should probably kiss more." I look at him questioningly. "You know, for the cameras and other houseguests. We can't have them thinking we don't get along."

I nod. "So kissing is okay, but no sex?"

He looks at me for a moment before he diverts his eyes. "Yeah, kissing is good," he says before walking out of the bathroom.

CHAPTER
five

Joshua

That kiss is something I'll never forget. Her lips are burnt into my memory. The way her fingers played with my hair made me feel like I was having an out-of-body experience. I've never felt shivers before from having my hair played with. I have to share a room with her later. We'll be in the same bed, under the same covers with possible body parts touching and the lights off. We're liable to move closer to each other as we shift in our sleep. Maybe a pillow between us will help us ward off any unexpected touching. I mean, if I'm sleeping I can't be held accountable for what my hand does, not to mention the morning wood I'll likely be sporting, and if it's anything like the hard-on I have now, I'm doomed.

My goal in this house is to concentrate, and I can't let some woman knock me off the rails, even if that woman is my wife and we have to live together and pretend we're in wedded bliss. So what if my wife is tall with a rocking body that I've only seen with clothes on and know my eyes will bug out of my head the first time I see any bit of hidden skin? Who cares that I *really* liked kissing her and want to do it over and over again?

I don't want to like her, at least not like that. Yes, I'm attracted to her. Who wouldn't be? First of all, I'm a red-blooded male, and chicks are hot. Second of all, she's sexy as hell. Not that hell is meant to be sexy, but I love that she's natural; no layers of make-up covering her face, no plastic added or fake tits being pushed up into her neck. No ozone-killing chemicals holding her hair in place. Those are the things that matter, especially as I'm standing here picturing my hands cupping her face and my lips kissing every bit of exposed skin.

Joey comes out of the bathroom, passing me without eye contact or even acknowledging me. That stings a little, to be honest. We have to show a united front, especially in front of the cameras. Next week when we win the master suite, we can be true to ourselves and sleep separately. I can take the couch, like every gentleman should. We just have to make it through this week as two people, who are married, trying to get to know each other. Unconventional? Yes, but doable.

I follow Joey and crash right into her, grabbing her hips just as she bends over to pick up her bag. I should let go and step back, but knowing that she fits perfectly against me has me holding on.

"Ahem!"

Joey springs up, almost smacking me in the face with her head. We both look at the voice to find Gary standing at the mouth of the hallway. I should let go of her hips, but I see the way he looks at Joey and everything is telling me to stake my claim.

"Already getting to know each other I see."

His words are like nails going down a chalkboard. He's not doing a very good job of hiding his jealousy. *Is he jealous that I'm here, or that she's married to me?* I pull Joey a little tighter to my body before I address him.

"We're married; why waste time?" I shrug and feel Joey stiffen. My comment will have to be discussed again in private. More ground rules we will need to define.

Gary looks around, as if he's not supposed to be here right now. "I guess it'd be nice if my wife felt the same way." He turns, leaving us alone.

I loosen my hold on her and she bends again to pick up her bag. However, I don't allow her to swing her bag onto her shoulder before I take it from her.

"I got this."

Smiling, she lifts my bag so I don't have to pick it up. "We should select a room before Gary goes to get Amanda."

I nod, figuring that Joey can choose the room she wants us in. I know I want the red room—it's sexy and alluring, not that she and I need that, but it would be nice to spend our wedding night in there. "I'll follow you," I say, motioning toward the two rooms that are waiting for us. When she turns toward the red room, I sigh in relief. I'm not sure I can stay in the white room. It's too bright and doesn't exude sexiness. Not that the word sex should be on my mind, but again, I'm a guy, it's there.

"Is this okay?" She spins on her foot and faces me. Everything about her posture tells me she's comfortable. Her arms hang near her sides instead of on her hips. She's giving me a choice when I gave her the go ahead to make the decision for us. I want to touch her, maybe hold her hand or tackle her onto the bed and tickle her. Either action would curb my curiosity on what it would be like to touch her, or to have her pressed against my body for a moment, until I need more.

"I think this is perfect," I answer, setting the bags down. There really isn't a need to unpack since we move from room to room every week. That is definitely something I don't like about this show. It'd be nice to have a private place that we're familiar with so we can spend some quality time with each other. Getting to know her will have to be done in front of the other newlyweds and the cameras.

I pretend to look around the room, anything to avoid making eye contact with her. I thought I'd be a little more freaked out about her revelation. I've encountered some crazy fans, and I never thought in a million years I'd be in the situation I am in now, especially with a fan, but it's safe to say she doesn't scare me. She intrigues me, though, and I like feeling that way about her. I want to know her more, inside and out. Find out what makes her tick and what defines the person that she is.

Truthfully, the fact that she isn't afraid of taking risks appeals to me though. When she jumped into my arms and kissed me, it felt damn good, almost *too* good, and I thought about taking things further. Unfortunately, sending the wrong message wouldn't be the smart thing to do. I have to maintain a level head at all times. When we're alone, the wall is up. The fortress is locked down and the bridge to cross the moat is raised. I can't let her in because I'm afraid if I do, I won't be able to get her out.

"I think we're supposed to get to know the other newlyweds." Her voice breaks through my inner ramblings, and I'm thankful. I think I could listen to her talk all day if given the chance. Turning to face her, I find that she's standing by the door with her hands clasped in front of her. I study her, taking her in. She looks like a runner with her long legs. They're toned with clearly defined muscles. I make a mental note to ask her to workout with me one of these days, but I'm fearful she may be able to squat more than I can. It's sad to say, but I'd be okay with that. Her smile isn't forced, but genuine and lights up her entire face. She's happy to be here, or happy that I'm her husband for the time being. Either way, I'm happy she's mine as well.

Walking toward her, I put my hand on her back. It's a

guise to touch her, not to guide her. I have a feeling she'd lead me anywhere I asked, and I'd follow without hesitation. I hope that, if anything, we'll be friends after all of this because even after knowing her for a few hours, I can tell it's not going to be enough.

We enter the common room, or as non-reality-television people would call it, the living room. There are three large couches, I'm assuming one for each of us, with a plasma TV attached to the wall. We don't have access to it, but I do remember last season's couples watching a movie or two. I'm thinking a horror movie might be in order, at least one night, so it forces the automatic cuddling rule. The common area is open and leads into the kitchen. We have a dining room table and also an island with bar stools. Aside from being outside earlier, we haven't been in the backyard. If they keep with the theme from last season, there's a pool, weights, a lounge area, and a pool table.

Thoughts of teaching Joey to play pool enter my mind. Having her bent over the table while I sidle up behind her …

My arm is suddenly yanked and voices become louder. Joey and I are in the middle of a conversation with Millie, and I haven't a clue as to what we're talking about.

"I just can't believe they let a movie star come on the show." That's Millie. Her voice is dreamlike, but has an edge to it. I have a feeling she's a lawyer or teaches high school students. You need major cojones to teach teenagers.

Joey looks at me, and I shrug. I'm sort of lost on the conversation and having a hard time focusing and keeping up. My shoulder is slapped and a bottle of beer makes it into my eyesight.

"Thanks, man." Taking the bottle into one hand, I extend my other to shake Cole's.

"Wow, this is all surreal," he says as he runs his hand through his hair, ruining the coif he had earlier.

"I know what you mean."

"I bet. You could have anyone, and yet you went on a dating show."

When Joey looks down at the ground and her shoulders slump, I smirk and call him an asshole in my head.

"It's not like that. I'm using this as an opportunity to raise awareness about the foundation I support. With the economy still in ruins and only beginning to rebuild, people forget about the smaller, less fortunate non-profits that lost funding. Everyone is focused on rebuilding big businesses and don't realize that most of our youth programs are still suffering. If Joey and I win, I'm giving my share to the foundation. Help them kick start their rebuilding efforts." They don't need to know that my mouth wrote a check that I can't cash and that I was drunk when I signed a contract to appear.

"Oh, you're so noble." A hand is placed on my forearm and it doesn't take a genius to see that it's attached to Amanda. She bats her eyelashes at me when we make eye contact, and I quickly look away. I also place my arm around Joey for good measure. Joey doesn't immediately relax into me, but we'll get there.

"So, Cole, what do you do for work?"

He moves to sit down, but Millie doesn't follow. She stands in front of us, making things a little too awkward for me. In this house, I want to be treated like any other newlywed, not the actor they've seen in the movies. That's not me. *This* is me, the real me. I'm not playing some part right now.

I add a little pressure to Joey's shoulder and motion for her to sit down across from Cole. As soon as we sit, Millie does as well, followed by Gary and Amanda. Looking at those two couples, it's easy to see that having Joey as a fan is working in my favor because she's sitting next to me while the other wives are at least a foot away. I definitely hope my fans are seeing this.

"Cole, as you were saying?" Even though he wasn't, since he never answered my question to begin with.

"I work in finance."

"Crunching numbers or are you the tax guy?"

He takes a long sip from his bottle of beer and smacks his lips when he's done. "Nah, more like corporate finance. I work long hours and that prevents me from dating. My friend suggested the show after my last girlfriend dumped me via social media. I didn't even see the message for two days, that's how busy I was."

I immediately look over to Millie, and she glances away. We're each taking risks by being here, marrying people that we may not consider adequate partners for ourselves, but it's a show and we have three months to learn about them and ourselves, and maybe make some lifestyle changes. Although, I'm not looking to quit acting, so I'm not sure what I can actually change.

"Gary, what do you do?" I ask him next.

"I work with computers mostly, web servers and mainframes. That sort of thing."

A hundred bucks says he runs a porn site.

"That must be challenging." I don't know jack shit about computers.

He shrugs. "It can be."

I nod and move onto Amanda, who tells us she's a kindergarten teacher and has been teaching for two years. I don't know if I'd want my children to be taught by her. Millie is a police officer. I was right about her; she is a bad ass. I have vision of her shooting the guys if they get out of line.

"And what do you do?" Amanda asks Joey.

Joey clears her throat and barely looks at me before focusing elsewhere. "I graduated a few months ago and haven't found a job yet." For the first time since I've met her, her voice is weak and lacking confidence.

"Convenient that you're married to a movie star, isn't it?"

I don't care if I'm a guy and we're from Mars; I know catty bitchiness when I hear it. Amanda's jealous, and her comment has just rendered the room speechless.

CHAPTER
six

Joey

We will not be instant friends in this house. I don't know how Joshua feels, but the glares, off-handed comments, and overall feeling that they're jealous is not sitting well with me. We have to co-exist, but being friends might be a little far-fetched for me.

I get why they're jealous. I would be, too. Joshua Wilson is every woman's dream. He's gorgeous, charismatic, his body is perfection, and the way he smiles—how his lips curve just a little off to the side—makes me weak in the knees. And I'm married to him, at least for the time being. I know I have choices while I'm in this house: I can shut off my heart, put up a wall and exist, or I can enjoy the moment, be his wife and take as many stolen kisses as possible so that when I'm out of here and back in reality, I have the memories even if I don't have him.

The six of us shared four bottles of wine and watched a movie, two of us on each couch. I sat somewhat close to Josh while the other wives had at least a cushion's space between them. One has to think that you're a bit of a risk-taker to come on this show. I think, except for my situation, sex is expected, but by looking at the other two wives, they seem uninterested. If Josh hadn't already set the boundaries, I'd probably try to cop a feel every chance I could. The other men aren't ugly by any means.

Gary is a little different. He's blond, not well built, and his hair is a bit too styled for my liking. His eyes are a darker brown than Joshua's, almost lifeless. He stares, and that's a bit creepy, but he's decent looking, same thing with Cole.

Cole looks like your average high school athlete who never gave up on his dream to go pro. As he sits next to his wife, his biceps flex as if he's trying to prove something. His hair is dark and his eyes are blue. He has a nice smile. Of these guys, I'd probably date Cole, or at least talk to him in a bar. With Joshua here, though, they don't stand a chance with their wives. And I don't stand a chance with my husband.

Earlier this afternoon, I stood in front of a mirror and looked at my hair that was styled just right, the dress I wore was beautiful and may not have been the one I had picked out, but I wasn't going to complain. Now I stand, facing yet another mirror and stare at myself. The make-up has been taken off my face, making my eyes look dull and almost lifeless. If it weren't for the deep purple negligee against my pale skin, I'd look like a washed-out vampire.

My hair is pulled up in a lame ponytail with the ends falling down in the back. I used to have long hair, down to the middle of my back, but in an effort to change myself after my engagement ended, I cut it. I regret that decision. I pinch my cheeks to give them some life. They flash pink but quickly fade. It doesn't matter which way I turn my head, the disdain I see in my reflection is how I feel about my mother right now.

When I opened my duffle bag to pull out my favorite pajamas, they weren't there. As I threw clothes haphazardly over my shoulder in the bathroom, I had the sickening realization that my mother had removed the security clothes I had packed and replaced them with satin negligees and matching panties. It felt like I just swallowed one of my Aunt June's potpies, and now it's pressing on all my organs. I'm so angry that I want to cry, and yet I'm standing here wondering what Joshua Freaking Wilson is going to think when I walk into the bedroom we're sharing.

Am I enough to turn his head? I wish. *Is he going to think this is some covert method of seduction?* Again, I wish, but yes that's probably what he's going to think. I don't have a choice. My clothing options are limited, and sleeping in jeans just doesn't appeal to me.

Taking one last look in the mirror, I sigh. "Suck it up, buttercup." This is my personal affirmation, one that's supposed to give me enough courage to step out of this bathroom and into the boudoir with one of the hottest bachelors in Hollywood. Well, I guess he's no longer a bachelor, but that little tidbit does nothing to ease my anxiety right now.

The hallway is bright and empty. All the lights in the house are left on for the cameras. Only in the bedrooms can they be dimmed. It's extremely creepy to know that viewers can pay to watch us sleep. That's taking peeping to a whole new level of stalkerism. The only noises I hear are Amanda and Gary talking. The two rooms are spread out, likely for added privacy, so they have to be speaking loudly. First fight and it's on their wedding night. That can't bode well for their future.

The future. I'm not a fan of thinking about what's going to happen tomorrow or even next week. I used to look forward to the future and planning what my living room was going to look like or what color I was going to paint the master bedroom. Those dreams, or whatever you want to call them, were shattered so easily and by someone who was about to vow to love me forever. Joshua hasn't made any such proclamations, so I should be able to live in a fantasy world without it crumbling down around me… said every female with hopes of dating a celebrity. I'm doomed.

When I get to our room for the week, I lean up against the doorjamb and stare at Joshua. I've spent years studying this man, but nothing has prepared me for this sight. If I didn't know better, I'd think he's shooting a spread for GQ magazine or something. His bare chest is visible, each ab muscle on display for everyone on TV to see. The dark red sheet is crumpled at his waist, and I don't need to be standing next to him to know that his hipbones are directing every gazing eye to what's underneath. I've seen this before in the many magazines he's been in. Joshua has never been shy about his body. I'm thankful for that, although unwrapping him would be a nice surprise.

No, what's making me weak in the knees, aside from the obvious, is the fact that he's in bed, reading, and he's rocking the sexiest pair of glasses I have ever seen. I let out an inaudible squeak that gets his attention. He looks up, setting his book down, and stares right back at me. This is do-or-die time—me in my every night face, with no make-up hiding my blemishes or chicken pox scars from when I was little. This is the *me* he'd get if we were living real lives.

I step into the room and pull the sliding door shut. I don't have the sexy catwalk his now-and-again girlfriend has. I definitely don't have any sexy moves. I stumble, hit crap and trip over nothing on the floor on my best day. Right now needs to not be one of those days. Taking a deep breath, I remind myself that if anything, we're friends and this is just a slumber party. No sex. No touching. But maybe some kisses.

Kisses lead to touching, and touching leads to more intimate touching, which leads to sex, and he said no sex so there should be no touching.

"Joey?"

Shit, he's calling my name and I'm staring at the wall like it's the most interesting thing I've ever seen. I turn, give him a fake smile, and step toward the bed. I scan the floor quickly to make sure there isn't something that is going to cause me to trip, and when my knees touch the side of the bed, I imagine myself sliding one knee onto the satin sheets, and setting my hands down to crawl toward him. He throws his book aside, but leaves on his glasses, pulling me to him.

In real life, I sit down and shuffle my feet under the covers without looking at him. Before my head hits the pillow, the lights in the room are dimmed and the bed is moving. My heart is beating so loud I can hear it over the hush of the room. He must hear it, too, but not care. I mean, why would he? He can have any woman in the world, and he's stuck with me for three months.

A small light comes on and I turn sharply to look in its direction. I'm met with his dazzling brown eyes. He's on his side, facing me with a smile that seems so tender.

"I thought we could talk some more."

He says all the right things to make a woman fall in love with him. He's smooth and sexy and so dangerous for my heart.

Mimicking his posture, I tuck my arm underneath my head. There's a space between us, which would be perfect for us to hold hands. I'm just going to have to picture that in my mind.

"You look good in purple. It makes your eyes sparkle."

My eyes close as I absorb one of the most romantic compliments I've ever been given. I have to diffuse the situation. I don't want to be attached, even though I already know I am. This is a dream come true.

"Thank you," is what I say instead of telling him to go to sleep.

"Who else is on your list?"

"Excuse me?" My list is something I don't want to talk

about, especially with him.

Joshua moves, closing the gap. "I want to know about that list you mentioned earlier. I can't be the only one on it."

I look at him like he has two heads, only to be rewarded with his laugh and a shit-eating grin. I shake my head ever so slightly, but he doesn't back down.

"I'm your husband."

"Low blow, Wilson," I say quickly. "I'd be careful with how you use that word because I might request conjugal visits."

"We're not in jail."

"Feels like it. I mean, sure, we can wear our own clothes and we have to pick up after ourselves, but we can't leave and the cameras are always on."

Joshua starts to laugh, and in the process gets closer to me. If this is the kind of sleeper he is—the bed hog type— it's no wonder he hasn't settled down yet. He probably gets kicked out of bed.

"Tell me who's on your list, Joey." This time when he asks, or demands, his voice is low and sultry, making my insides twist with excitement.

"Aside from you, David Beckham."

He blanches, but recovers quickly. I should tell him he has nothing to worry about, but I like watching him squirm. He should know that I don't stand a chance with Beckham, he's just very nice to look at and I definitely would take the opportunity if it presented itself.

"Why him?" he asks in a voice different from his earlier question.

He's insecure?

I offer a one-shoulder shrug, wishing we could change the subject. This is why I didn't want to tell him. "He's hot. He's very easy on the eyes. And he looks very good in his underwear."

"Is he number one or two?"

"What?"

Joshua moves closer, his breath tickling me lightly. "Who's number one on your list, Joey?" The sultriness is back, making it hard for me to concentrate.

"We should go to sleep." I ignore his question. I don't want to contribute to his ego any more than I already have.

"Why?" he asks.

I close my eyes, hoping he follows suit. I wait a full minute, which is probably more like thirty seconds and open them again. Joshua is staring at me, smiling.

"I thought you were going to sleep."

"I am. You should, too."

"I will," he says. "I want to watch you for a few minutes. Is that okay?"

Shrugging, I push deeper into my pillow and close my eyes. Tomorrow is going to be busy. We have a date competition, and I want to win. Not because I need a date with Joshua, but because I don't like to lose. The more I think about it, he's probably used to being up until the wee hours of the morning, which means he'll sleep in and leave me to deal with the others. Just when I'm about to open my eyes and tell him to get some sleep, he whispers into the air, "Joey, who's your number one?"

"You are," I tell him before I can hold the words back. I keep my eyes closed for fear of rejection. When he pulls my hand out from under my cheek and locks his fingers with mine, I know I just made his night. I can sleep happily knowing I did something for him.

Married Blind

"I'm Patrick Jonas, and welcome to another episode of *Married Blind*."

[Theme music plays]

"Tonight we'll join the newlyweds to check in with them and see how their relationships are developing, and we have another competition in store for them."

[Audience claps]

"I know I'm a little curious to see just how things are shaping up for Cole and Millie, who have just spent a week in the master suite. Let's take a peek at our newlyweds shall we?"

[Switch to the live feed]

"Hello, newlyweds."

[All respond]

CHAPTER
seven

Joshua

"Let's start with Joshua and Joey. Joey, you've been married for a week now, is it everything you've thought it would be?"

"And more!" Joey responds, and the audience laughs. I don't have a clear view of the people in the crowd, but imagine that most of them are women. Or maybe the producers make sure there's an equal and fair amount of both sexes being represented for the live tapings. I hope they see how I'm sitting, with my arm around her. I want them to see that I'm into this marriage one hundred percent, regardless of what Joey and I have agreed upon.

"For your fans, Joey, tell everyone what Joshua is like." Patrick Jonas laughs as he finishes his sentence. You can faintly hear people from the audience commenting and I wish I were able to hear exactly what they're saying.

Joey looks at me and her shoulders come forward in a small shrug as she smiles. She crosses her leg and her hands lock around her knee. She's wearing navy blue shorts with a white tank top. In the past week, she's been out tanning with the other wives and her sun-kissed skin agrees with her. We've had a good week—not great, but definitely something we can build upon. Everyone, for the most part, has been very nice, especially to me. They're all interested in how I became an actor and what it's like. Cole and Gary ask a lot of questions about my female co-stars and are very interested in how sex scenes actually work. I think they were slightly disappointed when they learned said sex scenes normally consist of me, the lead actress, and about thirty different crew-members looking on intently.

"Joshua is a pretty sweet guy," she says as she bows her head shyly. I pull her to me and she allows herself to be cradled. It's all for show and we both know this. The pads of my fingers rub small circles on her arm. Her goosebumps are instant, but she doesn't ask me to stop.

"Now to the question on everyone's mind … Cole and Millie?" Patrick's voice trails off as he says their name. It's his job to get the audience riled, and he does. There's a bunch of sick bastards wanting to find out if they did the deed or not. I know it's going to be worse when Joey and I win a week in the master suite, but I'm ready for it.

I glance at Millie who turns red and Cole stares at the television. I can see the tension in his jaw as he clenches his teeth together. You don't realize how invasive this show is going to be when you sign up. Well I did, but I'm assuming the others hadn't really thought that through. Sadly, everyone wants to know. He blindly reaches for her hand, a gesture that I find telling. If they didn't want the viewers to know, surely he would've kept his hands to himself. I turn my attention toward Patrick Jonas. He's smiling and likely imagining the show's ratings going up. The first couple to win the master suite wasted no time getting down and dirty. Three cheers for ratings.

Cole clears his throat and Millie glances at their joined

hands. When he looks at the screen, he's smiling. "One of the benefits of the master suite is that the cameras are off, so I guess whatever Millie and I did or didn't do is our business. I can say this though; Millie and I are getting to know each other as husband and wife and hope to keep doing so when the show is finished."

The audience ahhhs at Cole's words and I find myself nodding. I'm not looking forward to Joey and me sitting in the hot seat after we spend a week in the master suite. I don't know if it will be to our benefit or not. On one hand, my fans could get pissed, especially if Joey hasn't worked her way into their hearts. On the other hand, it gives us an advantage if people see that we're connected and truly in love. Joey already has a crush on me and I'm an actor, so that bodes well for us. Plus, Joey is hot. Hot as in if we weren't stuck in this house I'd want to know her. Sadly, we've met under the wrong circumstances.

"Newlyweds, your next challenge will begin in an hour." The screen goes blank, and it dawns on me that I don't have a clue what just took place after Cole gave his answer. I must've zoned out. Millie is the first to stand, quickly followed by Amanda. I can't see Millie's face, but I'm gathering that she's upset.

"Are you going to go with them?" I ask Joey, as she pulls away from me. The screen is off and the audience can't see us anymore, there's no need to pretend. Except sometimes I feel like I'm not pretending. I do enjoy having her in my arms.

Joey looks at me and back to where the other girls went, then back at me. She hesitates because Amanda in particular hasn't been all that nice to her. Millie has made an effort, but Amanda has been snide with her comments about Joey being married to me.

This past week we've all been able to hang out. The producers are giving us a chance to really get to know each other before they throw us into the depths of competitions.

Gary, Cole, and I have lifted weights, run a few laps, and spent hours watching the women sunbathe. At one point, I caught Gary drooling. I didn't ask him which girl had his attention because I didn't want to punch him in the face for staring at my wife.

Joey confides in me at night—which makes me believe we'll maintain a great friendship once we're outside the house—that Amanda feels as if she were robbed and that Joey isn't worthy of a guy like me. How Amanda knows that about Joey is beyond me. It's not like Joey chose who she would marry, the producers paired us up. It's a crapshoot and all about how you match up on paper.

Nights have been my favorite time in the house. I get to be me, and even though Joey has that crush, it doesn't define her. I'm fairly certain that the Joey I get at night is the same Joey I'd get outside the house. My favorite part is when she sneaks into my T-shirts when she thinks I'm not looking, or when we're about to go to bed and she comes in make-up free and even more beautiful.

"I don't know if I should," Joey replies with trepidation. Last year when I watched the show, catfights were a regular occurrence. It's not easy living with six people, especially when you're all fighting to be the best. Each of our competitions means something. We're vying for that elusive master suite or for cash and other household prizes. But when you get women together, who are trying to impress their new husbands, the gloves come off. I think Joey is trying to avoid situations like that even though they make for great ratings.

"I think you should go. The cameras are rolling and the more sympathetic you are the more my fans will become yours. We want those votes at the end of the show." I see her face fall before she can look away. She doesn't say anything as she stands and walks away. Everything in me is telling me to go after her, to tell her I'm sorry and I didn't mean it, but I can't become attached. It's only been a week and I'm already thinking about her outside the house. She's a distraction that I can't afford.

"What do you think they're doing in there?" Gary asks as he nods toward the back part of the house where the women disappeared. I want to say something sarcastic like making out, but I fear that he'd become overly excited and rush back there. I'm all for women having their time. Guys have it. We just don't like to admit it. There's many times where Rob and I sit around and discuss women. Mostly it's me trying to dissect my relationship with Jules and why we can't seem to make it work. I'm not even going to try once I'm out of this house. I have no doubt she hates me right now. I didn't give her a warning and I'm sure her image is taking a hit.

"I'm sure they're probably consoling Millie," Cole adds.

"I don't think any of us expected such invasive questions. I watch the show and even that question took me off guard," I say, hoping to put Cole at ease. I'm used to questions like this and the more popular I become the more personal they're going to get. You learn to shrug it off, or avoid the questions altogether, but sometimes you can't. Everyone here, aside from me, is not used to hiding what they're thinking. Most people wear their emotions; it's what the vultures of Hollywood strive on. Actors learn to act at the flip of a switch. When we're being asked about the week Joey and I spent in the master suite, I'm going to smile coyly, bow my head, and give them just want they're looking for without admitting it. Let them assume. It's what everyone is good at.

"I don't know how you do it." Cole leans back into the couch. Sighing, he runs his fingers through his hair before his hands move roughly over this face.

"I get it." I kick my legs out in front of me and almost mirror his relaxed state except my arms are behind my head. "It's not always easy, especially when they're talking about someone you care about. One thing to remember is that you don't care what *they* think. You don't have to tell them anything you don't want to, and most importantly it's your job to protect your wife." I point to the area where the girls disappeared. "She's your priority now, not the show."

"He's right," Gary adds. "We each need votes to win, so you have to show those women out there that you're a good guy."

Cole looks at Gary and shakes his head. "We're battling for votes and you're telling me to show the voters how sensitive I am?"

Gary shrugs and looks at me for guidance. I have none. I'm solely counting on my fans to come through for me. For all I know they could be hating on Joey and my plan could backfire. I'm praying that they love her, and find her a perfect match for me. It'd be nice if they hold off on the hate until after the show when I tell them all that marriage wasn't for me and that Joey is the most amazing woman I've ever met, that she and I will remain best friends. I can't let the media drag her through the mud. It wouldn't be fair.

"I just think … hell, I don't know what I'm thinking. We're about to go into a competition and I'm thinking of throwing it so Amanda and I don't win. I'm fairly certain the thought of me repulses her." Gary's frustration with Amanda is very evident when we're all hanging out. He's a clinger, and she's got eyes for me even though she knows I'm happy with Joey. It's all about how you act in front of others.

"You know the microphones are on and the producers will likely replay this for the viewers, right?"

Gary sighs heavily. "My wife is hot. I'm not. I know I have a lot to do to catch her eye, but three months isn't enough time to change this." He motions down the front of him. He's not out of shape, but compared to Cole and me, he's a bit portly. He's a guy who sits in front of a computer all day and most likely eats there; he could probably use a gym buddy.

"I can always help," I volunteer before I realize what I'm saying. I want to take it back because I don't want to be committed to helping him, but it's too late. Gary's eyes go wide with surprise and I know he's going to accept my offer. I would if I were him.

"Really?"

I nod, albeit reluctantly, but have no choice. He already follows me around like a puppy when the women are doing whatever it is they do. I'm the movie star and to him that means fast cars, lots of woman, and tons of cash to throw around at him. Two of the three I'm lacking. Women aren't the issue. "Sure, why not. I work out anyway, so you might as well join me. You have to change your diet, though. Don't be guzzling beer and eating chips all the time. If you don't take this seriously, it won't work. Watch what you eat, don't sit around so much, and be proactive. Amanda will start to notice."

Gary leans forward, clearly excited about our newfound friendship. "Do you think you can help with her?"

"I have my own issues to take care of." Rising, I stretch, hoping that the cameras are panning around. I rub my abs for good measure.

He scoffs. "Joey is so into you."

"That may be, but we're still getting to know each other."

I walk into the kitchen, grab a glass, and pour myself some water from the pitcher that is sitting on the counter. Gary and Cole follow. Cole goes for the water, while Gary grabs a soda. I tsk and he looks down at his hand and puts it back. He opts for the water, too, and while I know this may backfire, the fact that he looks up to me is a bit comical since he's supposed to be competing against me.

"Newlyweds, your next competition begins in ten minutes. Please change and meet out back." The voice clicks off and we stand there in silence. After downing the rest of my water, I take off toward the bedroom Joey and I have been staying in. Within the next half hour, everything is going to change and she and I will be in the master suite playing husband and wife.

CHAPTER
eight

Joey

The computer voice tells us it's time for our competition. I'm not sure if I want to win after witnessing the monumental breakdown Millie just had. Through blubbering tears, Millie confirmed what we all assumed— she and Cole had 'done it'. Her words, not mine. Amanda told her that she was lucky that she trusted Cole enough and she just wasn't there with Gary. I think she would be if she gave him a chance, but then again if he'd stop belching and rubbing his ever-growing beer gut, she might give him the time of day.

Not that I care.

I see her watching Joshua when he's working out. I don't blame her, but she should be focused on her husband, not mine. It's annoying when she prances around in her tiny bikini and asks him to rub lotion on her back. He looked at me one time for approval. He didn't and she didn't get his soft hands on her back. I probably would've cried if he had touched her.

He's mine.

For three months, less one-week, and then I have to give him back. Amanda has charted out our days, telling us how many are left, and I hate her for it. I don't want to know the end is near, that I have one less day to be his wife. I want to continue living in this fantasy world where nothing else exists. He doesn't leave me on a pre-determined date. We continue to be blissfully happy, sans sex, and I'm the only one he has eyes for.

"We should go," I say as I head for the door. We've been cooped up in the pantry for what feels like an hour. Millie chose this place because aside from the master suite, there isn't a camera in here. The producers can still hear us through our mics and will no doubt air all of what we discussed, but they won't see Millie crying.

As soon as I open the door, my heart jumps. Cole appears, scaring me half to death. He looks over my shoulder at Millie, and I turn just in time to see her sad smile appear when they make eye contact. He cares for her, it's written all over his face. He brushes past me, not even giving me a sideways glance, and goes to her. I long for that connection with Joshua. I want him to be the one to comfort me in my time of need or distress. I want to be able to hold him, cry on his shoulder when life is getting to be a bit rough and have him understand.

I have that now, plus the stolen kisses and stealth handholding. Most of that happens under the covers and I'm okay with it. I know the viewers can see when he's kissing me. Part of me hopes it makes them jealous while the other part of me wishes they could never see anything happen between us. The divorce, annulment, the end of my life as I know it will be messy. Joshua's fans are going to slay me on social media. I'll be branded the gold-digging whore the moment we step out of the house. I'm sure that's what I'm being called now, and it's probably a good thing all electronic devices have been taken away from us. I want to hope that Joshua will protect me, but like he's said, he's here to win the money. My feelings likely don't register with him.

Joshua is in the room when I walk in. I catch him pulling up his shorts and stifle a laugh when he yanks them a little too hard. His pained expression tells me everything that I need to know.

"I thought you were Amanda."

I pause and look at him. "Why would she be in here?" I don't want to be possessive, but damn it, he's my husband right now.

"She shouldn't be, but I can usually tell when it's you coming down the hall."

"How?" I ask, hoping that he can dig himself out of the hole he's starting to bury himself in.

Joshua doesn't tie the board shorts he's put on and it takes everything that I have in me to not pull him closer by those flimsy strings. He slides our door shut and comes over to me. We're almost chest-to-chest, the closest we've been all day.

"It's your perfume. I can usually smell it a mile away, figuratively speaking, and I've been waiting for you to get done with Millie. So when you walked in and I didn't smell you before you got here, I automatically assumed it would be Amanda."

Nice story, but not buying it, buddy. "Why was the door open if you were changing?"

"I've noticed that if it's shut, you won't come in. I'm not sure why, but sometimes I think you're afraid to interrupt me."

As I cross my arms over my chest, his eyes fall to my cleavage. He licks his lips, an act that I find enticing and sexy. Sometimes I think he's attracted to me and then other times I think he's a guy and probably horny. But he's right. If the door is shut, I'll go find something else to do and wait for him to open it. I don't want to bother him.

Joshua pushes my hair behind my ear and leans in. "I'm right, aren't I?"

When I don't answer him, he kisses me just below my ear. "Since we woke up, I've wanted to do this," he says in between kisses. My arms fall to my sides, giving him the opportunity to step closer. "I wish you'd open up to me."

"I can't," I cry out as my heart breaks a little bit more.

Joshua stands tall and places his hand on my neck. "Why not?"

Sighing, I look him square in his beautiful brown eyes. "It'll hurt when it's over."

He can't hide the frown that takes over his face. The words I just said hurt, not only me, but him as well. It's the truth and there isn't anything I can do to change it. He's said it from day one. I'm just reminding him that when this is over we go back to reality.

Reality sucks.

"You're right, but in here you're my wife and a wife walks in on her husband changing or when he's looking for a few moments of peace and quiet. A husband probably wants his wife to walk in, come lie in his arms, and pretend that we're not in a house with TV cameras following our every move. I may be an actor, but every now and again I need an escape."

I lean into his hand and fight the urge to kiss his wrist. It'd be so easy to give myself to him, but he doesn't want that. No sex, just kissing. My body is screaming for it, and even though he's not rejecting me, it still feels the same.

"We have a competition." I have to break up the sexual tension in the room. He's usually the first one to pull away, but today it's going to be me. I'm going to be strong enough to resist him.

"We have a game to win," he says as he places both his hands on my cheeks and kisses me full on the lips. His tongue grazes my lips, but before I can open and allow him in, he pulls away.

He wins.

He's always pulling away.

The six of us stand at the back door and wait for it to open. We see what our competition is at the same time so that no one has an unfair strategy. The door opens automatically, giving us each our own vantage point. When I see what's before us, today's outfits make sense. The guys are dressed in board shorts, each a different color, and only Cole and Gary wear T-shirts. My husband, of course, has opted not to put one on; either that or the producers didn't give him one. Amanda, Millie, and I are dressed in board shorts, much shorter than the ones the guys wear, and bikini tops. We color match, with Joshua and I being in Navy blue.

Outside, the backyard has been transformed into a mud pit. The guys rub their hands together when they see this and I can only imagine what is going through their minds right now. Mud wrestling is not something I've ever wanted to try.

Millie and Cole step out first, hand-in-hand. Seeing them together like that brings a smile to my face. There needs to be some blissful happiness in here even if it's not me. Well, it is me because, believe it or not, spending any amount of time with Joshua is worth what I'm doing to myself. When this is all said and done, and we walk out those doors, I have these memories that no one can taint or tell me it was wrong. No one knows the agreement we have, or rather the one he's insisting we have, so technically I can be as free to fall in love with him as much as I want.

Except I want him to fall in love with me, too.

Joshua reaches for my hand and I let him take hold. I welcome the warm tingly feeling I get when he touches me. Just that alone is worth the eventual pain. We walk to where the banner says 'The Wilsons' and all I can envision is our Christmas card, and then the immediate let down that we won't have one. I need to stop dwelling on what I can't change, and focus on something else.

Like making him fall madly in love with me.

"Newlyweds, welcome to the Pit of Doom."

The computer voice trails off, exaggerating the word doom as if it's supposed to scare us. Above us, the skies are blue and the sun is shining. Not exactly something I fear.

"You will enter the Pit of Doom and search for your name. But only one of you out of your pair may enter at any one time. When you find your name, place it on the board and then your spouse may enter. The first couple to retrieve the most names in less than two minutes earns a week in the coveted master suite."

Josh looks at me and smiles. "We can win this." I nod in understanding. He has a game plan, and it's in full effect now. He wanted to wait a week and let everyone settle in before he really started competing.

The bell sounds and I jump in first, shrieking at how cold and gross the mud feels. The mud is knee high and sloppy, making it hard to trudge through.

"Drop down to your knees," Joshua yells and I hate that I didn't think of that because now both Millie and Amanda have done the same thing.

"This is so gross," Amanda whines. I agree, but won't say anything. I'm focused on the task at hand and that is finding my or Josh's name. My fingers bump into something hard and I grab hold of it. The suction from the mud, air, and my arm pulling out is like a vacuum. I yank and free my hand, wiping the mud onto my arm and bingo, *Joshua & Joey Wilson*. I smile at the sight of our names together and hate that the only time I'll see it is in this house or on my annulment papers.

"That's my girl," Joshua yells when I stick the name card up in the air. I try to run using the high knee method. Joshua moves like he's going to help me, but stands back. He has to wait his turn and while I appreciate it, I don't want us to get disqualified. I climb out of the mud pit and run to the board, slapping our name up there and in he goes.

I turn around in time to watch Joshua jump into the mud pit. Millie is out now, but Amanda is still looking. Gary is trying to direct her to locations, but he's unsuccessful. They really ought to work on their teamwork. It's not all that fair to Gary.

Joshua is back in no time, and I'm slightly jealous that he had an easier time than I did. I jump in, drop to my knees, and trudge across the pit. My arms are submerged and my fingers are grabbing at anything and everything possible. The next card I pull out isn't ours and I bury it quickly in the mud. I want to win. I want that master suite because with no cameras maybe I can crack Mr. Wilson. The stolen kisses are nice, but I'm going to test him. I'm going to push his limits. I have years' worth of fantasies to play out in my head. I'm just hoping he's willing.

The next card I pull out is ours and I make my way back to the edge. I'm already breathing hard, but can't give up. I slap the card on the board and glance at the others while Joshua is busy finding another. All three guys are in now, but we're in the lead. Millie is cheering on her husband, while Amanda tries to wipe mud off of her arms. I really hope the viewers are seeing what I am witnessing right now.

"Come on, Josh. You got this, baby."

He looks at me surprisingly, but the grin on his face tells me otherwise. He liked hearing it as much as I liked saying it. He holds his hand up and tries to move as fast as he can to the edge. The countdown has begun over the loud speaker, ten ... nine ... eight ...

"Hurry," all three of us yell at the same time. It doesn't matter because Joshua and I are winning, but the support for your spouse could be a voting boost I suppose. I jump in Joshua's arms after he puts our name up and the timer goes off. He holds me, mud and all, to his body and kisses me.

I pull away quickly and he sets me down. "We won," I say, for lack of a better icebreaker.

Cole and Millie come over and congratulate us, as do Gary and Amanda.

"Well, I guess I know what you guys are doing tonight," Gary adds with a wink. I roll my eyes and deduce that he and Amanda are perfect for each other. She's vain, and he's crass. They complement each other perfectly.

"Come on, let's get cleaned up." Joshua pulls me toward the outside shower, taking it before anyone else can claim it. He pulls the curtain shut and turns on the water.

"One week in the master suite with a king size bed, Jacuzzi tub, and all the food you can eat. Technically we don't have to leave that room for seven days, except for our hospitality comp." Joshua takes the nozzle off the hook and starts running the water over my skin. The warm water feels good after bathing in mud for the past few minutes.

When he bends to get my legs, I use this as the perfect opportunity to shock him. "Millie told me that there's a bowl of condoms in there as well."

Joshua pauses, and I close my eyes. I know he finds me attractive. If he didn't, he wouldn't kiss me ... and he most definitely kisses me. I haven't initiated a kiss since our first night here in the bathroom. It's been all him.

"Sex will complicate things." He turns me around to face the wall and I'm thankful because he can't see the tears welling in my eyes. When his chest presses against my back, I've had enough for the moment.

"I think I'm clean enough to go inside now. The others are waiting." I slide the curtain over and walk away from him, keeping my eyes downcast so I can avoid whoever is looking my way. I don't want them knowing. I don't want them asking me questions that I can't answer. And I definitely don't want Amanda thinking she has a chance with him.

CHAPTER
nine

Joshua

As soon as Joey steps out, I peer over the top of the shower. The only one paying attention to us, or me for that matter is Amanda. I think it's safe to say I'll be adding her to the "watch out for" list when this show is over. I wouldn't mind spending time with these guys outside of here, except for her.

I glance at Joey, where my focus should be. She's facing the dark curtain that blocks us from going inside. I can tell from her posture that she's upset and all I can think is, *How am I going to fix this?* That shouldn't be my thought. I should be thinking about what the viewers are seeing, or what the producers are going to air to slant everything in their favor. They're paid to make the ratings higher, and Joey just set them up with a nice drama-filled segment. I slam my hand against the water dial to shut the water off.

They're purposefully keeping the curtain down and she's playing right into their game plan. This is what they want. And if I didn't know any better, I'd start to think Amanda is working for them.

As I step out, Mille and Cole step forward to take the shower. Gary lingers, not sure if he should walk over to Amanda or not. I remove myself from any plan he has and step in behind Joey, placing my arm around her shoulder. My lips find the crook of her neck and as much as she wants to fight her attraction to me, she can't. Her body sags into mine as we stand there with our backs to the other newlyweds.

"Please don't be angry with me."

"I'm not," she says with a hint of anger and disappointment in her voice.

"You are. I call feel the anger coming off of you in droves."

"It's because they won't open this damn curtain," she mumbles. The telltale click that the curtain is about to raise causes her body to relax.

Taking Joey's hand, I guide her into the house. We bypass the feast that has been set out on the table and go into the bedroom we've been staying in. As I pull the door shut behind me, I notice that our bags have been packed for us. Many thanks to the nice team of producers who have to venture into every aspect of our lives. In this moment, I'm bitter. I need to curb this attitude if we're going to win. What Joey and I are experiencing right now is just a small speed bump.

Joey sits down on the bed and slumps. I'm not even going to try and figure out why without asking, but I don't want to do it here. We need to be in the privacy of the master suite where we can speak freely.

Sitting down next to her, I pull her hand into mine. I never take my eyes off of her when I ask, "What can I do to make you smile?"

She looks down at our joined hands before meeting my eyes. "I wish this were real."

"It is."

"Everyone to the dining room please."

Joey and I both sigh as the computer-generated voice tells us what to do. She rises first without letting go of my hand. She looks down at me as she tugs. In this moment, I want to stand and kiss her into oblivion, but I know if I do, it'll just confuse her.

After we change, we walk out to the dining room where we're greeted with a round of applause. Cole pats me on the back and Millie hands Joey a glass of wine. I faintly hear someone comment that she'll need it. She probably will, but not for what they think. Besides, one would like to think that a man hasn't waited a week to consummate his marriage, but then again we're on a television show and privacy is lacking.

This dinner is too good to be true, just as most things in life are. We'll pay for this later, I'm sure. The guys, me included, lean back in our chairs and rub our bellies. All men do this, it doesn't matter who you are. It's our way of saying thanks to the cook for a well-cooked meal. The women laugh, and pour themselves more wine. This dinner had everything a five-star restaurant would have and more. The food: lobster and shrimp with tender New York Strips and the largest baked potatoes I've ever seen, along with the copious amounts of booze. At least that's how it felt.

I stand and start clearing away the empty beer bottles. Cole and Gary probably finished off a case. I nursed a couple of beers and made it look like I was keeping up with them. The last thing I need is to be drunk right now since it's what landed me here to begin with.

"You guys don't need to clean." It's Mille who speaks, and she winks at me as she passes.

"I think you ought to take your wife to your suite," Gary says, as he puts his hand on my shoulder. He laughs and ends up burping.

Real classy, dude.

I play along and yell out Joey's name. The onslaught of giggles tells me that the whole house has had too much to drink tonight, and I have a feeling I'll be warding off some very welcome, yet dangerous advances from my wife.

Joey comes up to me and our hands find each other right away. She tugs, and I follow. *I should tell her before it's too late that I'll follow her anywhere if she just asks.* That thought pulls me up short, and she snaps back into my arms.

"Sorry," I say, as she stumbles even though I caught her.

Her hand rests on my chest and she gazes into my eyes. I start to lean forward to kiss her, but the oohs and ahs behind us make me stop. Joey must sense this because she steps out of my grasp and pulls us up the stairs toward our suite for the week.

Joey gasps when she opens the door and I peer over her shoulder to see what caught her by surprise. The room is white and red; everything is pristine and crisp with just enough red to set off that romantic vibe. The white comforter is adorned with rose petals that also lead a path to the bathroom where I know the *Jacuzzi* tub is waiting. I shut the door and lock it, giving us our first bit of privacy since we got here.

"I didn't ask Millie what this room was like because I didn't want to spoil the surprise," she says with her back to me.

"They change it for everyone," I add, reminding her that this was done for us based on what the producers have learned about us.

Joey moves around the room with her finger trailing along the furniture. She then disappears into the bathroom.

"The water is hot, we should take a bath," she says when she comes out and faces me.

"Joey—"

She puts her hand up and stops me from denying her. Joey walks toward me with a glint in her eye. I have a feeling I'm going to be in trouble with her this week. "With our suits on, Joshua. I'm not going to ask you to do anything you don't want to do." Her hand finds the waistband of my shorts and pulls me to follow her. "You can give me this, at least."

Each step I take is with the intent on giving her just that. When I step into the bathroom, I see a dressing room off to the side. I remove her hand from my pants and kiss the back of it before disappearing into the room where I change quickly.

I hear splashing and know it's time I step out. I need to be the best husband I can be since I'm shortchanging her in the most important department. Leaning against the doorframe, I watch as she relaxes in the water. Candles are lit and there is some type of perfume smell washing over us. Whatever it is, it's making me feel calm. Her eyes are closed, but there's a smile on her face.

"Are you going to join me?"

Laughing, I push off the doorframe and walk to her. When my hand touches her wet shoulder she opens her eyes. Joey's smile never fades as she moves forward and I step in behind her. The water is warm and inviting, and the moment I submerge, I'm thankful that she invited me to join her. I probably would've been jealous if she hadn't.

Joey leans back into my chest and my hands roam over her arms, massaging as I do. "This feels good," I say, for lack of anything better. I push the button to turn on the jets and Joey starts to laugh. The way her body is moving against me coupled with the vibration of her laugh does things to me that I'm sure she can feel. When she presses against me, I know I have to find a way to curtail this moment, but for the life of me I can't bring myself to move. I can't leave her by herself on what the show calls our honeymoon. That is what the master suite is supposed to represent. If her former fiancé hadn't cheated, she'd already have had a honeymoon.

If he hadn't cheated, I wouldn't be here with her right now. She may be my short-term wife, but even in the few months we'll share it'll be better than that asshole could've ever given her.

I start to massage her neck, and the moan I get in return heads straight for my hard-on. "That feels so good. I think I want to live in this tub. I bet you have one, don't you?"

"Nah, I wish."

"Tell me about your apartment." Joey asking about me means the world to me. No one ever asks. They just assume that they know everything from the countless interviews and articles.

I dip my hands into the water, and when I pull them out I let the water drip off my fingers and onto her arms. I repeat this over and over.

"You know when you watch a movie about a young actor breaking into Hollywood and they show you where they live?"

"Yeah."

"My apartment is nothing like that," I laugh. "Rent in LA is extremely expensive and it seems like it's a waste until I'm ready to buy my own house. My room is barely large enough to fit a queen size bed. I had to buy one of those over the toilet cabinets to keep a few things in because my bathroom is tiny. I don't have a dining room table because I haven't bought one yet, so I eat on the counter. I have a roommate, but you probably already know that."

"How would I know that?"

"Well, I figured with me being your celebrity crush and all."

"You're not my only crush." Her voice is barely above a whisper and I want to ask her not to remind me, but I can't bring myself to say those words. Each second that I'm with her, I find another thing I like about her. Even the most mundane things, like how she brushes her hair fascinates me.

"I live with my parents," she adds, maybe sensing that I'm starting to feel bad for myself. "I wouldn't move in with Tony until after we were married. My room isn't anything on the grand scale, but I do have my own bathroom and my mom cooks dinner every night that requires us to sit down at the table. My mom, she's very proper sometimes."

"Hmm, sounds like I need to move into your house." She freezes momentarily when I blunder. "Anyway, everyone thinks that you're automatically rich when you become an actor and you own all these cars and houses. I'm not there yet, but maybe someday I will be. I have to pay my agent every time I get a movie deal or an endorsement, as well as my lawyer and don't forget the fact that Uncle Sam sure likes his portion, too. I'm investing for a future and not spending every cent I make."

The water starts to turn cold. We need to decide whether to run some more, or get out. I pick up her hand and look at her pruned fingers. "We should get out," I say, but don't move. If she wants to stay like this, I will. We can keep each other warm. I wrap my arms around her and bury my head into the crook of her neck.

"I don't know what it is about you, but I feel like I can tell you anything."

"It's because I'm your wife. It's the law or something," she laughs, and pulls away from me. I feel the loss of her immediately, but it's going to be short lived because I have every intention of holding her while we sleep. I stay in the water while she steps out. The bottom of her swimsuit has risen, showing off her ass cheek. I picture myself biting it as I pleasure her, but that will just have to be a fantasy. Joey disappears into the dressing room and I pull the plug, letting the water drain out of the tub. When she steps out, she's dressed in a black negligee, one I haven't seen yet. It's short and perfect, showing off her sexy, tanned legs. The valley leading to her breasts is inviting me to let my tongue explore. Teasing me about everything I'm missing and denying not only myself, but also the both of us. I swallow hard and start to stand.

She looks at me and shrugs. "All of our clothes have been

washed. I didn't want to dirty up one of your shirts."

I step out of the tub, letting water drip down my legs and onto the floor. My hands find her shoulders and then cup her cheeks. "You can wear whatever of mine you want, Joey." I place a small kiss on her lips. "I'll see you in bed."

I don't wait for her response as I move into the dressing room to change. My brain—the one below my waistband—is screaming at me to forget about the moronic rule I set and take my wife to bed.

CHAPTER
ten

Joey

I hate my life. Okay, not really, but the unfair life I'm leading right now is really starting to depress me. Yeah, sure I'm married to a Hollywood actor, the same one that I've had a massive crush on since he broke out onto the scene. I know there are hundreds, maybe even thousands, of women who would trade places with me in a heartbeat, but what they don't know is what makes my life so unfair right now.

Across the Astroturf lawn is my drop-dead gorgeous husband, shirtless. His body glistens in the sun after he asked me, with batted eyelashes, to rub him down with sunblock. I didn't hesitate as I rubbed my hands over every inch of his skin, trying to memorize all that I could before the moment ended. The contours of his chest and the ridges of his abs still linger on the pads of my fingers. He thanked me with a kiss.

A kiss!

I wanted more. I want more now, and every second that we spend together just increases my desire for him. The hand holding and random kisses are not enough to sustain me for three months. Last night in the bathtub I could feel that he wanted me, so I know attraction isn't the issue. No, the issue is his bullshit rule that we can't be married outside of the house. Does he not see how that makes me feel? I'm on this show to find my forever, like Millie. Not my temporary.

Joshua and I are nothing like Amanda and Gary. We get along and we want to spend time together. Those two are at each other's throats all the time and she can't keep her eyes off of my husband. It's annoying, and even though he and I will be done when the show is over, she doesn't know that.

I try to read the novel in my hands, but my eyes want nothing to do with the words printed on the page. No, they're focused on Josh and the beads of sweat that I imagine are dripping over his well-defined valleys and traveling over his hipbones. The V that every woman desires in her man is like a beacon in mine. I want to mold my body to his so I can feel him pressed against me, just one time.

The gasp next to me causes me to lose focus and look to my left. Thankfully, dark sunglasses cover my eyes and Amanda can't see my eye roll. When is she going to stop gawking at someone that will never belong to her? I shouldn't say that. Maybe Josh and her have a connection that I'm not aware of. I should ask him, but then again I'd really hate knowing she's his type and I'm not. That thought alone drives me deeper into my self-induced-let's-feel-sorry-for-Joey depression. I can't fault her, though. Of all the guys here, she sort of got the short end of the stick. Gary is that guy who didn't grow up around a lot of women. He doesn't know how to act. He's a bit crass and definitely rude, nothing like Joshua and Cole. It's easy to see why he's still single.

Millie comes out with three glasses of wine, handing one to Amanda and I. It's hot and I shouldn't drink, but what the hell? What's the worse that's going to happen?

A lot.

"How was last night?" Millie asks, as she sits down next to me, creating a Joey sandwich with Amanda on my other side. Amanda spins her legs around and faces me. Of course, she wants details. I look at Joshua and wonder how he'd feel if I made up a night of passion or if he'd want me to go with the standard "no comment" that he gives so many times when answering questions about his personal life. If we're not living a life outside the house, what does it matter?

I shrug nonchalantly. "I'm not sure I really want to talk about it. I mean, I didn't ask you, Millie." I decide playing coy is the only way to go. I don't want to lie, and I don't want anyone to know that he just held my hand all night. The less ammunition Amanda has the better, in my opinion.

"Huh," Amanda says before turning back around. "I never thought about that. I guess I wouldn't want you guys asking about Gary and me. I mean, Cole told everyone when he was asked. I suppose we just wait until the next live show."

Great, *she* has to be the voice of reason.

"Yeah true. It's just that Joey is living out a fantasy that we've all had, and I was curious if the hype is there or if he's a complete dud in bed."

I spit out the wine I had just begun to swallow and both of them start patting me on the back. My eyes meet Joshua's, and even from across the yard I can see the concern. I shake my head slightly, hoping he knows that I'm okay and that he doesn't need to come over here. I don't want the others getting a good look at his chest, even though he likes to go around shirtless. I think he does that to drive me nuts, to get my lady bits worked up only to be let down at the end of the night.

He has to know he's hot.

"Joey to the confession room."

I groan at the robot coming over the intercom. This morning we were told that our confession room sessions would start today. It's nice how the show has eased us in, and not thrown everything at us from the get-go, but the confession room is something I can do without. I don't have anything to talk about, and I have a feeling the questions or prompts will be invasive.

As I walk toward the door, Joshua stops me. His hand on my side sends waves of tingles all over my body. I take a deep breath, inhaling his cologne, and muster the strength to look at him. Big mistake. He's already tanning from the sun and his eyes are perfect. Beads of sweat sit on his torso are making me wish I were a towel so I could clean him up.

I need help.

"Remember, the viewers are going to hear this so you want to appease them."

My masked expression must relay enough so I don't have to answer him.

"Just be yourself. We're falling for each other and you want to play into the hands of my fans."

"Right, your fans ... And what? We're falling for each other?" *His fans*? *We're falling for each other*? I don't think anyone, other than myself, is falling anywhere and I'm heading down the *Alice in Wonderland* hole of fictional reality. This man ... I want him to fall for me. I want the fantasy that plays out in reality. I want his fans to know that their heartthrob found love on a reality show. Is that too much to ask?

He smiles his thousand-watt smile that makes me weak in the knees. "Of course, and we just spent our first night together. They're going to want to know. Just be yourself." He kisses me on my forehead and slaps me on the ass, sending me on my way.

When I step into the house, goosebumps rise on my skin. The air conditioner is on full blast and not a single soul is in the house. I hit the thermostat and shut it off. I know I'm not paying the electric bill, but unless we're in here to enjoy the cool air, there's no need to have it on.

The confession room is inviting, which makes it deceiving. The circular sofa is cream colored and littered with every color, shape, and size of pillow known to man. I choose to sit in the middle and on the edge of the cushion and slide my hands under my legs. I don't want to be comfortable.

"Hello, Joey. These questions have been submitted by fans."

The voice is female and still a computer. The producers really keep themselves hidden and void of any emotion when it comes to us. It wouldn't hurt them to just be themselves for once, but I guess that isn't how the game is played.

"Hi," I say in response. I already know I'm not offering up anything without being promoted. I'm not ready to confess, or break down for the viewers.

"You're married to one of Hollywood's rising stars. How does that make you feel?"

Biting my lower lip, I think about how it does make me feel. Special, stupid, lucky, like a failure—the list could really go on and on, but Joshua's voice in my head reminds me of what I'm meant to say.

"I'm blessed," I start with. "I don't look at him like he's Joshua Wilson the actor, but as Joshua Wilson, humanitarian and good person."

"You haven't hidden from Joshua that he's your celebrity crush. Do you feel that with him knowing, it makes things awkward?"

Of course they heard that confession in the bathroom and no doubt aired the audio of the kiss I gave him when I threw myself at him. I thought things would be awkward, though. I thought he'd think of me as a stalker and ask that he be removed from the show. But he didn't.

"No, I think it made things better for us. He doesn't have to worry about what I'm thinking when he talks about work and he gets to know what a fan of his is truly thinking."

"Do you think you'll be able to survive in Hollywood?"

No! I want to scream, but can't. *Stay poised and don't let the questions get to you.* Hollywood has already won where I'm concerned. Because of Hollywood, I won't have my husband, but a piece of paper saying that my once marriage doesn't exist. Although if we have sex, he'd have to divorce me and I'd get to keep his last name and be known as his ex-wife. Sex shouldn't be the answer to everything, but for me it is.

"Hollywood and I will get along just fine as long as it treats Joshua with respect."

"Thank you, Joey."

I can't tell if the camera is switched off or not as I sit and continue to stare at it. I know I should get up and rejoin everyone, but they're going to ask what the confession room is like. I'm the first one to use it and have a feeling I'll be the popular candidate considering Joshua's fan base. Maybe he and I need to sit down and go over the way I answer the questions. Make sure they're on point and acceptable to him.

My mind is made up when I hear Gary being summoned to the confession room. The last thing I want is to be caught in this room with Gary. The door opens as I stand. He smiles and my insides cringe. He's nice enough, but there's something about him that rubs me the wrong way.

"Your husband is a nice man."

I look at him questioningly. "Um, thank you?"

He nods and pulls his shirt up to rub his forehead. I turn away, not willing to even see what he has under there.

"He's helping me get in shape so I can win Amanda over, maybe get her to fall in love with me."

His words not only break me but also make my heart swell with pride. Of course Joshua would find a way to do something worthwhile in the house.

"Listen to him," I offer as advice when I pass by. "He may be onto something." I give him a soft smile, hoping to show him that I agree with him working with Joshua.

I walk outside and let the sun beat down on my face. Being on a studio lot, I give credit to the set designers and how they make sure we still get our daily dose of vitamin D. Even in the world of reality television, if it's raining we can go out and dance in the rain. I've never been kissed in the rain ...

Music is blaring while Joshua and Cole workout. Amanda is sunbathing and Millie is lounging on the outdoor couch with her hair piled on top of her head and her eyes covered in huge Liz Taylor sunglasses. I sit in the spot that gives me the best angle to stare at Josh. With his shirt off, each time he lifts his arms I can faintly see the muscles in his back move.

I sigh heavily when Josh bends over, earning a righteous laugh from Millie. I look away, knowing that if I keep staring he's going to catch me.

"God, you guys must have had some crazy monkey sex."

I can't help but laugh when she says that. In my head, yes, we're all over the place: bed, wall, dresser, bathroom counter, shower, stairs, couch, and kitchen chair. Any surface, really, and I can picture myself succumbing to his needs. Or mine, it doesn't matter really. I'm jealous of Millie and her relationship with Cole. It seems like they have the same connection as Josh and me, but they're getting the good stuff. Oh yeah, that makes me sound like a slut, but when you have man candy like Joshua Wilson kissing you, touching you, you tend to want to lose yourself and I so want to get lost in him, repeatedly.

"I need a drink," I say, changing the subject. I can't talk about the lack of sex we have. For one, we're always being recorded for those lovely *"hey look at what Joey did on Married Blind"* recaps. And two, admitting it out loud really stings. I said it in the shower and it hurt to say those words.

"Oh drinks would be fun." Millie stands, adjusting her suit before she turns to Amanda. "Wanna cocktail?"

"Did someone say drinks?" Gary asks as he steps out

into the yard, almost colliding with Millie. Beaming at him, Millie nods her head as she moves past him and into the house. I watch as Amanda walks toward Gary; she pauses and lifts her sunglasses to the top of her head. If I'm not mistaken, the shining smile she's giving him tells me that she maybe falling for him after all. Of course, it shouldn't have taken Josh's help, but whatever.

"Guys, I have chips, dip, and booze," Millie yells, getting Joshua and Cole's attention. I'm not sure what man would turn down chips or booze, so to watch them actually jog over here is comical. And to think, all I said is that I needed a drink.

"We should play N*ever Have I Ever*," Amanda suggests, and my stomach turns instantly. Depending on the questions I may have to lie. Like if Amanda were to say "never have I ever had sex with a celebrity?" The answer is no, but I can't tell anyone that. Amanda would ruin me. Her talons would come out and she'd scratch her way to my man.

"Sounds fun," Gary replies as he sits down next to her and I want to gouge his eyes out because no, this isn't fun.

Joshua sets up six red cups as our shot glasses and pours tequila in each of them. Cole slices enough lime to get us stared. I'm thankful to whatever producer makes sure we have ample booze on hand because I'm going to need it to get through this game. I have a feeling I'm going to be the winner.

Once the cups are ready, Joshua sits back, putting his arm around me. I take advantage and lean in. I mean, why the hell not, right? He's my husband so I should be entitled to touch him whenever I want. If someone would give him the memo on the rules of being married, I'd be forever in their debt.

Amanda perches on the edge of the couch, pushing her boobs out for Josh and Cole to see. I glance quickly at Josh to see where he's looking and I'm met with a piercing stare.

If I didn't know better I'd say he's happy to be sitting next to me, but I do know better. He's content and simply playing the game.

"Never have I ever ..." Amanda looks at all of us, pushing her blonde hair off her shoulders before shrugging in her attempt to be cute. It's not working for me, but maybe it does for Gary. "Touched my own boobs," she giggles but drinks, defeating the purpose of getting others drunk first.

"Stupid, that's what self-breast exams are." I lean over and lick the top of my hand and add the salt, slam my drink, and put the lime between my lips. "I hate this game already," I mumble as the tequila burns my throat.

"My turn," Millie says with far too much excitement. "Never have I ever been to a strip club." She drinks, much to my shock, and gives a little shrug. "What? I'm a police officer, it's a job hazard."

"Okay." Joshua and me are the only ones that don't drink. "I'm happy you're with me on that one," I tell him as he suddenly downs his shot.

"My turn," I blurt out, needing a break. I'm not a lightweight, but I haven't eaten and I'm afraid that it won't take long to turn me into a touchy feely unwanted wife. "Never have I ever had sex in public." Only Amanda drinks, giving us all a break.

"Never, huh?" Joshua whispers to me. I shake my head and keep my eyes locked on anywhere but him.

"Never have I ever been arrested," Joshua says, and this time it is just Gary who drinks.

"Do tell," Cole blurts out.

Gary blushes but tells that one night in college he was dared to go streaking and ran in front of a police officer. Millie tells us she's had to arrest a streaker before and it's not fun.

"Never have I ever had drunken sex," Cole says as he sits back, smiles, and watches the rest of us pound our shots.

And here I thought I was the prude one in the group, but even I've done that.

Our game continues and turns fun. I'm up to seven shots, or maybe eight. My tongue is numb and my speech is somewhat sideways, not slurred, but I'm actually enjoying myself. Joshua's hands have been roaming from my shoulder to my ear. His fingers play in my hair before he removes his arm and rests his hand on my bare thigh. His lips have touched my shoulder, my ear, and the back of my hand. He's killing me slowly, but it's worth it. It's worth having the memories of what I could've had if he didn't insist on living by his stupid rules.

"We should go to bed," he whispers as his lips move from my ear to my neck. He doesn't have to ask me twice.

I stand abruptly and announce that I've had enough. The fact that Josh laughs doesn't help because the snide comments start from Cole and Gary. I want to yell out "be jealous, bitches," but there really isn't anything to be jealous of. We'll kiss, he'll tell me no, but hold me while I sleep and fight the tears.

As soon as we're back inside the house, firm hands catch my hips and guide me toward the master suite. Joshua's chest is pressed to my back as we walk awkwardly to our room. I could stop and ask him what's going on, but the anticipation I'm feeling needs to be explored. I'm going to make a move once we're behind the closed door.

I open the door and he slams it shut. A smile creeps across my face when I hear the lock slide into place. Turning to face him, I rake my eyes over his body. I step closer, bridging the gap between us, and trail my fingers over his skin. A slight giggle escapes when I see him react.

"Joey." His voice is quiet, sexy.

My fingers find their way into his hair and his eyes close. Yes, the attraction is definitely there, he just needs to act on it. I wet my lips and place them on his chest, moving my way to his ear. "You're my husband. I'm entitled," I whisper as I tug lightly on his earlobe.

Joshua's hands grip my hips as he growls. If that's meant to discourage me, it's not. I kiss along his jaw to his other ear where I flick my tongue and his hands respond by pulling me closer. His hand slides up my back until his fingertips are touching the clasp of my bikini.

My head is screaming, *Yes, yes, yes. I'm winning.*

I'm afraid to pull away and look into his eyes. I don't want to see hesitation or regret. I trail my nose along his cheek and when my lips are in perfect position, I make my move. He has two options: let me kiss him like I did before, or push me away.

He chooses the former and plunges his tongue deep into my mouth, giving me what I'm asking for. I grip his hair tighter and grind my body against his. I'm pulled against him when he cups my ass earning a righteous moan. Joshua moves us toward the bed and I have to keep myself from pulling away and fist pumping out of happiness.

Everything about Joshua is just how I fantasized it would be. We don't plop on the bed, but glide down gently. He never lets go and our mouths continue to work against each other. Part of me wishes this were being televised so his fans could see that he's serious about me, but the other part is thankful this is being done in private so when he rejects me, only he can see my disappointment.

Joshua grinds his hips into mine making me gasp. He uses this moment to break away and lavish me with the most sensual kisses I have ever experienced. His hips move against mine as we rock into each other. My back arches when his tongue licks along the swell of my breasts. The tie of my bikini top falls away, the cool air making my nipples pucker. My hand moves the waistband of his shorts, pushing inside. He moans and I take that as a green light to continue. My hand moves up and down his shaft as my body teeters between reality and a stupid wet dream. In every fantasy I've had, we've done this, except we weren't drunk.

Drunk.

"Joshua," I say breathlessly as his tongue moves in and out of my mouth.

"I know. I want this, too."

Before I can come up with a coherent rebuttal, Joshua is pulling my bikini bottoms off and tearing open one of the thousand colorful condoms sitting on the nightstand, and as much as I want to gawk at his body, I can't. I'm afraid that this is just another moment in the insanity that lives in my head.

Married Blind

[Roll intro]

"I'm Patrick Jonas, and welcome to another episode of *Married Blind*."

[Theme music plays]

"It's time to crown another master couple this week and check in with our reigning couple. This week, the couples will compete for their first luxury competition. Tonight one lucky couple will win a date out, away from the other newlyweds. We'll find out more after this commercial break."

[Stagehands enter the house and adjust the microphones of the contestants]

[Break over]

[Audience applause]

"Welcome back. Now let's check in with our houseguests and see how their relationships are developing. I know I'm a little curious to talk to Joshua and Joey."

[Audience oohs]

"And find out just how things are shaping up for Cole and Millie and Gary and Amanda. I think it's time for Gary and Amanda to make a splash, don't you?"

[Audience cheers]

"I have a feeling they're playing it safe, but is there a need to?"

[Switch to the live feed]

"Hello, newlyweds."

[All respond]

"Well, the first thing the viewers want to know; Joshua and Joey, how is married life?"

CHAPTER
eleven

Joshua

I look at Joey, sitting next to me like a doting wife. When I woke up this morning … well, let's just say I was very confused. She was sound asleep on the couch and I was buck ass naked except for my … and he was snuggled up with a blue raincoat that was sticking to my leg. After a painful attempt to remove the sleeve, in which I lost a few leg hairs in the process, I hopped into the shower and tried to remember the activities from the night before. I want to say everything came flooding back to me as soon as the water hit my face, but only red cups, laughter, and a bottle of tequila gave me a glimpse of what we did. One thing is for certain— Joey and I had sex last night and now that awkward "is he going to remember" moment is happening.

Joey is cool as a cucumber and if I didn't know any better I'd say she's done this a million times. I'm supposed to be the actor, not her, and yet here she is poised and ready to take on the most invasive question possible in front of a live audience. I'm not sure what she's going to say. I mean, we had sex last night and even though I don't remember it, I felt pretty damn good when I woke-up this morning and I have no doubt that's because of her. I hate that we had to be drunk for it to happen, but my subconscious knew what I wasn't willing to admit. I want her. I just can't have her. Not like this and not in this house where our lives are dictated by time slots and ratings.

"Married life isn't what I thought it would be." She looks at me and shrugs. My stomach bottoms out with dread. "I mean, Joshua cleans up after himself, does his own laundry, and makes his own food. Aside from the ring on my finger …." Joey pauses and holds her hand out. My eyes close, I don't know what she's going to say, but it isn't going to be pretty or in my favor. "Well, let's just say things are different."

I'm suddenly angry and I don't know why. What the hell kind of questions are these and why is she being so coy? Patrick Jonas chuckles and for some reason I want to reach through the television and strangle him. My anger, for what it's worth, should be focused on Joey for not following our plan … my plan. I need to talk to her about last night and find out just how things got out of control. I know we were both drinking, but I didn't think she was that drunk and by all accounts she and I shouldn't have had sex, but we did and I think I liked it. No, I know I did because I have the urge to pick her up and carry her away so we can do it again, but this time sober. I want to know exactly what she feels like pressed against my body without the cloud of tequila being in the way. What happened last night or early this morning can't happen again.

"Are you saying that Joshua Wilson is a diva?"

Joey blanches, but recovers quickly, yet another feature that would do well in Hollywood. I don't know why I can find all these amazing things about her, but not give in. Apparently only my brain is the logical one since my dick has a mind of its own.

"Absolutely not. My husband is very kind and I'm a lucky woman for all the reasons I listed above." Joey glances over and smiles; her eyes light up and everything seems happy. When Patrick starts talking, her face tells a different story. She's acting, and I just bought it, just like I've been asking her to buy into my bullshit. Oh God, what did I do to her last night? I need this segment to be over so we can talk. It's the dreaded "this shouldn't have happened" talk that I never pictured myself having with her. She's going to be hurt and probably kick me in the nuts, and I deserve that, but I was drunk and the fact that I only remember bits and pieces of the night does not bode well for me. I can't even tell her that I enjoyed myself. I mean … it looks like I did and my body feels great, but I just can't remember.

"Gary, Joshua has taken you under his wing of sorts. How are you feeling with your new workout?"

All eyes are on Gary, and the man he was a few days ago is not the man sitting here now. He's taken my advice and is doing everything he can. I haven't seen him pick up a beer in a week and he's been pushing himself with training.

Gary smiles and he should be. He looks at Amanda, who has a small lift to her lip. There has been no mistaking her attitude toward him, but she seems to be warming her icy stance on them being a couple.

Amanda is much like me. She's just a bitch about it. I have my reasons for keeping Joey at arm's length. It's better for both of us if I do it this way.

"Josh and Cole have been a great support system and I do believe my wife is enjoying the fruits of my labor." Gary runs his hand down his chest and over his stomach, a slimmer one at that, but still a bit portly. Amanda blushes and the audience does their usual prompted oohs and aahs.

Cole starts clapping and I join in. Any confidence that we can give him is a boost. I meet a lot of people in my line of work and know that even the slightest amount of confidence can make someone feel as if they matter.

"Okay, newlyweds, you've been in the house a few weeks now, what do you miss the most about the outside world?"

"I actually miss my job," Millie answers first.

I don't. I'm happy for the vacation, but am afraid of what my bank account will look like when I'm out of here. I'm going to need to book back-to-back jobs just to catch up. I already have one set up in Alabama starting a week after we finish our press tour. That is going to be a good excuse as to why Joey and I can't work out once we're done with the game. We'd never see each other, and she needs a man who is going to worship her and be everything to her that I can't. I want to kick my own ass for thinking of such a lame ass excuse, but it's the best I got right now.

"Privacy," Joey says.

"Starbucks," Amanda adds.

"What about the guys?" Patrick asks.

"I miss my gym," I answer.

"My computer," Gary says.

I want to add his porn channels, but don't.

We all turn to look at Cole, who is staring at Millie. It confuses me as to why he's looking at her when the question is about what we all miss from the outside world. Millie whispers something and he smiles. A gesture that pains my heart a little, reminding me that I could have something similar with Joey if I weren't so damn stubborn.

"I miss the ability to take my wife on a date."

We can hear the audience members as they all audibly sigh and with one sentence he's put him and Millie in the lead. He's smooth; I'll give him that. And now I need to up my game. I can't have him stealing votes from my fans. The producers make sure we can hear the audience and their elation.

"Well, Cole, now that you've said that I'll tell you what your next competition is. Newlyweds, tonight is game night.

Outside you'll find three booths, and a trivia board. Up for grabs to the couple who gets the most questions right is: date night! Your competition begins in five minutes."

I quickly take Joey's hand in mine and all but drag her to the backyard. She and I need this date night so we can have some privacy to discuss what happened in our room last night. Short of getting into the shower with her—which I don't think is a very good idea right now—this will be our only option. Our booth is yellow. I hate yellow. My funk needs to change or we're going to lose this battle.

As soon as we're all in our respective booths, the questions start. The idea of the game is to be the first to answer, but we won't know if we've got the question right until the end. We have to be fast and efficient. I step in behind Joey and cage her in with my arms. I half expect her to step away from me, but she doesn't. Yet another reason why she's perfect. Despite her being on the couch this morning, she's showing the viewers that we're solid. But the whole couch thing confuses me and I need to ask her why she was there. Hopefully I didn't do a dickhead move and kick her out of the bed or something.

"Do want me to read the questions?"

"Yeah, babe, that works."

Joey turns her head slightly, but doesn't say anything about my slip and it makes me wonder what else I called her in the heat of the moment. The first question pops up:

What is the Invasion of Normandy also known as?

"D-Day," I whisper into her ear, not even looking at the options available to us.

What's the northernmost city in the contiguous United States?

"It has to be in Maine," I say when the options pop up.

"Are you sure?" she asks, hesitating.

"Positive."

Joey presses the button and we wait for the next question. The fact that the question is still on the board means that someone hasn't answered. I want to win, but I don't. I want to give her a date she'll never forget, but leaving the sanctuary of the house scares the shit out of me.

In which three cities can you find 'Sea World'?

This time there isn't any multiple-choice answer to pick from. Joey looks at me mouthing two of the three, but I'm not sure what the last one is. The clock ticks down as I shake my head. "Just press something because I don't know."

Her face falls and I know she's thinking that we just lost. She wanted to leave the house, too, not that I can blame her.

What does croquis painting mean?

"This is easy," she says as she presses the button. I don't have a clue as to what she just answered though.

"What's the answer?"

"To draw or paint a naked model." Her answer is so nonchalant that I need to know more.

"How do you know that?"

Joey shrugs. "I may have done some modeling early in college."

My mouth hangs open, completely dumbfounded by her admission. Joey steps back, getting my attention. Only she doesn't need to, she has it all. My eyes travel down her back and over her ass as images of her naked filter through my mind. I know I'm not doing her body justice. And damn if I don't want to try my hand at painting later.

"Do you know this one?" she hisses, shaking me from my daydream. I squint at the screen, even though I don't need to, and look at the question.

What actor plays Professor Charles Xavier in X-Men?

I press the button for Patrick Stewart and give her a 'what the hell' look. "You haven't seen X-Men?"

She shakes her head. I mean it's not the end of the world, but most women I know have the movies because of all the "eye-candy" as they call us men. Objectifying us every chance they get.

"Wow, I'm shocked."

"Don't be. My ex doesn't like sci-fi."

"Yeah well you're married to me now, aren't you?" Word vomit is what I'm suffering from. Joey stiffens and I know I've set her off again. I need duct-tape for my mouth.

"This is our last question," she reminds me. At this point I don't think we have a chance, but whatever.

What does RB stand for in football?

Joey pushes the button so fast I don't have time to finish reading the question. "Do you think we got that one right?"

"I know we did," she says confidently. I wish she'd turn around and look at me, but I'm getting the cold shoulder. The very cold one I deserve. Finding a way to fix my mistake isn't going to be easy. Joey wants what I can't give her even though I want to. I was never supposed to fall in love with her, or anyone for that matter.

Why'd she have to be so damn perfect?

"Newlyweds, it was close," Patrick starts. Right now I only want to win so we can have some privacy to talk. We have one more night in the master suite until our competition tomorrow, so I could man up and talk to her tonight. Or I can chicken out and hide downstairs with Gary and Cole until I know she's asleep.

"You're all separated by a few seconds. In third, Josh and Joey."

"Shit," I mumble. "It had to be that Sea World question."

Joey nods, not looking at me.

"And tonight's winner … Cole and Millie!"

"That was rigged," I say as they jump up and down, while the rest of us clap with little enthusiasm. Joey sidesteps me and goes to congratulate the winners. I tag behind her, with my tail between my legs, and wish them luck. Before Joey can escape, I grab her hand and pull her into the house and up our suite.

"We need to talk about last night," I say as soon as I shut

the door. I look around our room for any evidence that we got a bit freaky, you know with a painting hanging sideways or random contents on the floor. The floor … I look around the bed for the condom wrapper, but don't see one. Did she clean up after me?

"Josh, we got drunk and played a game. Games like that tend to teach you a little more about your friends."

"Joey, we had sex. Sex isn't a game. I took advantage of you, so if you want to hit me or yell at me, I can take it." I spread my arms out wide and close my eyes. When I don't feel the pounding on my chest, I peek out of one eye to find her staring at me confusingly. "What?"

Joey's arms are crossed over her chest and her lip is jutted out. If I didn't know any better, I'd say she's pissed.

"I don't want to hit you."

"Why not?" I ask, knowing full well that I deserve it for taking advantage of her. I know how she feels about me and should've never put her in this situation.

"We didn't have sex."

"Um … yes we did," I rebut her claim. She doesn't have to pretend like it didn't happen.

"No, we didn't," she says matter-of-factly.

I step forward and place my hands on her shoulders. "Joey, we did and I must've said something stupid to you because you ended up sleeping on the couch. What can I do to fix this? I don't want you to be mad at me."

Her eyebrow rises and there's a slight smirk creeping across her face. There's nothing but mystic and danger in her eyes. Whatever she's thinking, I have a feeling I'm not going to be able to say no.

Joey sets her hands my cheeks. "Joshua, you and I didn't have sex last night. When I came out of the shower, you were spread out like a five-point star and I couldn't move you so I slept on the couch."

"Joey, you don't have to pretend." I try to sound confident, self-assured. Maybe she doesn't remember, or she does and this is her way of telling me it was horrible.

"You're cute when you're flustered, but honestly, we didn't have sex so stop trying to say we did because I'm getting upset."

Joey starts to step away, but I grab her quickly and pull her back to me. I search for any sign that she's lying, but I'm unable to tell.

"I'm sorry, what can I do to make it better?"

"Kiss me."

"Kiss you?" I question.

"Kiss me like you mean it. Kiss me like I'm the only one in the world that makes you smile." Joey falls back into my arms. "Kiss me like I'm the one you want to spend the rest of your life with." She's now chest to chest with me and the sexual tension is heavy. Joey licks her lips and my eyes watch the slow motion of her tongue.

"Ah hell," I say before pulling her into my arms and crashing my lips against hers. I know we had sex last night, and that's a game changer. I just have to figure out why she's so hell bent on telling me we didn't. Everything with her is now intensified and turning her away from this point on is going to be extremely difficult. Maybe she knows this, or maybe this is just part of her game plan. Either way, I'm screwed. I'm done for. Joey Freaking Wilson officially owns me.

CHAPTER
twelve

Joey

In the past two weeks, I want to say that things with Joshua have stilled. That we don't talk unless the cameras are on. We don't kiss, touch, or make ridiculous eyes at each other. That would all be a lie. Everything changed after we had sex. While he sometimes initiates contact, he holds back a lot. I don't know if it's because he's unsure and now questioning his feelings or what. What I do know is he makes my knees weak, my stomach flip-flop, and my skin tingle. He gives me a headache, makes my heartbreak, and my imagination plots ways to cause him harm. I want to tell him what he knows, but saying the words out loud to him can only have one reaction—it was a mistake. I'd rather pretend that we didn't have sex than to hear those words tumble off his lips. There isn't any amount of kissing or subtle touches that would put my heart back together after that.

I love him, but won't admit it to anyone or say the words out loud. Saying them out loud makes everything seem real. I can barely admit it to myself on most days because I'm not sure if it's genuine love, or if it's the built up infatuation I've had with him for so many years. Either way, when he's in the room my senses are heightened, and after our drunken sexcapades, everything is off the charts crazy.

I finally feel like I fit in with the others in the house. Amanda's icy cold demeanor has changed to tepid. Not a great improvement, but better than nothing. Once Gary started to physically change, so did her attitude. I have to give him credit; he's worked out and watched what he's eaten all to impress her. I'm not sure that's something I would've done for someone, but he's proven that she's important to him. Amanda also curbed her wandering eyes for Josh and for that I'm thankful. Now she's taken to actually eyeing her husband, and I know he appreciates it. Josh says Gary gossips like a high school girl and I told Josh that there are some things I just don't want to know.

My husband is the one I want to be my everything, my whole world and every other clichéd analogy I can come up with. Every time I think about him and me outside of the house, my heart dies a little bit. Once we're off this studio lot, I'll never see him again unless I go completely fangirl and camp out at a premiere for a chance photo from behind the barricade.

If I have to be a fangirl, so be it.

I can't imagine being *that* girl, but who knows. Would he treat me like a fan? Sign my poster, pose for a selfie and move on? Or would he have his security team come get me and have me walk the carpet as his cordial ex-wife. With an annulment I won't be an ex, it'll be as if our marriage never happened. I can change that by telling him we had sex, but the outcome isn't favorable. Neither is being erased from history, and only having proof of our marriage available online or during next season's show, reminding viewers of what happened in this season. Dwelling on what's going to happen in two months will get me nowhere, fast. Taking life by the horns is what I need to do. That and meditate, and possibly walk around in my bikini more. I could bake a cake. Cake is always good.

The house is boring. We eat, sleep, lie in the sun, and go swimming. Twice a week we have competitions and once a day we go into the confession room and air our dirty laundry. Joshua says the best is yet to come, but I don't see how. He kindly reminds me that I'm not a fan of the show and that I can never let my guard down because at any moment they can change the way the game is played. He says I'm unprepared. I say he's too worried about winning. The only exciting thing that has happened lately is we named the computer monotone voice that comes on and tells us what to do. Her name is Linda, courtesy of Gary and him telling "her" to shut up because she reminds him of her mother. The name stuck even with Amanda mumbling something to the effect of how she's not so eager to meet his mother now.

That's something I envy about Millie and Amanda—they're going to meet their in-laws, not that I'd expect Josh to introduce me to his parents, but I'd like for him to meet mine. My parents would like him, and not because of who he is or what he does, but because of what he means to me. They won't, however, be entirely thrilled to find out about my impending annulment and I'm sure my mother will find some way to sue the show for fraud and whatnot. My mother loves to stir the pot, create drama where there doesn't need to be any. If she had thought about it, she would have sued McDonald's first for the "hot" coffee, but thankfully she missed the boat on that one.

Josh nestles in behind me, his arm resting on my stomach. From the outside we look like we're in love. He stands with me, holds my hand, and steals kisses. When I go to bed, he follows. When I take too long in the bathroom before going to sleep, I'm always rewarded with his sexy ass in bed, reading a book. I like to take as long as possible just so

I can burn that vision into my memory for the future. Most nights follow the same routine. If he's reading, he watches me cross the room all while closing the book and setting it somewhere near the nightstand. He pulls the blankets back for me and beckons for me to crawl into his arms. We'll make out until things get heavy and then he finds a way to get me onto my side so he can hold me.

This could be our last night in the red room, or the beginning of another week. It's his favorite. Not once have we spent a week in the other room. When we have to switch he runs and puts our bags down before Gary or Cole can do it. It's childish, and I love it. I want to be in the room where it all started.

It's competition day. Today will be different from the others. Technically, today is our one-month anniversary, according to Linda, who keeps us apprised of information like this. Being without television, our cells phone, and the Internet has been tough, but it's also been a blessing. I like the solitude that comes with being tech free, and I enjoy the time that we've all been able to get to know each other without the incessant ringing of a phone. Besides, I honestly don't want to know what people are saying about me being Josh's wife, or how the media is portraying Jules Maxwell, his ex. I don't want to know if they feel sorry for her.

Today's competition will be for a luxury item and master suite. You can win both, one, or nothing. I just want to win the master suite. The luxury items won't do me very well. I mean, what am I going to do with a designer kitchen?

My fingers move along his arm, gliding up and down in a rhythmic pattern. Josh pulls me closer, kissing me just behind my ear. "Why are you awake?"

I shrug and try to move even closer to him, earning a groan. I know what I'm doing, and have no doubt that he knows as well. "It's competition day, they make me nervous."

"Why? We can beat them."

"It's not all about winning. They're stressful. I hate that they're live and people can see us mess up or they will read into an expression we give each other. I feel like I have to be 'on' all the time. What if I want to drop the f-bomb or something?"

Joshua laughs, his chest vibrating against my back. "You saying fuck would be hilarious and the producers would probably let it go through if we weren't delayed a few seconds. Lord knows Amanda cusses like a sailor."

He sits up on his elbow and moves my face over enough to see him. "There's a team of people in this tiny room monitoring everything during the live network show. Only the people who pay for *After Midnight* get to hear your pretty little mouth swear."

"I don't swear."

"You fib. I've heard you in the bathroom." He pushes the hair that has fallen out of my ponytail away from my face. "When you think no one can hear you, I can."

I adjust slightly and stare down at my stalker. "Why are you lurking near my shower stall?"

Joshua blinks a few times as if he's clearing something from his eyes. He knows he's said something that he can't back out of now, and I'm not going to let him.

"Tell me," I plead with my hand resting on his cheek. I want him to trust me. Trust us. Day by day I work to take down his walls and I can see them crumble. He just needs to let me in. "It's just you and me in this room, whisper it to me."

When he leans forward, his stubble tickles my cheek. "Sometimes, I think about joining you," he whispers just before pulling my earlobe into his mouth.

"Newlyweds, please go to the backyard." Linda's annoying voice echoes throughout, killing the moment we were about to share. Joshua jumps up, leaving me shocked and speechless, and unable to get a better answer or even respond. Right now, I want to drag him into the shower and see just how serious he was.

Our room is quiet, even with him in the corner getting his team clothes on for the day. The old me would avoid the elephant in the room, brush it under the rug, but not this Joey. When this game is over, I want him to remember me as a formidable companion and teammate. He needs to remember that I didn't back down from any challenge or task put in front of me by him or this game.

"We'll talk about what you just told me later," I say, as I get out of bed and grab my clothes. Leaving the room is the last thing I want to do, but I need to let my words to seep in. "Let's go win. We need that master suite." I fight every urge I have to look back and see his expression.

As I enter the bathroom common area, giggling rings out from the stall. Millie steps in just after me and we both cover our mouths to stifle our own laughter.

"Oh my God," I mouth as we make our way to the faucets. I quickly brush my teeth and run a comb through my hair, pulling it back up into a ponytail. If I've learned anything about this game, it's not to take a shower until your comps are done for the day. Chances are they'll include something gross and you'll just end up in the shower again.

Stepping into a stall, I quickly change. I'm not shy about changing in front of her or Amanda, but with Gary in here there's no way. Even with him and Amanda connecting, he still gives me a funky vibe. When I smack my head against the sidewall I make a mental note to knock Josh silly for having me vacate our room to change. Although, if I bring it up with him, he'll remind me that I'm the one who left and that he never asked me to. He's too literal sometimes.

"Newlyweds, your game begins in three minutes."

Linda starts a countdown and I'm curious if this is for Amanda and Gary's benefit. When I step out, Joshua is leaning against the counter with his ankles crossed. His arms are folded across his chest causing his biceps to bugle out. The white tank top he's wearing makes me pray for a water competition today. I have two options: ignore him, or go to him and put this morning's comment aside.

The choice is easy. I step up to him and place a firm and lingering kiss on his lips, allowing my hands to trail over his muscles. His skin prickles from my touch and the inner goddess in me is doing a freaking cheer because of this reaction. He responds by gripping my hips, keeping me in place.

"Let's go win us the master," I murmur against his lips. He smiles and slides his right hand into mine. I leave my clothes on the bathroom floor, knowing it's tacky, but in my mind I'm getting some time with Josh that I really need right now.

We step out into the game ready backyard and I groan. Before us looms a monstrosity of hell. I survey the course and am thankful I chose not to shower yet. We have to slide down what looks like oil, fall into a pit of flour, and army crawl through honey. *Oh this ought to be so much fun.* Millie is going to kick all of our butts. Her police training has prepared her for this course. As I look at Josh to convey my worry, his response is to flex and kiss each bicep.

Freaking men!

Amanda and Millie step out, followed by Gary and Cole. The guys instantly start talking about oil and honey. The three of us roll our eyes and I pray this won't be what I think it is or what the guys want it to be. They seem to be forgetting that there is flour involved and it'll be in places they don't want to think about.

"You men are so transparent," Amanda says, with her arms crossed. For the first time in the show, I agree with her.

"Newlyweds, today you'll be vying not only for master suite, but also for a new hot tub!" Patrick Jonas is too excited for this competition. I know it's his job, but even he should feel a little remorse for us.

Everyone claps, but me. I don't need or want a hot tub. Where would I put it? In that imaginary house that Joshua and I are going to share in Barbieland?

"This is how the game works. You'll each climb to the top of the slide, with one spouse going first. You'll slide down and enter the pit, each of you looking for a letter. Once you have a letter, you'll crawl through the honey and take your letter to your board. Once the letter is placed on your board, your spouse may start their turn. The object of the game is to spell the longest word possible."

"Do you want to go first?" I ask as we make our way to the top of the slide.

"Yeah, sure," he replies. "Do you know what word we want to spell?"

I shake my head, not having the foggiest idea. "Let's just gather a few and see what we can come up with. We'll have to be smart about letter picking after that."

"I agree."

The countdown begins and Josh, Gary, and Millie are lined up on the line to start. All I can think as Joshua slides down is, *Wow, my man in oil, who knew?*

CHAPTER
thirteen

Joshua

Who is the sick bastard behind this competition? Give me oil and a hot babe, preferably the one I'm married to, any day. But when you throw in flour and honey, it's just a flat out mess. Don't get me wrong, watching Joey roll around in anything is a sight to see, but the fact that she looks like a stay puft marshmallow is a slight turn off. I know that's not saying much considering I look the same, but all men fantasize about watching their girl get all oiled up. It's just a total buzzkill when she face-plants in a pool of flour.

Joey and I are working well as a team. After three letters we agreed to go all out and spell 'happiness'. It was her idea, and I quickly agreed. She's clearly the brains of our operation since she was able to come up with our word with the letters a-p-n.

We look like crap. Our hair is matted and our bodies have this caked on composite that is meant to slow us down. My shoes are ruined, as I wasn't smart enough to take mine off like she was. This has been the worst competition to date by far. I trudge out of the vat of honey and slowly make my way to the board. Joey is already in the flour looking for our next letter. The longer it takes, the harder it is to move. The shower beckons me and I don't care if I drag this crap through the house, I'm not waiting for the outside one to become free. I feel gross and things are sticking to places they shouldn't be.

I make my way toward the stairs; each step seems to be slower than the last. As soon as Joey is at the board I look quickly to see what letters we need before climbing up the steps. We only need two more.

"This sucks," Cole mumbles as he tries to knock the goop off his hand.

"I know."

"Can't we just forfeit?"

I shake my head. "It's for the master suite. Someone has to win the room."

"I don't even care. We can just screw in the shower," he mutters as he leans against the makeshift wall. I don't want to think about him and Millie in the shower because one, it makes me jealous that I'm not doing that with Joey and two, I'm absolutely desperate for a shower.

"Here goes nothing." Sitting down on the slide I push off. Flour flies up into my mouth, making me gag. You'd think by now we'd have all the flour on our bodies, but it's procreating like magic. It seems like each time I get down here there's more and more white crap to make my life miserable.

The first letter I find is one we don't need, but it sticks to my hand. I shake it loose, only to have it fly and hit Cole in the back of his head.

"Sorry, man," I say as I move the flour around more, getting on my knees to search the bottom. I find another letter, an "F", and quickly look at the board. I've forgotten what I need. Joey is standing off to the side watching and if I could see clearly, I'd probably be able to see if she's angry and telling me to hurry up. I can't even hear well right now; my ears are clogged up full of crap. I reach down again and find another letter quickly. I pray that this is something I need because I have to get out of here.

My arm moves slowly, the flour fighting with the oil and many layers of honey. When it breaks free, an "S" stares back at me. The little boy inside of me rejoices and quickly cries when I get to the honey. I drop to my knees and then my elbows and army crawl my way through the thick amber goop. I used to like the smell of honey, but not anymore.

All bees must die after this.

As soon as I slap the "S" on the board Joey is already down the slide. She's moving so much faster than I am. I'm in shape, but this comp is kicking my ass. I walk to the edge and cheer on Joey while she searches for the last letter needed.

"Come on, Joey," I yell, hoping to encourage her. I let out a yelp when she jumps up and makes her way to the honey. I'd love to go in and just pull her through, but something tells me that I'd get in trouble and we'd be disqualified and there ain't no way I'm losing now.

Joey reaches the edge and crawls a little bit of the way until she can stand. I follow and help her start to rearrange the letters to make H-A-P-P-I-N-E-S-S. We step and try to link hands, but we can't.

"We did well I think."

"Yeah, it's a strong word." I look around and see that Cole and Millie are done, but they're hiding their word. Can't blame them, we did the same thing. It was Joey's idea to not put the letters up until we were almost done.

The bell sounds as soon as Amanda and Gary finish. I look down the line and see that everyone is as uncomfortable as I am, and I have a feeling we'll all be bitching about this for days to come.

"Well done, newlyweds." Patrick Jonas' voice is grating.

Usually I don't mind when he's on, but right now I want to strangle him. "Let's see what we have for words. Amanda and Gary, tell us what you have?"

Joey and I face forward and wait for them to announce their word.

"Patrick, we've spelt computer," Amanda answers, pride evident in her voice. It figures their word would be tech related.

I sigh in relief, knowing we've at least beat them by one point. Patrick calls on Millie and Cole next.

"Patrick, we've spelt reality," Millie says in defeat. She already knows that they've lost to Amanda and Gary.

I'm trying not to smile, but it's no use. Victory is ours, and it's much needed. We're going to need to use the jets in the tub to clean certain body parts and it needs to happen fast because I'm starting to chafe.

"Joey and Joshua, what did you spell?"

Joey stands tall and proud as she states, "Patrick, we've spelt happiness."

"And are you happy, Joey?"

"Yes, I am," she says without hesitation. I wish I wasn't questioning what part is making her happy. The part where we just won another week in the master suite and a hot tub? Or the part where I'm in her life? I shouldn't be worrying about how she feels toward me because I've told her that we're done once the show ends, but now I'm having second thoughts since we've slept together. At least, I think we did. Every now and again I have a déjà vu moment and can only chalk it up to us being intimate. I just can't prove it.

"Well congratulations, Joey and Joshua, you're in the master suite this week. And now for the hot tub winner, which was done by online vote. The winner of the hot tub, for your future home is ... Amanda and Gary, congrats on the fan vote and we'll see you in a few days with an announcement!"

Joey runs—well, as much as she can with flour patties

flying everywhere—to Amanda and gives her hug. Cole and I both waddle over to Gary and pat him on the back. No one is congratulating Joey and me for winning, but whatever. All I care about right now is a shower. A long, hot ... "Hey, Joey, let's go check out the master suite."

She looks at me oddly, but shrugs her shoulders. I wait for her by the door, but she doesn't come alone. Everyone is following. Last week when Millie and Cole won, the room was decorated differently. The girls became enthralled, while Cole, Gary, and I just stood there. Right now I just want to get her alone before I lose my nerve.

None of us care about the crap we're dragging into the house. Our shoes are ruined and it'll likely take multiple washes to get our clothes clean. Sadly, we'll have to clean the mess on the floor, but that can happen later. I reach the door to the master suite first with Joey right beside me. The transformation, if any, isn't as dramatic as the producers make it seem. When I open the door, I can't help the smile that I now have or the internal fist pumping going on in my head. The producers are evil and I love it. Our master suite is almost identical to the room I prefer downstairs with everything done in red and black, adding in white accents. I'm tempted to change the color of my bedroom in my apartment, if only it didn't violate my lease.

"Huh," Joey says, as she walks around the room. "I was expecting something different." She stands in the center, with her hands on her hips. I can't take her serious though because she has clumps of flour peeling off her skin right now. The zombie apocalypse is happening right before our eyes.

"Everyone out, and go clean up. Maybe we can grill tonight." I usher the others out of the room, picking up a few snickers about 'sex' and 'being eager' as they leave. If they only knew how well I've gotten to know my palm because I have a phobia of being married. I lock the door, testing the doorknob for good measure. Joey is still standing in the same spot, but her earlier defiance pose is now gone.

"We need to shower." I step up to her, wanting to touch her, but am afraid we'd stick to each other. I can't give her everything she wants, but I may be able to meet her halfway. Right now I'm willing to test my resolve and I hate that about myself. I should tell her to run far and fast before we step into that shower. Every day that I'm with her is chipping away at my walls. I hate that we've slept together and I can't remember it and that needs to change. I've gotten a foggy taste and need more.

"You can go first. I think I'll just use the tub."

I shake my head slowly. "You're going to need my help getting this crap out of your hair. We can shower together." I sidestep her and head for the bathroom, not waiting for her response. We've taken a bath together before and left our swimsuits on, this can be different. I start the water, testing the temperature before stepping in. I should holler to her, ask her if she's planning on joining me, but I don't. I've left the decision up to her.

The hot spray is a welcome reprieve. My muscles ache and need this relaxation. My heart beats a bit faster when I hear the shower door open. When her hands press against my back and her fingers work the knots out of my shoulders, I tilt my head back, letting the water rain down on my face as I bask in her massage. She doesn't have to do this, especially since I'm so cold to her half the time, but again she just keeps proving to me over and over again how much better she is than everyone else I know.

I shiver slightly when the cool liquid soap touches my skin. Her hands work the soap into a sudsy lather down my arms, washing away the concoction from our event. "Turn around," she whispers, just barely over the sound of the water. I do, and everything stops; the water rushing down on us, time, and my train of thought. Joey stands in front of me, naked and teasing me. When her eyes meet mine, I can see her fear, but only briefly. She continues her path as her hands move over my chest, down the front of my stomach until her fingers are gripping the waistband of my shorts. My hands clamp down on hers and she looks away.

Rejection.

Pushing her hands a little, I guide them until my shorts are loose enough that I can kick them into the corner of the shower. Joey tilts her head, telling me what she wants. One thing I know for sure is I enjoy kissing her. It's like an aphrodisiac of what's waiting for me, if I were to take it. My hand cups her cheek, my fingers tangling in her hair. Her eyes close in anticipation. Snaking my arm around her waist, I pull her against me. The moment her naked body touches mine, I jerk in response. All my rules are quickly flying out the window and I'm not sure I'm strong enough to stop them.

I brush my lips over hers, and she sighs, opening her mouth slightly. She's inviting me in, showing me that I can take her, that she's mine. I trace my tongue over her lips, her breath fanning over my mouth. "Joey," I whisper before closing the gap. Her nails dig into my skin, a pain I want to feel. Our tongues meet, in a slow and steady pace. My arm tightens around her waist as I pick her up and press her back against the cold tile. She arches into me as she wraps her legs around my waist and causes the most severe ache. Her hands roam, moving over my sore muscles, kneading and massaging as she moves against me. When her fingers push into my hair and pull, I think I've lost it. My mouth trails along her jaw, to her ear and down her neck, nipping at her collarbone as I hold her to me, rocking her body against mine.

We're close, too close, but I don't care. I want her. I've wanted her since I kissed her on the stage after we said our vows. From that moment, I knew she was someone special, but also knew that if I kept her, I'd damage her and she'd hate me. Joey pulls on my earlobe, causing me to groan. Her hand moves down my chest, reaching the small patch of hair below my navel. Everything I want and everything I fear is about to happen and I don't care. My eyes roll back when she touches me. Her grasp is firm and steady, and I fight the urge to pull her down on top of me.

Joey leans back, with one hand tight on my shoulder. "Stop fighting this," she says as her lips crash down on mine.

I need to listen.

CHAPTER
fourteen

Joey

Someone pinch me. No, wait, don't because if this isn't reality, I'd rather stay where I am. He's letting me touch him, freely and without reservation. He's not pushing me away, or asking me stop. Josh wants this, and he wants it with me.

The heat from the hot water intensifies everything that I'm feeling. Our bodies are slick and overheated, the anxiousness of what is about to happen seeping through. The cool tiles that are pressed against my back do nothing to curb the burning that I'm feeling. I kiss him hard, crushing my mouth to his. He growls as I stroke him; his hand grips my hips hard and I hope there are marks left so I can recall this moment. Pulling away, my forehead rests against his, our breathing labored, our mouths hovering over each other's. One slip, one push and he'll be in.

"Newlyweds, please report to the living room."

Joshua all but drops me onto the shower floor. My legs, barely down in time, catch myself before I land on my ass.

"We can ignore them," I plead, not wanting this moment to end. I stand up and face him, looking for any signs of regret. The only thing I see is torment. I don't know if he's still fighting an inner battle, remembering the other night, or about to kill the producers. We're getting so close and it's like they're watching us, trying to keep us apart. I want to cry, but that will make him think he's done something wrong, and he hasn't.

"Here, let me wash your hair." I want to bat his hands away out of frustration, but I don't. Being upset with him isn't going to help matters. I just need to keep reminding myself that we'll be alone tonight. His walls are crumbling, I can feel them coming down. Tonight, I'll start again.

If I weren't so upset about being cock-blocked by the show, I'd be getting lost in the massage Josh is giving my scalp. Right now, it feels like I'm floating on a cloud. I feel weightless and free. My neck rolls, guiding his fingers elsewhere, causing him to laugh.

"S'not funny," I say. "What you're doing feels amazing." He chuckles again and turns me around, letting the water rinse my hair.

"I didn't get a chance to wash you." He kisses me, soft and sweet, pulling away after each kiss only to come back again. This time his tongue traces my lips before he brings me to my knees with a searing kiss. Our tongues tangle; he groans and I'm back to where we were not even five minutes ago. I follow him when he pulls away with a devilish smile playing on his lips.

"Let's go see what they want. We're in the master suite, and I'd kind of like to see how this plays out later." He winks, stepping out of the shower. My fingers touch my lips, recalling the moment we just shared. Closing my eyes, I let tonight play out in my head, and how I'm going to get him to just let go and lose his inhibitions with me. With me ... he wants me. Every part of me wants to rejoice, dance a jig and fist pump like Arsenio Hall, but I have to keep my wits about me. He can't know I'm an eager beaver. That'll have to come later tonight.

I wash quickly, most of the crap from the competition melting away with the steam, and step out. Joshua is dressed and sitting on the couch, waiting for me. After quickly throwing on a pair of shorts and tank top, I put my hair in a wet, messy bun. No make-up, just me. The only one I need to impress is Joshua and I think we're finally on the page that we need to be.

"Do you wonder how long they stayed?"

"What are you talking about?" he asks, as he stands and reaches for my hand.

"The producers or whoever came in while we were in the shower." Joshua looks at me questioningly, so I continue. "How did our clothes get in here?"

Realization dawns as his mouth drops open. "Oh."

"Yeah, oh," I say for added benefit. "Creepy isn't it, thinking they could've been standing there, watching us the whole time?" This is one of those moments where I should've just kept my mouth shut. Joshua looks mortified. His hand goes slack in mine and I have to tug him to get him to move out the door. "Don't worry, I'm sure they sent a guy up," I say to ease his thought process. I know he's in actor mode now, trying to prevent *Married Blind Bathroom Gate* from happening. I've read enough of his interviews to know that he's always worried about people taking his picture or recording him at the wrong time.

"That doesn't help, Joey." He drops my hand and walks ahead of me. The small victory I achieved is now for naught. I shouldn't have opened my mouth about the clothes being in the room. He hesitates now when we're physical, if he thinks our privacy is violated, the walls will go back up.

When we get to the living room, we're the last to arrive. Millie and Amanda are sitting together so I chose to sit with them instead of Josh. It might behoove me to give him a little space right now although that's the last thing I want to do. I look across and each of the guys are mimicking each other with their arms crossed and scowls on their faces.

"Our men are pissy," I whisper to the girls, who both stifle a laugh.

"Gary wanted the red room, but Cole beat him to it."

"And Cole wanted to take a longer shower, but also wanted to beat Gary to the bedroom so his shower was cut short."

"They both complained at the same time," Amanda adds.

"And we didn't care," states Millie.

"Wow," I say. "I think the men of the house are pms'ing. Maybe we need cake."

Amanda and Millie look at me. Their smiles say everything. "And we need wine!"

"Hello, newlyweds." Patrick Jonas appears on the screen and we all give him our undivided attention. "Happy one-month anniversary! To celebrate, we thought we'd give you a few messages from home."

Millie and Amanda clap, but I stay reserved. My mother is neurotic and I can't imagine what's going to come out of her mouth. I'd like to hear from my dad. I miss him the most. The screen goes black and we wait with bated breath, for the first video to come on.

Gary groans when it starts and I quickly turn my attention to male talking.

"Wow, Gary, your wife is a babe. Does she know about your obsession?" he laughs, and Amanda stiffens. "Just kidding, G. Anyway, we miss you and can't wait for you to come back to work." The guy shows the "live long and prosper" sign from Spock before the screen goes blank. The room turns into an awkward silence where all you can hear is the clicking from the cameras above us. If this was to make Gary feel better about himself, it definitely didn't do the trick.

The next video starts and Millie immediately starts waving. "That's my mom and dad," she explains through a broken voice.

"Hi Millie, Cole, and the rest of the house. We just want to say that we're very proud of you and can't wait to meet Cole. We love you, Millie." Mille waves again and immediately gets up and goes to Cole, who welcomes her with open arms. I stare at them, jealousy seeping in because I want what they have. Cole strokes her hair, kissing her softly while she cries into his shoulder. They've fallen in love. They've done what the show is meant for.

My eyes turn sharply when a voice I know well starts talking. Jules Maxwell stares back at me, and only me, in all her perfection. "Hi Joshie," she says, as she waves her perfectly manicured nails at him. "I can't wait until this charade is over and you're home. I miss you. I'll be there at the finale, waiting to take you home. I love you." She blows a kiss before the screen goes blank.

My throat tightens and my eyes water. Screw being weak. I don't know what I was thinking. He warned me from the beginning, but I didn't want to believe him. Not with his stupid kisses and hand holding. I succumbed to him because of my unrealistic feelings. I thought that I'd be enough. We almost knowingly had sex and it would've meant nothing to him. Only a way for him to get his jollies because his hand isn't doing the trick.

"Joey," Amanda says softly. I muster up the best smile I can, trying to let her know that I'm okay.

"Excuse me," I tell the room before getting up. I walk out, without looking at anyone. I don't need to see their pity and I definitely don't want to see the look on Joshua's face. I don't want him to even acknowledge what just took place, and I don't really care if he's upset. His ruse is up. Everyone knows that our marriage is nothing but a sham.

I walk down the hall, unsure of where I'm going to go

and hide. The room I share with Josh is off-limits. The only safe place is the bathroom. As I walk by the towels, I grab one and walk as fast I can into the stall, locking the door behind me. My chest aches; I know what's coming and there isn't going to be anything I can do to stop it. I was stupid to believe that I could make him fall in love with me. I was stupid to think that I was enough for him, that we could be something outside this house.

My back hits the wall and I slide down, bringing the towel to my mouth as I scream as loud as possible. In the beginning I refused to shed tears over this, over a situation that I knew the outcome of, but I can't help it. Moments ago, we were about to finally connect as husband and wife, and now this. He never lied, but he led me to believe that we could be different. I should've just known that he and Jules weren't over. It makes sense, the no sex rule, because he doesn't want to cheat. But he did, he just doesn't know it.

Kissing isn't cheating in Hollywood.

I need to get out of here before people start to look for me. I stand and flush the toilet, even though I didn't use it. When I open the door I half expect Millie and Amanda to be here waiting for me, but why would they? Millie is blissfully happy, and Amanda wants my husband. As far as I'm concerned, she can have him. Maybe she's a better fit for Josh. One quick check in the mirror tells me that my eyes aren't puffy, so I'm safe there. I'm going to walk out there with my head held high and into the kitchen because I need chocolate. A cake must be made.

The room is quiet and the television dark. Everyone is still sitting on the couches, but Gary is with Amanda now. Joshua is alone. It's what he wants, so I'm not going to let that bother me. I step into the pantry and pull out the cake mix and frosting. Chocolate on chocolate ought to do the trick.

Chocolate is the only thing that will never lie to you.

I'm quiet and reserved, as I get everything out. I'm not

slamming doors or banging bowls onto the kitchen counter. I don't need to. It's my own fault for being naïve and thinking that someone like Joshua Wilson would want someone like me. I'm plain and ordinary. I have nothing to offer him or anyone like him. Actors don't fall in love with mundane people.

"Are you okay?"

I smile at Millie and Amanda, who both look forlorn. "I'm fine, just making a cake. We talked about having cake, right?"

"Right," Millie says with a forced grin. I shuffle around her while she leans against the counter. She could move, or help, either one would be nice. Just standing in my way though, is going to piss me off.

"Josh said—"

I put my hand up, motioning for Amanda to stop talking. "I don't care what Joshua said, or hasn't said. I'm fully aware of his feelings."

"But I thought—"

This time I stop Millie from talking. "I don't ask about your marriage, so please don't ask about mine."

The women fall silent and allow me to shuffle around the kitchen. I breathe a sigh of relief when they leave and the sliding glass door opens. I don't want to be coddled or pretend that our fake friendship actually means anything. I put the cake in the oven and lean on the stove. The warmth takes away the chill I'm feeling, but does nothing to take the weight off of my chest.

I cringe and step away when he touches me. I busy myself with washing the dirty dishes while he stands there.

"Joey?" My eyes close when he says my name, but it's not enough. I ignore him. We have nothing to talk about. If anything, he should be sitting at the counter coming up with a new strategy.

"Joey to the confession room," Linda says with her

impeccable timing as always.

After drying my hands on the towel, I check the timer. I won't be able to spend too much time in there or my cake will burn. I brush by Josh and avoid his hand when he reaches for me.

Sitting down with a huff, I smile into the camera. "What is it now? You've already embarrassed me, what could you possibly need to know? Are you curious as to why I'm not crying? Why I'm not begging Joshua to choose me over Jules Maxwell, a woman he has history with? This game is nothing more than a mockery of marriage. You can't expect people to fall in love with all your forced competitions and stupid confession room pranks. When all is said and done, we'll go our separate ways and think about our time here and how we could've done things differently. Maybe Millie and Cole will last, but the rest of us won't, and as producers, you should be ashamed of yourselves."

I stand, but hesitate. "What you did today just showed me that you only care about the ratings." I walk out knowing the producers aren't going to be happy with me. I don't care because in two months this show is over and I'll be back home doing what I do best.

Eating cake.

CHAPTER
fifteen

Joshua

My eyes widen when Jules appears on the screen. Staring intently, I try to fathom what the hell she's doing on there. The women in the room gasp and there's a slight wail. I don't need to look to know who let that out. Jules words sting as she solidifies for the people near me, and the viewers at home, that my marriage is a charade ... a joke. Anger builds within me, and my heart breaks for Joey. She doesn't need this. I don't need this. Jules Maxwell and I were not together when I signed the contract, or when I married Joey. We had broken up months before; it was yet another twirl on the merry-go-round that ended with one of us jumping off. This time I ended things and after meeting Joey, I'm not sure I ever want to get back with Jules.

As if in slow motion, I turn my gaze to Joey. Everything is telling me to get up and pull her into my arms, but I'm frozen. I'm not supposed to care about Joey, but I do. The last thing I want is for her to get hurt. That includes when the show is over. She and I need to end on amicable terms. I want to be her friend because treating her like my father treats his exes is out of the question. Joey and I will never share a child, but we share this ... this show, these moments captured on television.

As soon as Jules' message finishes, Joey springs from the couch and rushes down the hall. Millie and Amanda look at me, both throwing daggers, daggers that I deserve but not because of Jules. I didn't put her up to that, the producers did. She's just conniving enough to go along with it. I'll be happy to thank Rob as well. If he hadn't opened his big ass mouth, Jules would've never found out about my plan to annul this marriage as soon as I got out.

Mr. and Mrs. Mitchell appear next on the screen. Listening to them tell Joey how much they love her, makes me long for a normal set of parents. Mine, they probably don't even know I'm here, unless they called looking for money. But her parents, they sit together holding hands, showing me what a loving family she comes from. Joey says her mother is neurotic, but maybe that's her mom's way of showing Joey how much she loves her. At least, Joey knows her parents love her.

"Joshua, I wanted to shake your hand at your ceremony. I look forward to meeting you when the show is over," Mr. Mitchell says before the screen goes dark. My hands cover my face and run through my hair.

"Shit," I mutter under my breath. Thing is, I want to meet her parents. I didn't last month but each day that I get to know Joey more, the more I want to spend time with her outside this house. I still think ending the marriage is the right thing to do, but I want a chance to know her away from reality television. I want to see if we're compatible in the real world.

Both women get up and scramble into the kitchen. I catch a glimpse of Joey's backside as she cruises past us. A loud bang makes us jump, increasing the tension in the room. Right now I really despise the open concept of this house because there's no privacy and at this moment I need some.

"I thought my video was embarrassing." I tilt my head and glare at Gary.

"Huh?" I say sarcastically. "Really, Gary, your video was embarrassing?"

He shrugs and Cole mumbles something that I can't quite catch. My head rocks back and forth, and my lips are pursed. Now I'm just pissed. Heaving myself off the couch, I stalk into the kitchen. The women fall quiet and scatter, leaving Joey and I alone. Her back faces me as she busies herself. Anger rolls off her in waves. I've never felt someone's anger before, but I can feel hers. Joey leans against the stove; already the smell of something delicious wafts through the air. My fingers graze her shoulder. She flinches, trying to move away from me.

"Joey," her name falls quietly from my lips. I don't know if it's desperation, or nerves. Either way, saying her name not only hurts, but also makes me long for her.

"Joey to the confession room." Linda's voice booms over the speakers. Joey doesn't waste any time—she picks up a towel and dries her hands before walking out of the kitchen. Not once does she look back toward my direction.

"I'm so screwed," I say to no one and everyone who happens to be listening. I'm in a situation that I don't know how to fix. It's not going to matter what I say to Joey, or how many kisses I bestow upon her, the words that Jules said tonight will always stay with her. If we were to try a relationship outside the house, Joey would always wonder. I know I would if I were in her position.

All of this just proves that I'm not worth someone like Joey Mitchell. I can't imagine she would ever be as spiteful as Jules and do something as hurtful and embarrassing. I brought that on Joey, she didn't ask for it.

Cole walks into the kitchen and heads straight for the refrigerator. The clank of beer bottles is the only sound in the house. He hands me one, his expression telling me that he's sorry, even though it's not his fault. I tip my bottle toward him as a thank you before bringing the cool glass to my lips. I start with one quick sip, but quickly tip back the bottle and let the sweet hops coat my throat.

"Sometimes you just need a beer."

"No truer words said, especially right now." Setting my bottle down, I lean against the counter. "I wondered how long I'd be here, building a relationship with Joey, before it all came tumbling down."

He puts his beer down and sighs. Between him and Gary, Cole and I would be friends outside the house. Gary, I can see myself meeting him every once in a while for a beer and whatnot, but he'd be the one to brag to his friends about me. Cole, on the other hand, I want to catch a game with or have him over for a barbeque. He and I will be friends once the show is over.

"I don't have any advice." He shrugs. "Before I came on the show I had a hard time meeting women. It seemed that the only time I did was at a conference or when I'd be set up on a blind date. I wish I could pat you on the back and tell you what you need to do, but the truth is, I'm scared shitless. When the show is over, then what? How do I make things work with Millie?"

Running my hands through my hair, I breathe in deeply. "Hell, what do I know? I could walk out the door and ask an audience member on a date and she'd say yes. Not because I'm what she's looking for in a guy, but because of who I am. And look at me. I came on a reality show to get married."

"We all did," he reminds me.

I finish off my beer and grab us two more. I'm afraid to leave the kitchen, fearful that I'll miss Joey when she comes back. My plan is to stay here until she does and work some charm to get her to talk to me. I'm not stupid enough to think it's going to be easy, but I'm going to try.

"I think I love your wife," Cole says, causing me to spit my beer out all over the counter. He grabs the towel that Joey left behind, and starts wiping.

"What the hell, man?"

"I didn't mean it how it sounded. It was the aroma from the cake. It's going straight to my stomach, which leads to my heart. It smells really good."

"Yeah it does," I agree with him, quickly. Just as the timer sounds, Joey appears. I can't be sure, but I think she was eavesdropping. I'd be okay with it if she was, but she has to know I'd rather speak to her. Cole takes his leave when she enters, giving us a bit of privacy.

Standing out of her way, I pay attention to every move Joey makes while she moves around the kitchen freely. As soon as she has the cake pan resting on a wire rack, I reach for her hand. She tries to tug it away, but I tighten my grip, not allowing her to slip away so easily, and pull her toward our bedroom. The only thing that would make this more comical is if she'd set her feet firm to the ground so I could drag her, anything to lighten the mood around here.

Earlier this afternoon when we were in our room, we shared a very intimate moment, which was ruined by the scum ball producers. Now I need to make up for that. Once inside the room, I shut the door and lock it. Her arms are crossed over her chest in complete defiance. She doesn't want to be here. With each step I take toward her, she takes one back. We're back to the first days in the house, except she was happy then and right now I'd give anything to see her smile.

I hold my hands up in front of me, calling for a truce, or mercy. Whatever she's willing to give me.

"I'm sorry. I know those words are cheap and often misused, but you have to know that I didn't know that was going to happen."

"I know."

My hands drop in relief as I move forward, only to have her move back. "What gives then?"

Joey looks down at the ground, to the walls, the ceiling, anywhere but in my direction. Her eyes look wet and the thought of her crying because of me, because of Jules, angers and tears at my heart. When I'm out of here, Jules isn't going to like what I have to say.

"Joey?"

She shakes her head, pulling her bottom lip between her teeth. Hours ago, I would've used my thumb to caress her lip, but now I'm too afraid.

"Why did you tell her your plan?" Her voice breaks, stabbing me in the heart.

"I didn't. I wouldn't do that to you, or to anyone. I know how vindictive she can be. I didn't even tell her I was coming on the show."

"How does she know?"

"Rob," I answer. "He knew. Gave me shit for it too. Said I was wrong. My agent and lawyer know, but they don't work with Jules." I pause and take a chance at moving closer to her. When she doesn't step back, I consider it progress. My fingers tentatively touch her elbow, tugging slightly to bring her closer.

"Joey, what happened out there today was the cruelest form of humiliation. I can't imagine what's going through the producers' minds or what Jules did to get her face on the show. For her, it's publicity. But for us, it hurt us deep. I don't want to see you hurting like this, especially because of me. This is what I've been trying to shield you from, the nastiness of Hollywood. You're too good for this type of crap, the constant drama of the next person trying to bring you down.

"I like that you're pure of heart, and sweet. I even like that you're my number one fan. What I don't like is the fact that people on the outside want to hurt you and I can't do anything about it. I'm no good for you out there. I'm afraid you won't like me, or that I'll ruin you. I need for you to truly understand why I feel this way."

Joey takes a step back, squares her shoulders, and glares at me. Her finger stabs me in the chest, not once, or twice, but three times, each one stronger than the previous.

"Ouch," I say, bringing my arms up to defend myself.

"Joshua Wilson ..." She stops and shakes her head. "You know what, it's our anniversary. I made cake. Let's eat cake."

Joey doesn't give me a chance to respond, and I'm not really sure what just happened, but she's left the room and I'm just standing here like a moron utterly confused. Here I am pouring my heart out, trying to explain my feelings, and she wants to eat cake.

I play the words over in my head, looking for a spot where I screwed up. Everything sounded perfect, but now that I recall them, it's complete shit. No wonder she couldn't reply, I didn't make any sense.

Rushing to the kitchen, I discover she's behind the counter with a knife in her hand. She holds it up, and it scares me a bit, even though it's covered in frosting. Cautiously, I take a seat at the bar and wait. If Joey wants to celebrate our anniversary, who am I to stop her? Right now, I don't think I'm allowed to argue with Joey, there might be some husband code I'm missing. To be on the safe side, I clasp my hands and rest them on the counter and keep my gaze forward. I don't want to get caught staring, at least not right now.

Joey starts humming as she flitters around the kitchen. I try to imagine her in mine, but the images aren't that great. My kitchen is small with one counter. She'd hate it. In fact, my apartment isn't anything great, but its home.

A heaping piece of cake is set down in front of me. I lick my lips in anticipation as I pick up the fork that's sticking out of the middle.

"This looks delicious."

"Are you saying I can't cook?"

Her question confuses me because all I said is it looked delicious. I fear it's a trick. The best answer is avoidance, so I stare at my piece of chocolate cake. I really just want to eat the cake.

"You know we never got to feed each other cake at our reception." Joey comes around to my side, resting her hand on my shoulder. I lean over and kiss her on the cheek, thankful that she's so forgiving.

"We really didn't have a reception, but we could definitely do that whole cake thing now if you want."

"That's what I want." Her voice goes quiet as she gazes into my eyes. I don't see the hurt that was there earlier, but I'm not stupid enough to believe that it's gone. It'll come back, probably tonight like a bad dream. I'll be there to hold her, to kiss away the demon known as Jules Maxwell.

Joey has a nice big chunk of cake nestled between her thumb and fingers. I shift slightly, preparing myself to take a bite of her offering.

"I'm so happy to be your wife." Those are the words I hear as chocolate frosting and cake are rammed into my mouth, up my nose, and over my face.

"Don't even think about sleeping in my bed tonight. You may think you know me, and what I'm feeling, but you're wrong. I've never been so humiliated in my life, and on national television. It's one thing to be your wife and to stand by you, but for her to make a joke out of me is inexcusable."

Joey waits while her words sink in. Through my chocolate haze, I see a lone tear fall. I try to reach for her, but she backs away, shaking her head. I jump when the door slams, leaving me in the kitchen with cake smeared on my face, and a heart beating so rapidly I can't tell if it's because I'm anxious, or if it's because I'm upset that she's hurting.

I have cake, though, and according to Joey, cake makes everything better.

BLIND *reality*

Married Blind

[Roll intro]

"I'm Patrick Jonas, and welcome to another episode of *Married Blind*."

[Theme music plays]

"Tonight our newlyweds will be playing for their first luxury vacation. Who will be crowned victors for the eight-day stay in Tahiti? Also tonight, we'll learn of a new twist. One that is sure to rock the house and make the spouses think twice. When we return, we'll join our favorite newlyweds and see how they're doing."

[Make-up fix]

[Check lighting]

[Break over]

[Audience applause]

"Welcome back. When we last left our houseguests, Amanda and Gary were getting cozy in the master suite."

[Audience oohs]

"Let's go live to the house to see how life is treating them, and to see if everyone is ready for tonight's competition."

[Audience cheers]

[Switch to the live feed]

"Hello, newlyweds."

[All respond]

"Gary and Amanda, how are you enjoying married life?"

CHAPTER
sixteen

Joey

"Well, Patrick, the jetted tub in the master suite is to die for. I don't think I ever want to leave," Amanda's reply is a bit too bubbly for me. She's bouncing in her seat right now, happy to be the center of attention. Not that I blame her, it is nice when the focus is on you, unless you're me. I'd rather not be the focus of anyone's attention until this stupid game is over.

"Oh yes, I hear it's fabulous. I may have to come in and try it."

Creeper!

I feel like yelling out that they should try the shower, but it's probably not appropriate and would likely lead to more questions, like "how are you and Josh?" Me and who? Oh yes, my husband ... the one who told his roommate his devious plan to wed and not bed, on national television so he could win half a million dollars to save the community center where he grew up. He's noble, I give him that, but the rest of him needs work.

Patrick Jonas carries on, while I tune him out. You can tell who his favorite houseguest is, and right now it's Amanda. It could be because of her clothing. She's taken to altering the "outfits" we're given to wear for competitions, and made them more ... well, Amandaesque. The tops are cut to show off her ample, and likely fake, breasts and her shorts are rolled so high ... You get the picture.

Amanda has also resumed the former and now active hobby of staring at Joshua, all the time. At first, when the show started, it bothered me because she was so nasty to me. Making snide comments about how I didn't deserve someone like him. She'd touch him, running her fingers down his arms and he'd laugh. He placated her because it's his job. But now, now that she knows Jules Maxwell has rocked our boat, she thinks she has a chance with him. Her new daily routine consists of doing yoga while he's working out; making sure her rump shaker is facing him. I applaud her ability to bend and twist, but for the love of all things holy, no one wants to see your beaver dam, especially not Josh.

If there's one thing I know about Joshua Freaking Wilson it's that he doesn't do plastic, and Amanda is as plastic as they come. Sad to say, but I'd much rather he ends up with Jules instead of Amanda. But my opinion doesn't matter. Once the show is over, I'll never see him again. Right now, I can't even fathom being friends with him. It's not worth the heartache.

Joshua taps me on the shoulder, getting my attention. I smile at the creeper, Patrick, and listen to him explain what we're competing for.

"Tonight you'll compete in your first luxury competition. The winners will be flown to Tahiti for an eight-day excursion."

Everyone in the room claps or let's out some kind of excited squeal, except for me. I don't want to win. There's no point.

"So if we win, do I get the trip?" I whisper into Josh's

ear. He looks at me out of the corner of his eye, but doesn't appease me with an answer. Needless to say, our relationship is not what it was before the video messages were shown to us. I know it's not his fault that Jules said what she did, but it definitely drove the final nail in my proverbial coffin as his wife. I had been hanging on by a thread with breaking down his walls and getting somewhere in his heart. I had hoped that when the show was over, he'd take me into the green room and profess his undying love for me by ripping up the annulment papers. That hope no longer exists. It's not going to matter what I do, I'll be single in a few shorts week.

Jules Maxwell made sure of that.

"Newlyweds, we'll meet you out back."

Everyone is in a hurry, rushing for the door, except for Josh and me. I don't want to win, there's no reason to. We won't be taking the vacation together so I'm not even sure why we're playing.

"We should be the first out," I suggest. "No reason to even compete." Standing up, I turn and face him, giving him a shrug. I feel like a mediocre person in this game, like it's not going to matter what I do or what competitions we win because it's all for nothing. It's all over for me once the final vote comes in.

Joshua stands and run his hand through his hair, he forehead wrinkling as he frowns. Is he frustrated? Maybe, but this is what he wanted, minus me willing to lose. "I don't want to throw the competition, Joey."

"So I get the trip?"

"I told you I'm sorry about Jules."

I scoff. "This has nothing to do with Jules. You want an annulment at the end of the show. I want a vacation and I have no intentions on taking one with an ex."

He shakes his head with narrowed eyes. He opens his mouth to say something, but quickly shuts it. It's a victory for me, another wall going up to protect my heart, until it isn't.

His lips are against mine before I have time to flinch. Fingers grip the back of my neck, intensely. I let out a small whimper because dammit, I want this. I want him.

But he doesn't want me or maybe he does, but my heart can't take it. I've had a taste of him, and yes I want to feast on his platter, but he'll be the death of me.

Pushing him away, I run the back of my hand across my face, slowly and with emphasis. "I think it's best if we don't show any affection when people aren't around," I say as I walk away from him. The need to protect my heart is greater than receiving delicious kisses from Josh. Even if they're toe curling and goose bump inducing.

The backyard is transformed into a mini Tahiti. I instantly hate it. I'd love to see Joshua and me sitting on the beach under the sun. Relaxing by the cover of shade trees and eating dinner under the moonlight. Midnight strolls, hand in hand, along the beach with waves crashing over our feet. Waking up under white gossamer with the sun filtering through the open window and the smell of the sea air making us feel calm. It's all a dream that I thought was within my grasp.

"I made you a drink, Joshie." Amanda bounces up to him, making sure her breasts are on full display. I glance at Gary who looks defeated. I'm not sure if I feel sorry for him or not. He likes her, maybe even loves her, and at one point she liked him.

That is until Jules happened.

I raise my eyebrow at Josh, who looks green. "I'll take it," I say, grabbing the red liquid filled glass from her hand. Without hesitation, I bring it to my lips and drink solidly, downing most of the cocktail. "Hmm, this is good. Want to try it, Joshie?" I add emphasis the "ie". At most, I called him Josh and thought about calling him honey or babe, but never Joshie.

"I'll take anything you give me," he replies, taking the

glass from my hand. His eyes never leave mine as he drinks. When he pulls away, he leans forward and kisses me with his cold, but flavored lips. Amanda huffs in the background; her annoyance matches mine where she's concerned. Maybe I should use Joshua to help Gary out. The only problem with that is I'll get hurt in the long run. I have too much to lose, even if I don't have him now. Dignity costs a lot in my eyes.

Josh pulls me behind him to where our names are listed in front of the wave pool made to look like an ocean, complete with sand. The producers have gotten fancy and have the sound effects of the beach playing overhead. It's as real as it's going to get for me unless I figure out a way to put my stupid anger aside and play this game to win. A half million dollars is enticing, and could be well spent on a whirlwind vacation. Who knows, I could go to Italy and meet my dream guy.

Except my dream guy has me wrapped in his arms with his mouth dangerously close to my ear while we listen to Patrick Jonas explain the rules.

"Each couple will take their place on the surfboard. One spouse must stand the entire time, and neither may touch the water. The last couple will be crowned the winner. Please step onto your surfboard."

We do as we're instructed. The board wobbles a little, and Josh stills me with his hands on my hips.

"If we're both going to stand, I think we should hang onto each other. We'll take breaks sitting down."

"Or we could just jump in now and get it over with," I offer the easiest solution.

He cups my face, shaking his head. "We're not losing. If we don't go together, you can have the tickets."

Except in the end, we lose to Amanda and Gary. I'm not sure how it happened, but it did. I was standing against Josh, my head on his shoulder and with my eyes closed. The sun had already set, and we were soaking wet. He was holding me, trying to provide some warmth, but it wasn't working. I was shivering, and we lost our balance. The surfboard started to wobble, and when a gust of wind was blown on us, Josh slipped with his foot going over the board and touching the water.

Ten hours of standing and we lose.

After a long hot shower, I'm somewhat warmed from the chill. I crawl into bed, in the white room, and close my eyes. The bed dips and I feel Josh get in beside me. He pulls me close so that we're spooning. We haven't done this in weeks, not that I've allowed him to touch me. I missed this, though, even if I couldn't admit it to him.

"Please stop ignoring me," he whispers against my skin. For a brief moment, my heartbreaks at the pain I hear in his voice. I don't have a choice. I'm not like him. I haven't been trained to be able to shut off my emotions like a light switch. I've liked him for so long that when I found out I was married to him, it was a dream come true. Sure, it's a fantasy type dream, but nonetheless it was my dream and it was happening. Regardless of how long our marriage lasted, it was my fairytale. And yes, he shattered that fairytale early on, but he never shut me out. Josh treated me like I was his equal; his friend and partner.

I wish I were the type to tell him how I feel. Aside from him knowing that he's my celebrity crush, he doesn't know that I genuinely like him and I've fallen for him while we've been in this house. He doesn't know, each day, up until the fateful date of the video messages I hoped and even prayed we'd walk out of this house hand in hand and into his waiting car. Destination unknown, but we'd be together and willing to start a life with one another. The only thing he's willing to start is a past. Again, I don't know if I can be his friend after the show.

Two options are in front of me. Pretend I'm already fast asleep, or tell him how I feel and what I want, even though I know he'll never be able or willing to reciprocate the feelings.

I keep thinking that if he knew me, the real me, he'd see that I'm more than a woman whose mother thought she was so desperate that she put her on national TV to find a husband. I can be the wife he needs if he'd just open himself up to the chance of falling in love with me.

My mind is made up for me when my body turns in his arms. His beautiful brown eyes are sad. The usual spark of life seems to be missing. I trace his frown lines, hoping that they'll magically disappear with my touch.

"I wish I could be enough for you. I wish that when you looked at me you saw your future, not someone temporary. When I see you, I see the stars lighting our path through life. I see us doing something great and magnificent. I don't care that you're famous because that's not how I see you anymore. To me, you're the one who makes sure I'm warm at night. You make me feel like I matter, and I want the opportunity to show you that *you* matter to me as well."

His eyes glisten and he pulls me closer. No more words are exchanged as I kiss him lightly on the mouth before snuggling into his chest. His breathing lulls me into the most perfect dream ever, one where he and I are together in the future.

CHAPTER
seventeen

Joshua

"Hey?" I tap her lightly on the shoulder, but she doesn't budge. Her shallow breathing tells me she's asleep and quite comfortable nestled into my chest. She hides her face to block out the camera that remains on for the midnight perv watchers. This is why I prefer the master suite so much. I enjoy my sleep and being in the white room is particularly hard on my sleep pattern. It's too bright in here.

I have so much to say to her, but I'm a coward. I want to look into her light blue eyes while I open my heart, but I'm afraid of her reaction. It's not that I think she'll tell me no, it's what comes next. What happens when I'm not enough anymore?

My mom once told me that eyes are the road to someone's soul and that you can tell everything about someone just by looking into them. You can tell if they're lying, sad, happy, or even full of mischief. When I'm given the opportunity to look into Joey's eyes, I'm searching … searching for the answers that I need in order to survive both her and this game.

I contemplate waking her up. It's been an hour since she laid it all out there and I've been here thinking about all of the things I want to say to her. When my parents started fighting, I learned to keep everything bottled up. Neither of them had time for my problems because they were dealing with their own personal fallouts. To them, I was just a piece of property that they were fighting over. No one ever asked what I wanted except for Gene, the director at the community center where I started spending all my time. He's the reason I'll gladly give up my winnings. The center needs it. The foundation, doors, and windows are in need of repair, not to mention all the furnishings are beyond ruined. Flooding did a number on the building and I want to help them get back on their feet. Gene, he saved me and now I need to save him. The money I give yearly covers supplies, but not the repairs.

Joey stirs in my arms, and instead of letting her go so she can roll over, I pull her closer. The faint scent of her perfume lingers, reminding me that I love the way she smells. Not everyone wears the right perfume, but Joey does. It complements her and puts crazy thoughts in my head. Like the need to spill my guts even though she's sleeping.

"Joey," I whisper, hoping to wake her. When she doesn't stir, I know that if I don't say what's on my mind, I'll never get the words out. "When I look at you, I ask myself why you're not enough for me, and the truth is, you are, but I'm not enough for you. My world is hectic and ruthless. It's not very stable. It's demanding, the hours are long and I can be gone for weeks on end. I like the fact that you see us doing something great and magnificent because that means you see the real me, not the actor or your celebrity crush.

"When I see you, I see a woman who can accomplish anything. I see my future slipping away because we met on a reality television show. Before I even arrived, my agent had the annulment papers already typed and ready for your

signature, but that doesn't mean I don't want to see you after the show ends. I'm just afraid that once we're in the real world, you'll see how ugly my life truly is. I'm afraid of losing you to Hollywood."

I thought I'd feel better after saying those words, but no such luck. I know the words need to be said to her, when she's coherent and can understand them. Our eyes need to meet, maybe our hands will connect and the words can just tumble out of my mouth. In my fantasy world, she slaps me in the face for waiting so long and shuns me the rest of the show, making our annulment a piece of cake. In reality, at least what I'm picturing as my reality, she jumps into my arms and kisses me so passionately that I'm left with the choice of either pushing her away or taking her to bed.

I so desperately want to take her to bed.

When Barry called, reminding me of our agreement, I had to tell my agent, Matt. I believe he had a heart attack as he ran through every scary life-changing scenario and suggested the no sex rule. I agreed, because the last thing I wanted was to be attached to someone I didn't like. It was my lawyer, Jason, who added the annulment. Matt agreed. I didn't fight them on it, since they're paid to look out for my best interests and protect me. I'd give anything to get one of them on the phone and explain to them that I'm falling for the girl. That what I'm feeling is real and that maybe the annulment isn't such a good idea anymore.

They'll be angry, sure, but it's worth it for me. I want … no, I need to spend some time outside of this house with Joey. Seeing her in my life, on set and whatnot, can either make or break us. I have a feeling that Joey is resilient, but maybe not against the likes of Jules Maxwell.

Before I know it, all the house lights are on again signaling daylight and Joey is turning in my arms. She stretches, opens her eyes, and graces me with a smile. I don't want to let her go, but forcing her to stay cuddled up against me like a caged animal probably isn't the best way to hold onto her. And just like that, we're awake and starting a new day.

I'm starting the new day without any sleep, since my mind wouldn't shut off long enough for me to relax and shut my eyes. Behind my closed eyes, all I saw was my life without Joey. Me living on the streets of Venice bumming coins from tourists while she's off gallivanting with some über famous actor who not only stole my lead, but my lady. It's farfetched, I know, but it could happen. Of course, I have people in place to make sure that never happens, but it could. My heart could break so bad that I just give up.

"I'm sorry for staying in your arms all night. I must've been tired."

She's apologizing for being comfortable? I made her feel like she has to do this, it's not right.

"I didn't mind."

"Right," she murmurs as she gets out of bed, leaving the room. She's wearing one of those undershirt tank tops with shorts. Adorable, yet too overdressed for bed in my opinion. Although, being in the white room, we aren't left with many options for clothing. If we were to strip down, our goods would be all over the web in minutes and my manhood would probably have its own twitter. Funny as that may be, I don't think my lawyer nor agent would appreciate it as much.

Joey returns and raises her eyebrow at me for still being in bed. Would she do this if we were at home or would she crawl back into bed with me? I offer a small shrug and get up reluctantly. If I had my choice, we'd stay in bed all day and order room service, except that doesn't exist here, or at my apartment. I make a mental note to whisk us off to a hotel as soon as the show's over so we can have some time to ourselves without any outside interference. I think for me, I need to see where this can go.

I reach for her hand as I pass her, holding her finger with mine briefly. I have to find a way to tell her how I feel before it's too late. I should tell her before the end of the show, but I don't want to cheapen things by telling her in the house where everyone can hear us.

After I brush my teeth, and run my wet hand through my hair, Joey and I are called to the confession room. When I enter, she's sitting on the couch, staring at the camera. This is our first time in here as a couple, as we tend to be called in here by ourselves. Maybe the lovely jackass producers will fill her in on what I said, making me look like a bigger ass for not being able to tell her while she's awake.

Sitting next to her, I put my arm around her and lean back. I'm lounging with no shirt on, and the shorts I slept in. At least Joey is looking respectable enough for the both of us.

"Are they going to ask us something?"

"Dunno. Is that what they usually do for you?" I ask her.

Joey turns, bringing her leg up underneath her. She's wearing workout clothes, reminding me that I should ask her if we could exercise together. Exercise could lead to pool time, or the shower.

"Last time I was in here, I yelled at them for being jerks. They haven't called me since. I wonder why they've done it now."

Because your husband is a moron and professed his love to you while you were sleeping and is too much of a chicken shit to tell you how he feels while you're looking at him.

"I don't know. We could make out," I offer, shrugging as if making out is no big deal. It is, especially now that I'm able to admit my feelings to myself. All I want to do is make out like horny teenagers and see where it can lead. Again, the shower would be nice, but since that day we haven't even ventured in that direction. I don't blame her. Jules ruined the moment.

"Josh and Joey, tell the viewers what you miss about the outside world."

I glance at Joey and she looks at me. We both shrug.

Honestly, living in the house is nice. We don't have to grocery shop and I already do my own laundry. I guess I miss work the most.

"Freedom," Joey blurts out and I have to agree with her. Being confined to the house does have its drawbacks, but I also enjoy the privacy in the sense that fans are not hounding me all the time.

"I agree with Joey. It'll be nice to get outside and not be surrounded by walls all the time, and I'm looking forward to going back to work. I have a few projects coming up that I'm eager to work on."

"What's the first thing you'll do as a couple once the show is over?"

We glance at each other again and smile, but it's me who talks to the camera. "A honeymoon would be nice, but we'll have to see what my schedule is like."

"The light went off," Joey says as she points to the camera.

I lean closer and sure enough the red light is non-existent.

"Now what?" she asks because usually they call in the next person or couple and I'm not hearing anything over the loud speaker.

"Do we stay?"

Joey shrugs. "I'm not sure that's what they're looking for?"

"What if it's what I want?" I wiggle my eyebrows and receive a slap across my leg, giving me a great idea. "What if we fight?"

"Fight?" she questions.

I shrug. "Yeah, you know, play boxing. I'll even let you kick my ass."

Joey stands and places her hands on her hips. The look she's giving is full of sass. I struck a nerve, just like I planned. Standing, I mimic her stance. She glares and I poke her in the shoulder.

"What do you mean, you'll let me kick your ass? What makes you think I can't do it?" She steps closer, her chest almost touching mine. Logic says to step forward so her breasts are touching me, but the child inside says to provoke her. Help bring out her wild side.

"You're a girl. I'm a guy. Laws of nature dictate that you can't."

Just as the words leave my mouth, her leg rears back and connects with my leg. The kick to my chin stings and I have to hold back a hiss. I don't want her to know she hurt me, even a little bit. I wasn't expecting her to do it or I might have prepared better.

"Did that hurt?"

"No," I lie.

This time she pinches my arm. It isn't a normal pinch either. It's one of those where she grabs arm hair and twists. My mouth drops open, but I hold back the 'ow' that wants to escape.

"What about that?"

"Are you trying to hurt me?"

"You said you wanted to fight. So I'm fighting."

"I don't think I like the way you fight," I tell her, much to her displeasure.

"How do you suppose we fight?"

"Like this," I say, and without hesitation, I capture her lips. Starting off slow, our lips dance with each other. I have no doubt we'll be explosive when we can be together. My tongue traces her bottom lip, while her mouth opens slightly, telling me that she wants more. Hell, I want more. The moment our tongues touch, she becomes alive. Her fingers are pulling at my hair and the sharp pain is worth it. When she moans, I just about come undone. I could kiss her all day and night if she'd allow me to. I leave her lips, kissing my way along her jaw to her ear, pulling her lobe lightly. Her neck beckons me, begging me for attention. Her soft whimpers spur me on, so

I pull her closer, showing her what she does to me.

My lips trail over the top of her breasts, and to the other side of her neck. She pulls my hair, bringing my mouth back to hers. As soon at our lips touch, I pick her up and she wraps her legs around my waist. Sitting us down, I grip her hips, moving her back and forth. I need this with her. I can't continue to hold back if I'm going to try something with her outside of the house.

We need to win master suite because I need her.

"Amanda and Gary to the confession room."

We both pull away, and lust filled eyes bore into mine. Our breathing is labored. I smile at her, and kiss the tip of her nose. I need to make my move before it's too late and I've shut her out for good.

"That's the best fight I've ever had," she says before standing up. She takes my hand in hers, and walks us to the door. I think I like the confession room now.

The women are teasing us. They're in the pool bouncing up and down while tossing a beach ball around. My gaze is focused intently on Joey, in her white and blue striped bikini. Every now and again, she looks over and smiles, sending my heart into a shit storm of emotions.

My reasons for not being with her are quickly becoming excuses. At best, they're weak ones. She's an adult and should be able to make her own decisions on whether she wants to be with me or not. Just because we're married doesn't entitle me to make them for her. I can only tell her how I feel, but ultimately it's her choice.

When I finally accepted that I'd be on this show it was my intent to guard my heart, win as many competitions as my partner and I could, wow the viewer's so we can get the votes, and walk out a winner. But that's all changed.

Before I entered the industry, I told myself and anyone who came along that I wasn't getting married. Growing up in my house wasn't an enjoyable experience. My childhood isn't something I like to remember and I never wanted children to be a product of my situation. I know I can be different from my parents, but the fear that I'm not lingers in the back of my mind. When Jules and I broke up, it's because she was caught a few too many times with Bronx Taylor—a man that I can't stand for multiple reasons. One being he sleeps with whomever he can to get a part. Sure it's common, but when I'm losing parts because of it, it strikes a nerve. I've taken Jules back because she's an easy pattern to fall into. I loved her once and can easily say that I don't harbor any feelings toward her because of my wife; the one I married blindly and without reservation and felt an immediate draw to, the one who has put up with my crap—my back and forth bullshit on how I feel and she has never wavered on her feelings toward me—she's the one I'm in love with. Now I just have to find a way to tell her, but it has to be done right, and not in front of the cameras for everyone to see.

Joey's laughter brings me back to reality. Her smile is infectious and I find myself grinning like a lovesick fool for no other reason except she's smiling and happy. I'd like to think I make her happy, but I don't. Not yet at least, but that's about to change.

"What's so funny?" Cole asks as he sits down next to me with a plate of nachos. I've been so immersed with thoughts of Joey I hadn't realized he had left. I look at Gary, sound asleep and snoring lightly. If I didn't know any better, I'd think this house is boring, but that's far from the truth. At any given moment, we have to be ready to compete.

"Just watching Joey," I say, taking a chip off his plate.

"She's beautiful. I think you and I got lucky. Not sure how Gary puts up with Amanda."

Cole's right, Joey is beautiful. She's everything I've been

looking for, but didn't know I was. I needed a TV show and a blindfold to help me find my happiness.

I stare at Joey as she climbs out of the pool and walks toward the house. I want her to come over to me, but she won't. She doesn't cross the boundaries too much and I respect that. Once we're behind closed doors, though, she definitely likes to test the waters.

"Where ya going?" I holler out as she passes.

"Shower," she replies without stopping to talk.

"I think that's my cue." I don't care if Cole knows what I'm about to do. For all he knows, Joey and I have been intimate this whole time. Even when Jules ousted my secret, I played it off like she's a scorned ex.

Cole mumbles have fun as I walk by and all I can do is chuckle. I like that everyone is outside, although it won't take long for people to start filtering in. We wouldn't be the only couple caught in the shower, but the last thing I want is for Joey to be embarrassed.

I quickly undress and step into the shower as quietly as I can. She stands there with the water cascading over her body. Her long, toned legs and her perfect ass beckon me. Stepping forward, I mold my body to hers as if she were made for me. She's the perfect height. I don't have to bend over to kiss her, but I do have to lean. I can nuzzle her as we stand side-by-side and tangle my feet with hers when we sleep.

"What are you doing in here?" she asks as her ass moves just enough to cause friction.

"I thought we could shower together. You know, to conserve water and all that other environmental bullshit everyone is always spouting off." I like that with the shower running we're barely audible. We can't wear mics in the water, and as long as we stay near the nozzle, the overhead mics can't pick up what we're saying.

Joey turns to face me. Her blonde hair is now dark and slicked back away from her face; her eyelashes wet and highlighting her beautiful gray eyes. I don't know why I've waited so long. She searches my eyes for a clue, a truthful answer to her question. The words rest on the tip of tongue, but my mouth can't open and my voice can't seem to make the sounds necessary to tell her that I'm falling for her or that I have already fallen. It's a deep seeded fear of rejection that must be preventing me from telling her. What if she tells me that I'm no good for her, or she doesn't believe me?

"You want me?" she questions, knowing that I've given her the impression that I don't.

"You have no idea."

"What's changed?"

I pause and let her question sink in. I know I need to open the floodgates and tell her everything, but doing that could have repercussions, and this isn't the time to talk.

"You've changed me, Joey. You see the real me."

Trailing the backside of my fingers along her cheekbone, I move in stealthily when she closes her eyes. My lips graze hers, pulling away slightly before taking her bottom lip in between my teeth. This feels right. It feels natural being with her like this.

"Please don't start something that you can't finish."

"Oh I intend to finish, Joey," I say as I gently back her into the wall. She hisses from the contact the cold tile makes with her warm skin. The water hits my back as I tower over her. There's a look in her eyes, a look of want and need. I trail my lips over her shoulder, my tongue blazing a path over her skin. Her taut nipples beckon me as I bring one into my mouth, pulling lightly with my teeth as her back arches. If I don't act fast, I'm going to not only run out of time, but also have a middle school mishap and let go too soon. While lavishing her breast, my hands cup her ass, lifting her gently so she can wrap her legs around my waist. I groan when I come into contact with her pussy.

"There are so many things I want to do to you, Joey, but

that'll have to wait until we're in the master suite," I whisper as I enter her. "Right now, I need to feel you wrapped around me again." She doesn't correct me, confirming what I already know. This isn't our first time together and as much as I want to be angry with her for not being honest, I understand why she did it.

My hands grip her hips as I slide her up and down my shaft. Joey rocks into me, creating a rhythm that belongs only to us. I watch as her eyes close and her head rests against the shower wall. Her heels dig into my ass, spurring me on to be faster. At the first indication of a moan, my mouth is covering hers as I slam us into the tile, my hand clutching the lip above to give me more leverage.

This is not how I wanted our first coherent round of sex to be, but I can't wait any longer. I have to know what it feels like to be lost in all things Joey. And I am lost, especially now as I feel her tighten around me. I want to hear her scream, call out my name, but not here. We're rushed, and the privacy is lacking. I swallow her cries, matching each and every one as I thrust into her, harder and faster. Her legs squeeze me, locking around my waist as I push into her one last time.

"Look at me, Joey." When she does I lose all sense of what I was going to say. She gives me everything, and does so without hesitation or reservation. She never asked to be married to me, and given the chance, I'd choose her time and time again.

The words are there, but I'm not sure if I can say them. I'm confident that she feels the same way, I'm just questioning if this is love that I'm feeling, or if I'm lonely. The way I feel when she walks into the room is nothing like I ever felt with Jules. My gut is telling me to follow Joey to the ends of the earth. To take her by the hand and profess my love to her, but I'm too afraid.

Instead of telling her anything, I kiss her. I kiss her hard and fast, deep and crazy, as I hold us to the wall. When I pull away, the lust is there. The need and want is evident in her features.

It's time to man up.

Married Blind

[Roll intro]

"I'm Patrick Jonas, and welcome to another episode of *Married Blind*."

[Theme music plays]

[Cut to commercial break]

"Welcome back. Our third season has seen some fantastic competitions, we've witnessed a couple fall in love, a man transform for his wife, and a Hollywood romance take shape. Its day sixty and things are heating up between our newlyweds. Our online polls show the favorites right now are Joshua and Joey. I'm willing to bet it's because of that steamy fight they had in the confession room, wouldn't you? Let's hear what the audience thinks about the latest developments."

[Camera pans to audience members]

"Tell us who you think will win?"

[Audience members stand at microphones]

"Well, I think Joshua and Joey will win, but Joshua is leading Joey on. He's in love with Jules Maxwell, and rumors are she's planning their wedding."

"Interesting thought, thank you for that. Let's hope that's not true for Joey's sake."

[Pause for new member]

"Who's your favorite?"

"Definitely Millie and Cole, you can tell they're in love."

[PJ faces camera]

"So there you have it. You've heard the views of some of our audience members, but we'd also like to hear what *you* think. Go to our website and take part in the latest poll to let us know who you think will win *Married Blind*. We'll be back after the commercial break."

[Make-up fix]

[Check lighting]

[Break over]

[Audience applause]

"We think our newlyweds have had it a

bit too easy, don't you?"

[Audience cheers]

"For the remaining thirty days, our houseguests will compete not only against each other, but another couple as well. We'll be introducing another couple and ... well, let's say things are about to get interesting."

[Audience oohs]

[Switch to the live feed]

"Hello, newlyweds!"

[All respond]

"How is everyone tonight?"

[All respond]

"With only thirty days left, you must be excited for the finale?"

[All respond]

"Well as you know, we like to twist things every now and again, and this season is no different. This year, we'll be introducing another couple into the house and they will also be eligible to win the grand prize."

HEIDI MCLAUGHLIN

[Camera on newlyweds]

"I'll be back later today to introduce them."

[Cut]

CHAPTER
eighteen

Joey

I stare blankly at the screen as it fades to black. The last image we saw was Patrick Jonas smiling at us even though not a single one of us smile back. I'm trying to process what he just said, 'another couple moving in' and none of its making sense. Why wait until the show is almost over to do this? It's bothersome that they have a chance of winning after only being here for thirty days. How is that possible? *We're* the ones who have put in the blood, sweat, and tears for the past two months, and they get to waltz in and participate in a few competitions and what, win the game over the rest of us? I don't think so.

As I look around at my housemates, I have a feeling my expression matches theirs. Most of us have been in bliss the past two months and that's not great ratings. They want drama, conflict, and probably catfights. Believe me, there have been many times where I've felt like yanking out Amanda's extensions, but I refuse to stoop that low for ratings.

Josh grabs my hand and pulls me from the chair. He all but drags me down the hall and into the bathroom. He wants to talk without an audience and this is really the only place we can do that aside from the master suite and in the shower with the water running. He still doesn't trust that no one will be able to hear us. He pushes me up against the wall and crashes his lips to mine. Our tongues move together and my body sags against his. Ever since he came to me in shower, things have been more intense. We haven't been intimate since and I thought I'd feel disconnected from him, but that's not the case. The once subtle touches and stolen kisses are a thing of the past. He's full-on romantic, and I love every minute of it, but dread the show being over soon. I sigh when he pulls away and am met with a quiet chuckle.

"What was that for?" I ask, breathlessly.

"I just wanted to be able to have one more kiss before the house erupts into chaos."

"I think chaos is a harsh word."

Josh shakes his head and leans in. "No, I don't think so. This game is ruthless and the producers have something up their sleeve. They're bringing in another couple to stir things up in the house. I'm just afraid our edge is gone."

I roll my eyes even though he can't see me. "You know, I think Millie and Cole have a leg up on us."

Josh pulls back and squints. "Do you not have faith in us? I'm hurt," he says as he covers his heart and gives me an overly forlorn expression.

I cover my mouth and stifle a laugh. "Just think about it. You can see that they're in love."

"We could act like that," he proposes, but I shake my head, because I don't want to pretend. I just can't let my heart believe that Josh and I are there yet. Could we be, yes, but we've been avoiding the elephant in the room—what happens after the show. Right now, I'm in wedded bliss and I don't want to know that he hasn't changed his mind.

"We can't and you know it. We have a good thing going right now and if it's not enough then so be it. I don't want us to change our game play because of the producers. I'm not like you. And I don't want to be misled. I can't just shut my heart off when the game is over. I'm not trained in the art of hiding my feelings."

"Joey—"

I put my finger against his lips. I know what he's going to say and as much as I want to pretend that we're this amazingly happy couple who are looking forward to the future, we're not. I've finally accepted the fact that at the end of this month, I'll be single again. It is what it is and I have no regrets. I'll walk away with my head held high and with the knowledge that for ninety days, I was Joshua Wilson's wife.

"You know what I want, but I'm not asking you to change your mind. I don't want you to pretend with me either, not for the cameras. I already know that I'll be checking into *The Joshua Wilson Rehab for Heartbreak Center* when the game is over."

He looks at me funny with his brows furrowed. His grip on my sides tightens, and he averts his gaze. I hate seeing the torment in his eyes. Sometimes I feel like he's about to burst out in song and dance, telling me loves me, and when that doesn't happen, I'm surprisingly okay. I can't force him to change his views. That has to be all him. I don't want to ask him for anything other than what he's offered. Right now, he's given me two months of some of the best memories of my life. In a few years, I'll be forgotten. I won't even be a blip on his radar and he probably won't even remember me.

Josh opens his mouth to say something, but closes it quickly and sighs. "Whoever comes in this house, we have to make sure they know we're in this to win."

"Are we not doing that now?" I question him.

"We have to be better, stronger." I know he wants to win, but I'm not sure I do. I don't want to be on the reunion show, which happens a year down the line, where they check in with us to find out how we're doing. I read the contract. I know we'll be in the same room together, sitting on the same couch. We'll have to answer questions and that's not something I want to do. I don't want to give people the chance to take pity on me or make a mockery of our marriage. I chose to live these months in as much happiness and naivety as possible.

"Okay," I say, agreeing with him.

"No, don't just agree with me. I have experience with douche bag producers and they're putting this twist in for a reason. Something's happened that they don't like and they're not able to change the outcome of the game in their favor. Remember what they did with Jules?"

"How could I forget?" I say sarcastically as I roll my eyes. He knows how I feel about that little stint, so a reminder really isn't necessary.

Josh pulls me into his arms, enveloping me in his warmth. I could live here, if allowed. Society frowns on this much physical attachment, although his movies would be interesting. My fingers bend into the back of his shirt as I hold him to me.

He kisses me lightly on the cheek before he pulls away, looking into my eyes. I wish his eyes matched mine and showed me that he's scared of what our future holds, but they don't. His are full of strategizing and game play. He's trying to figure out how to win over the fans, especially after the Jules incident. I try to win them over by eating cake, not knowing if that even works, but the thoughts are there. I know I'm scared, scared of the unknown. Maybe I need this shake-up to keep me grounded because his eyes alone make me feel like I'm floating and that will get me into trouble.

I push his hair out of his eyes. It's gotten longer, and he's in need of a cut, or maybe not. He could like it. I know I do. I like him for who he is on the inside, not the celebrity he is, or what he looks like. Those feelings have changed ... no, they've gotten stronger since I've gotten to know him. I'm forever going to be his number one fan.

I'm not gonna lie, I've been wondering if I've been blinded by stupidity as far as this game is concerned. It's felt too easy, like they're just dangling a million dollars in front of us and it's ours to lose. Maybe that's where I fail at this game because I never watched the show.

"I'd like for us to win the master suite comp," I say, looking for a reaction.

"Oh yeah?" he questions in a husky tone as he leans in to kiss me. The exact thing I was looking for.

"Yeah, I miss you," I mumble against his lips, putting myself out there for him to crush.

"I'm all yours, Joey." His fingers thread through my hair, holding me to him. I refuse to read into his comment, but will totally live in the moment.

"We should get back out there," I tell him.

"What for?" he asks as he leans in, kissing me again. If we weren't in the bathroom stall, I'd be all over a serious make out session. For the past couple of weeks, I haven't been playing to the best of my ability because simple looks and shy touches from him turn me into a puddle of goo. I can't be like that if we want a chance at winning. I need to be strong. I don't want to let him down.

"Let's go kick some *Married Blind* butt."

Josh gives me a reassuring smile that doesn't quite meet his eyes. He's nervous and I'm not sure why. It's just a game, and while the payout is large, it's not like he can't make that in a big hit movie.

"Whatever this game is, we'll get through it together," I say, trying to reassure him.

"Together," he replies as we walk out. I glance in the mirror and hate that I'm not standing there fixing my make-up or hair. Everything is as it was when we walked in.

Walking back into the main part of the house, Gary can

be seen sitting at the table with a beer in his hand and sweat rolling down his face. My guess is that he and Amanda had another fight. One day they fight, the next they're making out on the couch. I have to use a lot of Lysol when I clean. I pat Joshua on his chest and motion for him to go speak to Gary. I think this new mystery couple has everyone on edge.

I sit down next to Millie, who tries to smile.

"Are you okay?"

She nods, but tears fall. I pat her hand, hoping to convey that I'm a great listener if she needs an ear.

"Yeah. I'm just worried."

"Do you want to talk about it?"

Millie shrugs and dabs at her eyes with her tissue. "I watched the first two seasons, so I knew what to expect when I came on the show. Last year, they brought on everyone's exes and it put the house into a tailspin. I'm really praying that it's something different this year."

"Oh," I say, trailing off. I agree; the last thing I want is to spend time with Jules, but maybe it's better to end things now than on the final show. If Jules Maxwell shows up, I can guarantee that Josh and I won't win. Honestly, I'll likely leave the studio.

"I'm in love with Cole, but we've never discussed our past. We're happy. Well, as happy as you can be living your life while being on national television."

"I don't mean to interrupt, but they said a couple. They'll be married, like us, and they're going to compete. Patrick didn't say anything about exes."

Millie looks at me completely distraught. "What if?"

"No, I don't play the 'what if' game because if I did I'd be in my room packing my bags. If they were going to bring in an ex, you know they'd bring in Jules. Sadly, I don't think I'll exist if she's in the room."

She looks over my shoulder and shrugs. "I think he sees you just fine."

When I scoff, she shakes her head.

"I don't know why they're doing this," she says.

I answer with, "Ratings," and she rolls her eyes.

"It's just a game."

She's right, it *is* a game. We signed on the dotted line to get married in front of a live television audience to people we don't know. Who does that? The six of us apparently, and we did it for a reason. Each of us has our own history, but that doesn't mean it's for the producers to bring out of us until we're ready.

"We gave them permission to own us for three months. So we roll with the punches and be sure to kick their butts in our next comp and show them whose boss." It's easy to say, but it is what it is. We signed up for this; it's time to deal with it. Besides, it's only reality television. No one will remember any of this next season, let alone next week.

She laughs, making me feel a little bit better.

Leaving Millie to tend to her own demons, I wander around the house memorizing everything from the colors in the painting on the wall to the design of the pillows that sit on the couches. Josh has warned me a couple of times that one of our competitions will be about our surroundings. He's tested me and I've failed. I promised to get better.

Hour after hour, we wait. Dinner is quiet with only the clank of our silverware hitting our plates. I want to yell out it's just a game, but my heart is pounding in my ears, waiting for Jules Maxwell to walk through that door. Ever since Millie brought up the ex-factor, I've been thinking that Jules is going to come in here, married to some unsuspecting guy.

I don't know what Josh would do. They have history, years on their side. We have days, a marriage he plans to annul even though I believe we have chemistry. But it'll never be enough to compete against her. I'm probably worrying for nothing.

Jules is my scapegoat for any and everything that can go

wrong with Josh. When he leaves me it won't be because of me, but because he loves her more. It's easier that way for me.

"I hate this waiting," Cole says as he puts his fork down. "How have we given a show so much power over us?"

"Because we signed our lives away," Amanda adds, earning sighs from all of us.

"Don't be so dramatic. Its reality TV and they need to keep the viewers entertained," I add, pushing my plate away.

Amanda glares at me. I deserve it. "What if it's someone we know?" Millie asks.

I look quickly at Millie, who is resting her head on Cole's shoulder.

"Do you think they'd do that?" I ask to everyone at the table.

The guys mumble and Millie nods. "It's what I've been thinking since Patrick told us," she says.

"I think it's someone to rock the boat, so to speak," Amanda adds. I don't want to tell her that I agree, but I do. We're not spicy enough for the viewers.

"I'm sure we're freaking out for nothing," I say.

"How can you say that? Two people are going to walk in and take away your chances of winning a million dollars," Gary snaps, completely disgusted with what I said.

Joshua reaches under the table and squeezes my leg, his way of letting me know that he agrees with me, but it does nothing to curb my anxiety. The longer we have to wait, the more it builds.

Millie starts to clean off the table and I stand to help her. Amanda doesn't budge, but its fine. We've grown accustomed to doing most of the work around the house while she sits there. She's someone I won't miss when this show is over.

When the doorbell rings, I freeze and Millie drops a dish in the sink. From behind me I can hear the chairs scraping against the floor, the clear sound of everyone else standing. Mille dries her hands and I wait for her before we walk over to the rest of the houseguests where we stand in a united front. I clasp Joshua's hand, a show of solidarity, or just staking my claim. Either way, he makes me feel calm.

Our monitor comes on and we're greeted with Patrick Jonas staring back at us. "Good evening, newlyweds. As I said earlier, you'll be meeting a new couple tonight. They already know you, and you'll have five minutes to get to know them before your next competition begins. The winner of tonight's comp will win the right to stay in the master suite."

The door opens and I take a deep breath. I tell myself, *Whoever it is that walks through that door, it'll only be for a few days.* Those are the words I repeat as the first person walks in.

I squeeze Josh's hand and set my eyes on the foot of the door, watching for their shoes first. Two sets of legs come into view. Everything looks normal. They're both wearing black shoes. The woman wears a skirt and her husband, slacks. Their hands are clasped; clearly they're not afraid to touch, and it makes me wonder how long they've known each other.

The audible gasps make me look up and I wish I hadn't. The couple in our doorway isn't Jules or Millie's ex, but none other than Bronx Taylor with his dirty blond hair styled perfectly and begging for fingers to be run through it. His smile is tilted and I finally meet his hypnotic hazel eyes, eyes that are piercing mine. I swallow hard and hear Joshua very clearly drop the f-bomb. Josh is no longer the only Hollywood hottie in the house.

Bronx steps forward at the same time I do.

"You look fantastic, Joey."

"Thanks, you too," I say as he envelops me into his arms.

Did I forget to mention Bronx Taylor and I were study partners in our first semester of college before he dropped out to pursue acting? By the growling I hear behind me, yes I did.

I step back and take a nice long look at Bronx only to

realize that he's going to be living here … without a shirt, and I have a feeling Josh isn't going to like this one bit.

This definitely calls for cake. I think I *really* need cake.

Married Blind

"Houseguests, let me introduce you to Mr. and Mrs. Taylor."

[Audience cheers]

"Bronx and Rebekah, meet the newlyweds of Season 3."

[Switch to live feed]

CHAPTER
nineteen

Joshua

"Oh you've got to be [bleep] kidding me with this [bleep]," I say as soon as I make eye contact with the douche that is known as Bronx Taylor, while he stands there with a brash smile on his face. His eyes are focused on Joey like she's some sort of ... some sort of goddess! Like she's what he gets in place of his Oscar. His upper lip rises into a smirk, which I'm sure is meant to mock me, but it just pisses me off.

Joey pinches my side and hisses, "We're live, watch your language."

I raise my arm, pointing in Bronx's general direction in protest, but Joey just shakes her head. "What?" I grit. "He ... this ... you ... ugh!" I throw my hands up in frustration. Joey glares at me with disdain. I have a feeling I'm in a losing battle when I shouldn't be. She's happy he's here and I don't understand why. *I'm* the one on her list, not him, unless he's on there and she didn't tell me. She has to know about his relationship with Jules!

"I officially *hate* this game," I mumble, earning a jab to my side. I try not to flinch, but when Bronx chuckles I know my acting skills aren't up to par.

"Rebekah?" Her name is mumbled from one of us, and I'm positive that it came from Gary. I angle myself slightly and see him running his hands through his hair. I glance a look at the new wife in time to see her smile shyly and wave.

If I didn't know any better, I'd say this is a set-up to not only boost ratings, but to rock the two marriages that don't seem to be that strong. Those marriages would be Gary's and mine. And some jackass producer has brought in the one guy who could make me lose my cool.

The way Bronx is watching Joey and not his wife, who is making stupid eyes at Gary, leads me to believe that they know each other. But how? Not once has she mentioned anything about knowing this slime ball and I would think that their friendship, or whatever it is, should've been forthcoming.

I should've asked her more about her list and who was on it. Maybe she hid him for fear that I would freak out, like I'm freaking out now. He likes her. I can tell by the way his eyes are following her and how they lit up when she fell into his arms. His eyes are smizing and here I thought only chicks knew how to do that.

"We'll give everyone a few minutes to make introductions," Patrick says from behind the comfort of his teleprompter. If he were in here I'd be strangling his neck, even though he's not to blame. He's just the patsy.

Bronx takes Rebekah's hand in his and they introduce themselves, starting with Amanda and Gary. Amanda snorts when Rebekah holds Gary's hand a little too long. "Don't worry, I feel ya," I want to holler out to her, but I refrain. The child in me wants to take Joey and run down the hall with her yelling neaner neaner neaner, but somehow I think that will be frowned upon.

Cole and Bronx chat it up a bit and it annoys me that I can't hear what they're saying over the stupid music that is coming out of the loud speaker. Seriously, cut to a commercial already.

When Bronx and Rebekah step in front of us, I'm rigid and no amount of pinching from Joey is making me any less so. He hugs her again, lingering longer than what I'd consider appropriate. I need to get her alone and quickly. My mind is racing, and while I don't suspect they've slept together, the thoughts are there. Call it jealously, but I like knowing that I'm number one on her list, but if he's also on there, we're going to have a problem, especially if she didn't tell me. And if this is a ploy by the producers to step up my game, so be it. If I have to fight for Joey's affection, I'll do it. I refused to do it for Jules, but I will for Joey. It's because there's more at stake with Joey, Jules can't hold a candle to the beauty that Joey has in her.

Aside from meeting Joey, I'm regretting the decision I made to be a part of this show. *Who in their right mind would try to put a wedge in between a married couple?* My own question makes me pause. This is exactly how life is and they're just making that abundantly clear to us. I just sure as hell wish that it were with anyone other than Bronx Taylor. Couldn't it have been Joey's ex? Him, I could handle, but not this. It's bad enough that I have to interact with him on a work and social level.

My hand clenches as I stare him down. *This* man ... I have no words for how much I despise him. Don't get me wrong, I'm all for a healthy competition among peers—it keeps you real to your craft—but when you purposely try to sabotage an audition or gloat about a part you landed over said peer, that just makes you a sleaze ball. And I'm not even considering that Bronx Taylor is the reason Jules and I broke up for good. She didn't cheat, that much I do trust about her, but he pushed her to and that was enough for me to call it quits.

"Newlyweds, if you'll head to the backyard, we can start our next master suite competition." Patrick Jonas's voice is grating on my nerves and I have to bite my tongue to keep from lashing out. I roughly grab Joey's hand in mind and all but drag her to the backyard. She crashes into my back when I pull up short. The backyard is a large *Hungry Hungry Hippos* game board with skateboards and laundry buckets. This is going to be interesting.

"Oh you've got to be kidding me?" I throw my hands up in the air and groan.

"What is your problem?" Joey asks as she pushes me toward our pink hippo.

"It's pink," I say, pointing to the stupid ugly hippo that has a flashing hot pink sign in its mouth that's blinking our names.

"That's your problem because our," she points at our hippo, "is pink?"

"Yes! I hate pink. I think it's stupid and dumb and—"

"Hey, Joey. How about we do lunch when the show's over?"

My blood boils as Bronx steps forward, taking Joey's hand in his, and raises it to his mouth, kissing the top of it. Her eyes flutter and her cheeks turn pink. Pink! My hands clench into fists as I maneuver myself to stand in between them. I puff my chest out and square my shoulders causing Bronx to back-up. His hands are up as if he's trying to back down from a fight. This isn't some audition for a street gang movie, but real life ... the reality television version of it anyway.

"I'd love to."

"You're busy," I spit out.

"I am?" she questions me as her hands land on hips in defiance.

"Somehow I think she'll be free." He winks as he walks

toward his station.

"What the hell is going on?" she asks as if she doesn't already know.

"Couples, to your stations."

I don't have a chance to say anything because she walks away. Bronx is watching and laughing. I have a feeling he knows why he was sent here, and he's succeeded in a matter of seconds. Everything we've been building on is crumbling faster than the Berlin Wall and there isn't jack shit I can do about it right now. We have to win this competition so we can hash everything out in private. And while we're arguing and hopefully making up, Joey and I will need to discuss boundaries later. I know she doesn't like Amanda and I've respected that. She'll need to do the same when it comes to Bronx. At least I hope she will.

With my luck, she won't. I've already told her we're done at the end of the show so why should she respect my feelings? She shouldn't, and I don't really have the right to ask her either. I've been sentenced to thirty days in purgatory all because I'm a dumb ass. Telling her that I don't want to be done now will only look like a desperate ploy on my part. Thank you very much, *Married Blind,* for screwing up my plan.

Bronx and Rebekah laugh, as they stand ready at their red hippo—the hippo color I wanted—but not before he turns and winks. Is he winking at Joey or me? I can't be sure, but either way that gesture is enough to piss me off even more.

"What the hell is wrong with you?"

In this moment I want Joey to take ahold of my shirt in her fist and yank me to her. I want to hear her tell me I have nothing to worry about. I want to feel her lips press against mine in a gesture meant for only us. But she doesn't. Joey stands in front of me matching my posture with an angry scowl on her face. I know I'm in the wrong, but refuse to admit it.

"I told you I don't like pink."

"Since when?"

I shrug and look away, acting like a disinterested child.

"Unbelievable," she mutters as she turns away from me.

I have feeling that any progress we've made these past few weeks is now swirling down the toilet and it's not even Bronx's fault. He's the just catalyst for my self-destruction.

"Listen," I say when I come to stand behind her. I press my body into hers and she goes rigid. "Joey?" I try to sweeten my voice, to show her the desire I feel when I'm near her, but she doesn't budge. "Let's win this one, okay?"

Joey doesn't respond. She just stands there waiting for our instructions even though the game looks fairly self-explanatory.

"Now that everyone has met each other, let's begin." Patrick's voice over the loud speaker annoys me, but I can't let that show on my face. It's game time and even if Joey doesn't want to win this one, I do.

As soon as everyone is at their colored hippo, Patrick continues. "Welcome to the live action version of *Hungry Hungry Hippos*. One of you will lie flat on the skateboard and hold out your bucket while the other pushes you by your ankles. The object is to collect as many matching balls as you can before the buzzer. If your hand touches the ground, you're disqualified."

"Newlyweds, take your positions."

"Do you want to be on the bottom?" I wiggle my eyebrows at her and am instantly rewarded with a smile, even if she does shake her head. I'm just relieved to see that smile.

"You have no idea," she mumbles as she gets down on her knees and climbs onto the skateboard. Seeing her like that, on her knees, makes me wish we were somewhere else, and unless we win the master suite the only place we can be alone will be in the shower. Everything we've done has been in the shower, minus the one time in bed that is completely foggy as hell. My no sex rule was really, really stupid, but it was a necessary evil.

"You're going to have to lean when I say right or left," I instruct as Joey gets situated on the board.

"I know, Josh." Her voice is stern, telling me that she's annoyed with me. It's funny how you learn so much about someone in such a little amount of time. Joey bends her legs up so I can hold onto her ankles. I grab them firmly and give her a slight push.

The timer starts ticking down; giving us fair warning that the game is about to start. I look over at Gary and find him staring at Rebekah. When we're done, I need to ask him what the deal is between them because they definitely have history. When I glance at Bronx, he's staring at Joey, fueling my anger toward him and this situation.

The buzzer sounds and I hesitate briefly before lurching us forward. Joey works the game like a champ, leaning in the direction she needs me to go. We bump and collide with others as she tries to capture all the pink balls that she can, and as much as I want to look and see how the others are doing, I can't. My focus has to remain on Joey.

At the sound of the horn, I drop her legs and fall to my knees. I didn't think it would be exhausting, holding her ankles like that, but it was. I crawl over and sit next to her, waiting while she counts how many pink balls we were able to capture.

When she's done, I stand and pull her with me. I put my arm around her, tugging her into my side. She relaxes into me and I use this opportunity to place a kiss on her forehead. "You kicked ass," I tell her, praising the job she's done. I'm not sure I would've been able to stay on the board.

"Thanks. I just hope it's enough to win."

"Me too."

"Newlyweds, was that as fun to compete in as it was to

watch?"

I want to say no, but I grumble a somewhat positive response.

"Cole and Mille, how many yellow balls do you have?"

"We have eighteen yellow balls," Millie replies as I look at our bucket. I'm confident we've beaten not only them, but Gary and Amanda as well. When I look toward Bronx, he's smirking. We can't see into each other's buckets, and that's a bit unnerving to me. All I know is that we need to have just one more than they do.

"Joshua and Joey, how many pink balls do you have?"

I chuckle like a child because it seems like Patrick Jonas likes to draw the word out longer than he needs to.

Joey glares at me before clearing her throat. "We have twenty-four pink balls."

I bite my tongue when she answers for fear she may end up stabbing me later on when no one is looking. There's an audible sigh as Cole and Millie walk off the game platform.

"Josh and Joey, you're currently in the lead." I throw a fist pump into the air just for the viewers.

"Gary and Amanda, how many green balls do you have?"

"We have twenty green balls." As soon as Amanda answers, they're stepping off the platform before Patrick can go through his spiel. Now all eyes are on Bronx and Rebekah. My thinking is that they wouldn't want to win the first competition because that could pit the house against them. But this is Bronx Taylor we're talking about, and he doesn't care who he steps on to get to the top.

"Bronx and Rebekah, how did you enjoy your first competition?"

"It was lovely, thank you."

"She seems very prim and proper," Joey whispers and I nod agreement, but not before I wonder why Joey cares.

"Tell us, how many red balls were you able to capture?"

Rebekah looks over her shoulder and beams at Bronx,

causing my stomach to lurch. "We have twenty-five red balls," Bronx states all too smugly for my liking.

"Crap," Joey mutters as she takes my hand to walk us off stage. I tune out Patrick and his celebratory congratulations to the happy couple. Rebekah's squealing is enough pain for my ears.

"Houseguests may return inside." The black screen starts to lift as we wait to go back in. None of us are in the mood to talk to Bronx and Rebekah, at least those of us who are of the male species. Amanda is yapping his ear off and all I can think is thank heavens it's him and not me right now.

When we step in, the house has changed. The couches are gone, having been replaced by loveseats and, in addition, the first picture taken of each of us as married couples are on the wall. Millie walks over to hers and traces around the edges.

"They're going to survive this," Joey says as she walks over to the photos. I want to tell her that we will, too, it'll just take some work, but I don't think she'd believe me.

I wander down the hall and into the red room. I'm hoping Joey and I can just stay in here since we never packed our belongings. I'd rather not fight for a room tonight.

A room?

Stepping back into the hall, I walk toward a new opening. Sure enough while we were playing outside, they somehow brought another room into the house. The wonders of Hollywood magic never cease to amaze me. This room is green and reminds me of grass; definitely not one I want to be in.

I turn at the feeling of a hand on my shoulder. Bronx is standing behind me with a smug look on his face.

"What?"

"Tsk, tsk, Wilson. I'm here to win," he says as he walks away. Before he rounds the corner, I swear I hear him say *your woman*.

CHAPTER
twenty

Joey

"I can't believe you're here," I exclaim as Bronx pulls me into his arms. I know to viewers it's going to look like I followed him down the hall, but the hall just happens to lead to the bathroom and that's where he found me. He sets me down, brushing lose hairs away from my face.

"I didn't know you were on the show until they made me watch every episode."

Bronx and I spent hours studying for exams and writing papers together. We had three of our four classes together our first semester. I had a crush, but when he left it faded.

"I can't believe you're married," he says, stepping back and apprising me. "It really agrees with you."

I want to tell him thanks and that I'm in love, but admitting the latter is far too painful so I shrug and hope my facial expression tells him everything he needs to know.

"You're married, too!"

"Yeah, Rebekah and I have been married for about two months." I don't know if it's game play or not, but it seems odd that we've all been married the same time.

"I'm so happy you're here. It'll be nice having a friend in the house." I sit up on the counter, watching as he looks everything over. When he dropped out he said he'd keep in touch, but never did. It didn't take long for him to make a splash and cause a few waves, but it's a go big or go home type of world. "Tell me about your wife."

He shrugs, and stands in front of me. "Met her at church."

"You go to church?" I ask, raising my eyebrow.

"I did while I was filming my last movie. It looked inviting, and I found it to be so much more."

"Interesting." I hop down when I hear voices starting to filter down the hall. The last thing I need is to be caught in a compromising situation with Bronx. Since his arrival only hours ago, Josh's demeanor has changed. I know there's a story there, and it has to do with Jules. At one point, Jules was rumored to be dating Bronx and another guy, but by the time the rumor started to stick, she was with Josh only to not be with him again. Honestly, their relationship has been nothing but a Hollywood train wreck.

Amanda and Millie come in, both eyeing me. I turn to face the mirror, better to watch my back that way, and pretend to fix my hair. Amanda is all over Bronx, touching his arm and chest, laughing as if he's said something funny. I don't want to watch her fawn over my friend. I'll leave the daggers and hair pulling to Rebekah.

I follow Millie out and into the backyard where Gary is in the corner talking to Rebekah. It only takes her a second to realize that people are watching before walking toward us. "Everything is odd with Bronx and Rebekah here," Millie says as she sits down. Cole walks out with two pitchers of daiquiri, pouring a glass for Millie.

"I know." Before I can get comfortable Bronx steps out, followed by Amanda. She sits down in a huff and pulls a full pitcher into her lap.

"Wanna talk about it?" Millie asks. I'm curious what Amanda's problem is, but I don't care enough to ask.

"Gary and Rebekah have some sort of history. I mean, look at them." She blatantly points to the corner where they're talking. From an outsider's view, yes something is going on, but it's not like Amanda cares about Gary.

"What if he cheats?" she whines, earning an eye roll from me.

"Automatic annulment, didn't you read the contract?" I ask.

"Yes, but what about my heart?" she answers mid drink and just in time for Rebekah to head our way. Awkward doesn't even begin to describe us right now.

Yeah, I don't know about that because I'm in my own pickle. Josh walks out with a plate of meat and what looks like potatoes wrapped in aluminum foil. This is why we're a match. When life stresses me out, I make cake. When he's stressed, he cooks.

Bronx walks over to Josh and pats him on the back. I sigh at the sight of both of them standing side-by-side. I'd like to see them in a movie together, but I doubt that will happen any time soon. There's no mistaking that I'm a fangirl through and through. I watch all the awards shows live with my own predictions of the winners written down and a bowl of popcorn in my lap. I buy the all the magazines, even the tweenie bopper ones with the pullout posters. I've camped out, waiting in sub-freezing temperatures just to get an autograph or a chance at a selfie. I'm there at midnight, watching the latest new release and returning the next day to watch it again. I've had unrealistic fantasies about the two men standing yards away from me. One is and has always been, since he came onto the scene, my dream come true. The other was short lived and even when he became famous did nothing for me. In my eyes, Joshua is the catch and Bronx is just the side dish.

If my marriage weren't ending in a few short weeks, I'd be rushing to buy a lottery ticket in town because the odds are definitely in my favor. They have to be.

We drink in silence, watching as the men filter around the yard, not giving us a glance. It's nice to stare and not worry about being caught.

"How did we get so lucky?" Millie asks as she brings the glass to her lips. The three of us are on our way to getting drunk. Her eyes are so focused on the scene across the yard that her mouth is seeking the straw. I stifle a laugh before turning my gaze back to the man candy section of the backyard. Bronx is staring at us. Holy hell does my body sigh when I look at him and say his name. Time has been very good to Bronx. If I weren't married to Joshua, I'd become Amanda and start making some moves, but alas, I have the better one out of the two.

Josh hasn't said anything to me since the competition ended and right now he's over there with a beer in his hand talking to Gary and Cole, avoiding Bronx. He's shirtless and laughing. It's a far cry from the disposition he was showing earlier. The whole freak out over the pink thing was a bit ridiculous and definitely something we'll have to talk about later.

Rebekah sits down, but doesn't pour herself anything to drink. Give her a week and she'll be guzzling right off the bottle. You sort of need the liquid courage to keep up with the drama and stress of living with people you don't truly know, not to mention the marriage part. And she's not even looking at the guys. I mean come on, two very hot guys, one good-looking and one who is definitely working himself to make his wife happy, are standing outside shirtless. You'd have to be a saint *not* to take advantage and look at them.

"They're all freaking shirtless," I say, reminding the girls of the obvious. "You know, even Gary isn't looking that bad these days."

"He's definitely trying," Millie adds as she passes me the pitcher of strawberry daiquiri. I top off my glass and pass it onto Amanda.

"But look at Bronx," Amanda sighs as Millie and I turn to look at her. "What?" she shrugs. "It's not fair. First you with Josh and now ..." Amanda glares at Rebekah who is sitting at the end of our large couch. I'm not sure if she can hear us or not, but Amanda doesn't care either way. "Why couldn't I get paired up with someone like that?" She points directly at Bronx.

"It all has to do with your application," Millie tells her. I wouldn't know since technically I didn't apply.

"Obviously, but what's on my application that doesn't match up with Josh, but makes me compatible with Gary?" Amanda asks as her frustration level grows.

"I don't know," I say honestly. I don't know what types of questions were asked, or how they were answered. I'm in the dark and chances are if I had answered my own, I'd likely be with Gary. If Josh and I win, I'll have to buy my mom a new car because if it weren't for her, I wouldn't be here right now.

The three of us sigh when Josh and Bronx both turn and face us. Gary and Cole are in between them and it looks like Gary is hanging onto everything Bronx is saying. The guys are far enough away that we can't hear what they're talking about, but Josh looks pissed. His hand, the one not holding his beer, is flying animatedly through the air. There's a lot of pointing in Bronx's direction, coupled with head shaking.

"Excuse me?"

Our heads move together as if they're on a rope as we all stare at Rebekah, who has moved closer to Amanda. We don't respond, but Amanda and I both decide drinking is acceptable in this moment. The sucky thing is, Rebekah is smiling, all soft, sweet, and very innocent looking in her flower print dress with half her long brunette hair pulled up in a ponytail and matching ribbon—she doesn't have a clue that we don't want her here. Or maybe she does, but was told not to care. We've been at this game for two solid months and as much as Bronx is welcome eye candy, they're intruders.

None of us speak, and even though the sound stage is loud and there are airplanes flying overhead, you can hear each of us breathing. Millie, Amanda, and I are just staring at her, waiting for her nose to grow and for her face to turn green. Yes, I know that's a rude assumption, but she's here to steal our money, and our fans. In the words of my eight-year-old cousin, 'homey don't play dat'.

"Are you always so perky?"

I had a feeling Amanda would be the first one to crack, and bravo to her because I'm not sure I would've done it. I don't want to know Rebekah. Millie and I are friends and will keep in touch once the show is over. Amanda and I, we may meet each other for lunch if we happen to be in the same city at the same time, but it's not as if we'd go out of our way to meet up. I can't see myself ever seeing Rebekah outside of this house. She's not part of the original three.

"I have a very positive outlook on life," Rebekah says as she juts her chin out.

"Is that why you married a stranger and came onto a reality show to win money?" Amanda blurts out as I stifle a laugh. It's not funny, it's what we did, but I'm not sure any of us had a positive outlook on life except for Josh.

I glance quickly at him as he and Cole grill the streaks for dinner. The sun was blazing today and the night air isn't much cooler. I wouldn't mind a dip in the pool with Josh later, but that's not likely going to happen if he's angry with me. We still need to talk about the arrival of Bronx, which I have a feeling won't go very well. My eyes travel over to Bronx, who is looking over here. Is he staring at his wife, or the three of us?

"Why are you here?" I ask, barely tearing my gaze away from Bronx, and when I do Rebekah is still smiling sweetly at us. Her hands are clasped and resting on her knee, showing off a dazzling rock. I tuck my hand under my leg and square my eyes at her, waiting for her answer.

"I'm here, just as you are, to win," she replies as she stands, presses her dress down, and walks across the yard. Amanda begins to mimic her until she sees Rebekah talking to Gary. That alone is enough to get Amanda off her ass and over to where Gary and Rebekah are now in deep conversation.

"I'll be back," Millie says as she gets up and disappears into the house. I continue to suck on the straw that feeds me my delicious ice-cold cocktail while I lounge sloppily on the couch. Bronx is walking over to me and I know this isn't going to be good.

"Hello, Joey."

I start to sit up, and am assisted by his warm hands on my back and arm helping me into a decent position. Putting my drink on the table, I sit back and appraise him: no shirt, sun-kissed skin, and beads of sweat pebbling his chest. Everything in me is telling me to stop staring, but I can't. Having him and Josh in the same general area with the freedom of touch, in the non-creepy way, should be a sin, a sin that I'd be willing to commit over and over again if forgiveness was easily given. To the hell with forgiveness, this house has two of the hottest up and coming actors and I want to sin. Badly.

"You're staring like you've never seen me shirtless?"

"I haven't. I mean, not really. Watching you play pick-up and having you sit next to me are two very different things. And you've changed ... a lot." I give him a once over before forcing myself to avert my eyes.

"Have you missed me?"

"Eh." I shrug. I have, but haven't. It was one semester of fabulous studying. "You've done well for yourself."

"I try. Are you happy I'm here?"

I glance at Josh, who seems worried. He shouldn't be.

"Like I said earlier, it's nice to have a friend in the house. Are you happy to be here?"

"Oh I'm very happy to be here," he says, leaning closer to me. I can smell his cologne as it wafts over me. He smells like the sun and ocean. I'm temporarily mesmerized until he laughs and leans back.

Bronx takes my hands in his and starts to trace the lines in my palm as I fight my body's need to shiver.

"This line here says you'll have a long life."

"Did you learn that from one of your movie roles?" I already know the answer, but only realize it after I've blurted out my stupid question. His mother is some spiritual guru and his dad is a banker. Bronx's parents are still married, making his life vastly different from Joshua's.

"No, my mom—"

"I know what your mom does and your father, too. We've spent countless nights studying, remember?"

I close my eyes and pull my hand away when I finish that sentence. I'm such an idiot and need a filter for my brain. I half expect Bronx to get up and go find Millie so he can impress her, but he doesn't. He doesn't even slide back to his spot, opting to stay next to me. When I open my eyes, I'm reaching for my drink, taking a long pull through the straw until the glass is just about empty. I really need a refill.

"What's it like being married to Wilson?"

"In my mind, perfect. I'm a fangirl ya know."

"Oh I remember when you threw a party in your dorm for some awards show."

"Shut up, you came and loved it."

"Yes I did," he says as he puts his arm around me. Any other time, any other place, and I'd snuggle right into him.

"How does Wilson like you being his stalker?"

"Oh I'm not a stalker," I say, as I shake my head. "I'm factual in knowledge." It's a crock of shit, but I'm not going to admit to stalking anyone. Besides, stalking would indicate that I know where he lives, and I don't. I've never been to Hollywood and somehow I doubt he's on the bus tour that takes you to all the stars' houses. They only show you where Hugh Hefner or David Hasselhoff lives.

"Well enlighten me, Joey. What makes you a fangirl?" Bronx leans in, his cologne inviting me to nestle into the crook of his neck. I back away, not wanting to give him the wrong idea, or for me to actually lean in and a take a whiff. How embarrassing would that be? The answer is extremely, not to mention wrong on so many levels. I'm a married woman.

"What are you going to do with the money if you win?" I ask, changing the subject.

"I'm not sure. I haven't really thought about it, but winning is pretty much guaranteed."

"Is that so?" I look at up the sound of Josh's voice. He's scowling, not at me, but at Bronx. I'm surprised when Josh reaches for me before he sits down and taken back when his lips pepper kisses on my cheek and neck. He's putting on a show and I'm not sure if I like it or not. I'm pulled into his side as his arm locks around my shoulder. I can't move, even if I wanted to.

"Why don't you just piss on her?" Bronx snarls in Josh's direction.

My mouth drops open, but Josh is quick with the comeback. "You should probably worry about your wife before you worry about mine."

Bronx scoffs, but doesn't say anything. After a moment of awkward silence, Bronx gets up, leaving us alone. I use this time to my advantage and test Josh by letting my fingers dance over his bare chest. We really needed to win, and failed at doing so. I'm not sure I can get freaky in the room knowing the cameras are on. The shower is one thing, but the live feed scares me.

Dropping my hand I nestle into him. "Why do you think

they're here?"

Joshua sighs and relaxes into the couch. My stomach rumbles, knowing there's food to be eaten. "Should we go eat?"

"No, I want to know what the sigh was for."

Josh groans as he runs his hand over his face. "Bronx and I ... let's just say we don't get along."

"That's been obvious since he walked in the door, but tell me why." I don't want to assume it's because of Jules. The last thing I want Josh to think is that she's all I think about when it comes to us.

"Tell me why're so chummy with him."

"Bronx was my study partner my first semester of college. We had classes together, so it just made sense. I had a crush, but never did anything about it because he was a friend. One day, he says he's leaving for Hollywood and that was that. Never heard from him again."

"And you just welcome him with open arms?"

"Sure, why not?" I shrug. "He followed a dream. No one can fault him for that. Now tell me why you don't like him," I ask as I thread my fingers through his hair.

"Ugh ... I know I should've told you this the first night we talked, but Bronx is my competition and in more ways than one."

"What does that mean?" I ask as I turn to face him. I push his hair out of his eyes and smile softly at him. "You can tell me."

When he looks at me, his eyes are pained and confused. "You've read my interviews, you know about Jules, but what you don't know is that at one time I was in love with her, then Bronx came along and she ... well, she thought she wanted to love Bronx, too. Since then I've forged a battle with him for every part we're both being considered for, and now I see him making moves on you."

I shake my head. I want to tell him that my heart belongs

to him, but the pain that comes with that is too much. So instead I tell him I'm sorry.

"Don't be," he says as he leans in to kiss me. "But please stay away from him."

CHAPTER
twenty-one

Joshua

Nothing is as it seems because as I look around the room, I feel like an outsider. Cole, a man who I'd consider a friend, is buddy-buddy with Bronx and in deep conversation with him at the kitchen island. It's probably not a bad thing to get to know your competitor, but he hasn't come looking for me today. Neither has Gary, Amanda, or Joey, the latter of which bothers me the most.

I knew I screwed up last night when I asked her to stay away from Bronx. I didn't consider her feelings or their past relationship and I put her in the same category as Jules, but without the commitment. I'm an idiot to think she'd listen. I've offered nothing but an end when the game is over.

When she came to bed last night, I knew something was wrong. From the day we entered the house, we've always gone to bed together. Sometimes we'd fool around, but each and every night, even after I've been a complete ass, she'd let me hold her. Last night was different. When I told her I was ready for bed, she said she was staying up to read. I didn't push the issue because I knew I had messed up.

The dip of bed hours later, the sleeping in sweatpants and on top of the comforter told me everything I needed to know. And this morning when I woke up, the chatter of a late night game with Bronx hit me square in the chest. She spent time with him, instead of me. I get that they're friends, but I'm her husband. Am I deserving of the title? No I'm not, but I'm trying to be.

"Josh to the confession room." I ignore the embodied voice that commands us to do things around the house because I'm not done observing. I'm not done watching everything I've built for the past two months slip away because some money hungry executive is afraid he's losing his job and needs a rating boost.

Instead, I'm leaning against the entryway that separates the bedrooms from the main living area. Everyone is either sitting on the couch, cuddling in the corner, or in the kitchen. No one turns to see where I am, to give me the 'I'm sorry you've been called to the room' look. It's as if I don't exist.

I turn my gaze back to the cuddling couple and shake my head. It's Gary and Rebekah, and while they may not be touching, they're definitely what I'd consider too close for comfort. I've deduced that they know each other and I'm going to make it a point to figure out how and why Gary thinks she's here and how she ended up with the likes of Bronx Taylor.

Amanda is oblivious to where her husband is because she's too busy making eyes at Bronx. First me. Now him. How come Gary isn't enough for her? After everything he's done to impress her, she tosses him away like yesterday's news. Although he doesn't seem to care right now, so why should I?

"Josh to the confession room." Linda speaks again and no one stops to see where I'm at or why my name has been called twice now. The one person who should care doesn't.

She's too busy making a cake. This is just perfect. My bubble has been burst. It's not even a pinprick giving me a slow leak. We're talking full blown pop.

Pushing off the wall, I take the few steps necessary to the confession room. I try to slam the door behind me, but it's on hydraulics and even I'm not that strong. My last few times in here have been with Joey, and we've used this room as our personal make out room. We both knew the viewers were watching, but we didn't care and I'm stupid enough to believe that that was enough to show her that I care, but now I know that's not entirely true. I have to find a way to let it be known that I want her, that I want to see how things go with us once the show's over. I never meant to fall for her, but I also never meant to meet anyone like her. I'd be stupid to walk away.

Sitting down, I rest my elbows on my knees and look into the camera. Do the viewers see my pained expression? Are the fans that Bronx and I share seeing what I'm seeing, even though he's only been here for a day? Have Joey and I done enough to secure a victory?

The red light blinks, my cue to start talking. There are no questions today, nothing fun. We're in serious mode and the producers have seen what I was going through out there so the next logical step is to bring me in and confess my fears.

"I'm a coward," I say to the viewers. "My fear is that I don't know what love is and my inability to recognize what's going on in here." I put my fist over my chest and pound once. "It's going to be my downfall. How do you know when you're in love? Is it when your body craves that person?" I'd say yes because when I finally gave into everything I had been fighting, and made love to her in the shower, I felt like a new person.

"I want to spend all my free time with her, and make time that doesn't exist be time for just the two of us. I never want to get up in the morning for fear that I'll be cold because her body keeps me warm at night. I find myself watching her comb her hair and it's fascinating. I love that she wants to workout, but not willing to give up her cake. She's real, not a plastic filled human trying to be someone she's not.

"My fear is that I'm tainted by the ugly of the world and can't see the beauty that is in front of me. My hope is that I'm enough for her, but the angry, bitter man inside of me says I'm not and I never will be. My stubbornness is going to drive Joey away and I'm not sure that I know how to stop it. I made a mistake. From day one I've told her something that I can't take back."

I sit back and stare off into the dark space, hating myself for being in this mindset. If I hadn't let her break down my walls, I wouldn't care that she's talking to Bronx, but I do. I'm angry and I'm hurt. The sad thing is, I deserve it. I have to own everything that she throws at me because I created the divide between us. The rules I put in place were meant to protect her, not hurt me.

"Tell us about Joey?" The voice is male, different from Linda. I cock my head toward the camera. I should get up and leave. I've already said too much, been too open with the viewers and with myself. The actor in me is saying—fake it. Give them the goods and play this whole situation off, but I'd be lying to myself, and if I can't be honest with who I am, what good will I be to Joey?

"Joey …" I say, remembering the first time I kissed her. Even with the blindfold on I felt something. It took no time for her to work her way into my life without even trying, even when I was fighting her every step of the way.

"The way she smiles can bring me to my knees," I tell the camera. The viewers. Her parents. Jules. What I don't tell them is that the way she says my name in those passionate moments we've been sharing makes me crumble. My knees shake at the thought of her lips touching mine. My resolve has weakened and honestly I'm not sure how much longer I can survive her unintentional onslaught. I need her not only physically, but emotionally as well.

In hindsight, this show was not a good idea for me. I never expected to develop feelings of longing and lust for someone I barely know, and now that I have I don't know how to make things right for her, or for us.

The last time I felt like this was with Jules, but even when I saw her on screen and heard her tell me that she can't wait until I'm home, I knew I had fallen for Joey, even with all my barriers up. With Jules, things were different. I didn't seek her out for companionship or to be my girlfriend. We just fell together. It was easy and convenient, until it wasn't. When Bronx made his presence known, I knew I was on the same path as my parents and I didn't want that. It was too easy to go our separate ways, even if we end up back together every now and again. She knows I'm not serious about her, but refuses to accept it.

I seem to be the one who can't commit, or follow though. Maybe it's out of fear or I have to learn how to open myself up more and realize that when I have a beautiful woman standing in front of me, one that is willing to be my partner through the most unconventional circumstances, I need to take the bull by the horns and seal the deal. I'm just not sure I can. What Joey wants from me, I don't think I'm capable of giving.

Again, I'm a coward.

When I signed the contract, I never thought Barry would follow through with having me on the show. When my agent informed me that I had to fulfill my obligations and appear on the show, he was angry that I got him and myself into this mess and asked if this was a ploy for money. It's not about that at all. It's about me wanting to make a difference in people's lives, which is why I'm giving my winnings to the foundation; the very center that helped shaped who I am today. I told myself that I'm here to win, not fall in love.

I may be lying to myself right now.

My lower lip feels raw and there's blood on the tip of my finger after rubbing where I've bitten through without any cause or concern for the pain. I didn't even know I was chewing on it until now. Who knew a question like this would send me into a diatribe in my head, justifying why I'm here and what I'm feeling for Joey?

"Do you want to continue?"

My head cocks to the side as I focus on the camera. I hate the detached feeling of this room. I don't care if the couch is comfortable and there are throw pillows everywhere. It's cold, unwelcoming, and invasive. I can't tell the viewers what I think about my wife because I'm not sure I can say the words out loud.

"Joey is unlike any woman I have ever met before. She makes me laugh and I have a feeling she'll be the one to make me cry." The words tumble out of my mouth. I can't stop them. I don't want to. If I can't tell her, I'll tell the viewers, the fans. I'll give them some insight as to how I see her. I want them to fall in love with her.

"Are you looking forward to a future with her?"

"Do I even have a future with her?" I ask the voice behind the dark screen. "The producers seem to think otherwise or they wouldn't have pulled that little stunt with Jules Maxwell, or have brought in another man from her past. Honestly, I stand a better chance with her ex in the room than I do with Bronx."

"Please answer the question, Joshua."

In this moment, I want this show to be over. I want to get out of here and start dating Joey to see how we are in real life. I want her to experience the Hollywood premieres, after parties, and nights alone on my couch. Can she keep up? Will she complain?

Does she know that the moment she steps out of my apartment, the cameras will be back? That people, fans, will watch her every move? They'll track what she eats, wears, and where she goes every single day. Will she smile for them like she smiles for me? Or will reality hurt her, much like reality is hurting us now? Does she burp in public? Is she the type of girl who is constantly in her stretch pants and a tank top because it's today's norm on what dressed up looks like?

What does she look like dressed up in a fancy gown with her hand resting on my arm? How will she react on the red carpet? As my wife, the public expects her to be there and what if she can't? Joey didn't come on this show to marry a celebrity; she just got lucky, or unlucky in her case. She also wasn't expecting to have her marriage annulled once the show stopped airing either. I feel sorry that she got stuck with a bastard like me.

Running my hands through my hair, I sigh heavily. It's good for the ratings, me contemplating my answer. It gives others a hope they didn't know they were looking for, that they could snag someone famous. Joey, even though she wouldn't want this, is the poster girl for all women who have celebrity crushes.

"Yeah, of course, but shouldn't the question be whether or not she's looking forward to a future with me?" I stand and leave the confession room before they can ask another question. Being put on the spot is not something I enjoy. I don't know many who do, but usually I'm prepared with a "no comment" or I can offer a smile and a slight shake of my head and that usually gets the reporters off kilter enough that they move on. Not this time. I can't look them in the eye when they ask, and that bothers me.

The house is empty when I step out. The sound of laughter is faint and coming from outside. It's too nice to be inside and when you have walls surrounding you, tensions seem to run high. Walking through the house, I look in the rooms for Joey as fear runs through me, wondering if I'll find her with Bronx. I don't think Joey is that type, but he is. He has no qualms weaseling his way into an existing relationship and I have no doubt he'd do the same with Joey, given half the chance.

As I step outside, the California sun blinds me. Immediately, my arm is up, covering my eyes as I try to adjust and work past the dark spots. Amanda and Millie are sunbathing. Gary and Cole are working out. My stomach drops as my eyes travel to the laughter and I find my wife and enemy in the pool together, with his wife watching. I think I'd be okay if Rebekah was in the water, but she's just sitting there, in a dress while Joey is in her bikini, sitting on Bronx's shoulders.

If absence makes the heart grow fonder, it's working. I want what I cannot have, what I pushed away. I had her, and she's slipping through my fingers. I don't know if it's just pure stupidity or my ego getting in my way, it doesn't really matter because right now all I can see is Bronx screwing up my life again.

I have to ask myself if the money is worth it because right now, the answer is no.

CHAPTER
twenty-two

Joey

I've never seen the look of jealousy on a man before, until now. Sure, Tony would scoff when I professed my undying love for Joshua when I watched him on TV or saw him in a magazine, but he knew it was just an infatuation and something that would never come to fruition. Looking at Josh now, as he watches Bronx and I in the pool, tells me that he's jealous, but of what? Is it the fact that I have a friend in the house or the fact that my friend is Bronx? Neither should really matter because he's already tossed me out like yesterday's trash. The end is looming for us. It's flashing like an airport beacon getting ready for a plane to land. Even after we've been together, he hasn't said things are different. Words are usually spilled in the heat of passion, but not from Josh.

I can't change Josh's mind. I've tried repeatedly and have only continued to hurt myself in the process. Would I rather be with him right now, and not when we leave this house? Yes, in a heartbeat, but he doesn't want that. He has Jules waiting for him on the outside and I don't care what he says, he'll end up with her. He always does.

I tap Bronx's shoulder, letting him know I want to get down, but it's not soon enough. Josh is already back in the house with a weak attempt at slamming a sliding glass door. I don't even know why I was up there to begin with, or why I didn't ask to be put down right away. When he swam under my legs and lifted me up, it caught me off guard, but I thought it was all in good fun. Seeing Josh's expression, though, tells me that he finds nothing funny with this situation.

"I should go find Josh," I state as soon as my feet touch the bottom of the swimming pool. Bronx holds my waist and allows tiny water droplets to fall onto his face without a care in the world. I find it rather annoying myself, but whatever. His hazel eyes make up for my annoyance and there's no mistaking how women can become lost while looking into them. Maybe it's an actor thing and part of the mystery of being so sickeningly beautiful. I'm not sure, but looking him in the eyes is dangerous and should be avoided at all times.

"I'm sure he's fine." Bronx half slants his head toward the door and as I glance around, I notice that Josh is the only one inside, and he's alone. Normally, I'd be an eager beaver and go running to find him especially since I haven't seen him all day.

"I have to go," I say as I step away from his grasp. Even though his fingers linger on my skin when I move away, I don't turn back as I rush out of the pool and into the house. As soon as I step inside, I regret not grabbing a towel because the air conditioner is on full blast and the house is freezing. I cross my arms over my chest and run toward my bedroom where I find Josh packing his clothes.

"What are you doing?"

He doesn't stop or look at me as he continues throwing his clothes into his bag. I'm half wondering if he emptied the contents, and this is his way of organizing his things, since neither of us have actually unpacked due to always changing rooms.

I find a towel and quickly dry off the water and step into a pair of sweatpants, slipping a T-shirt on over my head before placing my hand on his.

"Josh?"

His gaze meets mine and I wish it hadn't. His eyes are on fire; he's angry with me. He rips his hand away from underneath mine and continues to throw his clothes in his bag.

"Joshua," I say his name again in hopes that he'll at least talk to me.

"Don't. You don't get to talk to me right now."

"Excuse me?" I commit the most childish act known to mankind and pull his bag away from him. He sighs and drops whatever piece of clothing he has in his hand.

"Joey, I don't want to fight."

"Well I do, so let's have it." I cross my arms in defiance and stare him down. Maybe this was the problem with Tony. When he said he cheated, I accepted it. I didn't try to fight for us, not that I would have, but I was so indifferent with everything. Yes, my heart broke and I shed far too many tears but I didn't call him, text him, or even answer his emails. Once he said the words, I ran and never looked back.

I can do that with Josh, too, because we're ending. We have an expiration date, as much as I wish that weren't true, it is. However, I'm not willing to end on bad terms. I want to say that things were happy and fantastic for the ninety-days we were married. I don't want to walk out of this house with regrets.

Josh runs his hand through his hair and offers up a pained half ass grimace. If I didn't know any better, I'd think he's got a broken bone or something with the way he's looking at me.

"I don't want to fight, Joey." His voice has changed. He's not angry, but sounds defeated, almost sad.

Did I do this to him? If so, it wasn't my intention. The last thing I want to do is hurt him even though he's hurting me. He'll never know it, though. I'll never be able to tell him how much it hurts knowing he's walking away from me, from us, before we're even given a chance.

I sit down on the edge of the bed, pulling my leg up under me. "I'm not looking for a fight either, but we need to talk about what you saw outside."

He shakes his head and sighs. When he walks past me I think for a moment that he's leaving me here, but he's just shutting the door to give us some privacy from our housemates. I can't take my eyes off him. He's showing me a vulnerability that is often hidden behind the walls he keeps up.

Joshua sits next to me, keeping the standard "friend" space in between us. "I know I made a mistake last night by asking you to stay away from Bronx. I didn't mean to piss you off."

"You didn't," I say, slightly confused as to why he thinks he did. I try to reach out to him, but he shies away. Any progress I was making in bringing down his walls has evaporated.

"I must've because you didn't come to bed last night—"

I hold up my hand, telling him to stop talking. But before I can finish, Linda instructs us to all go to the living room.

"Figures," he says as he gets up. I expect him to wait for me, but he doesn't. The door slides open fast, and he's muttering something as he disappears down the hall. I follow behind and by the time I reach the living room, he's already sitting on the love seat.

I take the seat next to him thinking he'll lean into me like he usually does, but he's still angry, even more so now that we were interrupted. As soon as everyone's in the living room, Patrick Jonas appears on the screen. His smile is creepy and I'm starting to despise him.

"Newlyweds, how are we all doing?"

Bronx and Rebekah are the first to answer with a rambunctious 'super'. I roll my eyes and try to focus on Josh. I can tell his teeth are grinding by the twitching in his jaw. His leg is bouncing up and down, and it's obvious that he's eager to get the hell out of here.

"We have a luxury competition for you tonight, a night out at the movies. Before you get too excited—this is a singles competition. One husband and one wife will win. You will not be competing as teams in this one. Everyone to the backyard, please."

"What the ... are they ..." Josh grabs his hair in what I can only guess is frustration and lets out an awful sound. It's a cross between a grunt and scream. I don't know what to do to because aside from how ridiculous this game sounds, he wants to win, and that's what we usually try to do together—as a team.

"Come on, let's go win," I say as I grab his hand and pull him outside. As soon as I see the setup, it's clear that the producers have upgraded this particular game to obnoxious levels and it's complete and utter crap.

"This is so cool," Gary yells out as he claps his hands.

"Do they really expect us to fight each other?" Millie asks, standing next to me.

"No, they expect Bronx and I to fight, and for the rest of you to pick sides." Josh walks toward the ring that is set up in the middle of the yard. Hanging from eight different hooks in different colors are sumo suits. I've seen these in videos—they might look fun but it's something I've never wanted to try.

"I'm going to ruin my nails." I look at Amanda and shake my head. Millie and I walk toward the hooks with Amanda and Rebekah on our heels. We stand there, inspecting the awful plastic looking suits that they expect us to climb into.

"Oh God, I'm going to chafe."

"You know, for once, I agree with you, Amanda." I give

her a wink. She's right, we're going to chafe, and it's not going to be pretty.

"Well, you could always just lose," Rebekah suggests as she takes her suit down from the hook.

"Oh the hell we will," Millie replies as she grabs her suit.

"I'm not going to like this," Amanda says, and for the second time today I agree with her. I'm going to hate this game, but there's no way in hell I'm losing. Even though we aren't competing with each other, Josh has to feel the same way. That's been our goal from the beginning, to win. Win the competitions so we can win the fan votes. Sure, we've lost a few, but the effort has been there.

"Look on the bright side," I say to Amanda as I pull my suit down.

"And the bright side would be that I can kick your ass and not get kicked off the show?" She smirks, which only fuels my desire to whack her upside her head.

"If you're lucky, you may end up with a night at the movies with either Josh or Bronx," I reply with a highly sarcastic tone as I lean into her. "But be careful, neither of them like women who pick their seat."

Her hand moves forward, away from her butt check so fast I have to catch myself from laughing. Instead, I bat my eyelashes and step back to my spot. After I step into my suit, Josh is there to secure the back. It's ridiculously big and uncomfortable, but I have a feeling, that despite my earlier reservations, I'm going to have a lot of fun.

"We did this on the force as a team building project. The trick is to knock your opponent off their feet and fall on top of them. Just try not to fall," Millie tells us as she wobbles toward the ring.

"Now that everyone is set, we'll announce the match-ups and rules. All rounds will be three-minutes in which you have to successfully knock your opponent off their feet and pin them on the ground for three seconds in order to move on to the next round."

"Told you," Millie whisper yells as she attempts to jab me, but is met with sumo plastic.

"You must win at least two matches to advance to the final round. Rounds one through four will be qualifying rounds. Round five, if necessary, will be a battle round used to determine who will be in the championship. Round six will be the final round and one husband and wife, not necessarily yours, will win. We wish you the best of luck. Up first are Amanda and Rebekah."

We watch as Amanda and Rebekah roll into the ring. Gary and Bronx are there to help them stand. I pull on the rope to test its durability and lean into Josh.

"If you fall, roll to the rope and use it to stand up."

He nods and pulls on the rope to test my theory. "Don't fall," he says, making it sound like it's my intention to put my fat sumo self on the ground. I know I used to play with Weeble Wobbles when I was a toddler, but the idea of being an adult one doesn't exactly appeal to me.

The bell dings and the only thing missing is a woman clad in a string bikini walking around holding up a sign announcing that it's round 1. I'm kind of sad that she's not here because that would make this display of human suffering all the more enjoyable. Patrick's voice booms from the loud speaker telling Rebekah and Amanda to get ready. Out of the corner of my eye, I see Millie wobble over to me with a mischievous look on her face.

Millie leans into me, her sumo boob touching mine. In fact, as she tries to get closer, they rub together and I catch Josh looking at us with his eyebrow raised. I roll my eyes and earn a nod from him. "I heard Rebekah and Gary talking last night. They know each other," she says a little too loudly because she can't reach my ear.

"Interesting," I reply as Amanda and Rebekah prepare to face off. Both Gary and Bronx are with their respective spouses, each taking a corner.

Amanda attempts to jump up and down, moving her head from side to side. Her feet barely leave the mat, but that doesn't seem to bother her. She's trying to intimidate Rebekah, but by looking at the latter's face, it's not working.

The bell dings again signaling it is time to fight and Amanda is full on trotting to Rebekah, but Rebekah sidesteps her and Amanda goes tumbling, bouncing off the mat.

"Ooh," Cole exclaims as he claps.

"Come on, Amanda," Gary shouts words of encouragement at her while he pulls on the ropes, jumping up and down.

Rebekah wastes no time falling onto Amanda, preventing her from getting up. Patrick starts his count of one, two, three and calls Amanda out by count. We're not sure if we should clap or what, so we just stand here, thinking about our fate.

Don't fall down, I repeat in my head over and over again. That seems to be the sure fire way to lose. And I don't want to lose. I want to spend a couple of hours cuddled in Josh's arms without any disturbance from the others.

Rebekah seems to stay on top of Amanda longer than what I'd deem necessary and it isn't until Amanda lifts her head that Rebekah starts to roll off of her and out of the ring. Once she's standing on the ground, she's trying to pump her extremely fat arms into the air.

"Next up, Gary and Joshua."

"Woohoo," I cup my hands around my mouth and holler for Josh. I waddle over and help him into the ring and he takes me by surprise when he kisses me. I smile sheepishly and pray that he wins this battle, putting us one step closer to a night at the movies.

"Come on, babe," I yell as the bell rings and he thunders toward Gary. By all accounts Josh could easily take down Gary, but when you're ballooned out and covered in plastic it's a bit hard to be yourself.

Millie and I laugh when the guys bounce off each other. Neither of them falls as they continue to grapple for some type of leverage.

"You know, this would be so much better if we were watching you ladies wrestle in oil."

Millie and I both turn and glare at Bronx, who shrugs as if he hasn't said anything to irritate us. I'm not stupid, I know men do that sort of thing, but come on we're on national television.

"The viewers don't want to see that," I say. "They want to see you and Josh in Speedos while you roll in oil." I don't even look at him, not willing to take my eyes off Josh.

"He doesn't love you," he says low enough for only me to hear. My body stiffens, but I refuse to look away from Josh as he battles Gary for the win. Their match is lasting much longer than Rebekah and Amanda's and is much more entertaining.

"You can ignore me and the thoughts going through your head, but you know it's true. You know I wouldn't lie to you. And I know you. I know you're questioning what it's going to be like when you walk out of here. Wondering whose car he'll get into when the show's over, yours or Jules'. She'll be waiting, Joey. Just prepare yourself for when he chooses her."

Bronx doesn't wait for my reaction before he takes his fat sumo ass away from me. I bite the inside of my cheek to prevent myself from crying. He's right, but I'm not willing to admit my thoughts to anyone. What I think about my future with Josh, or lack thereof, is my business. Right now, I'm a happy wife with an amazing husband and we're going to win.

"Let's go, Josh," I yell a little louder as I pull on the ropes. That seems to encourage him because as the clock counts down, he's energized. He lunges for Gary, knocking him down and falling on him at the same time. Patrick counts to three before announcing Josh as the winner.

I throw my chubby arms up in the air and try to dance a

little gig, but my fat suit doesn't even move.

Josh rolls out of the ring and tries to give me a hug. We bounce off each other a little and settle for handholding.

It's round two and Millie and I are up against each other. I attempt to blow Josh a kiss with my oversized t-rex arms before heading toward the ring. Josh helps me in and I want to think the slapping sound I just heard is from him tapping me on the butt.

I stare Millie down, but she smiles and we both start laughing. We know we have to take this seriously, but she's my friend and I have a feeling she's going to make me suffer. She's a pro. She's done this before.

We circle each other, both of us not really willing to make a move. The guys catcall from the corners, encouraging us to wrestle. I'm starting to think Bronx's idea would be much better. Not only am I sweating like a pig roasting over a fire, but I also itch and can't reach inside my suit to take care of it. A sudden onset of panic starts to set in and I rush toward Millie, catching her off guard. She falls and I jump on top of her, pushing down with all my might. When Patrick says I'm the winner I roll off of her, telling her that I'm sorry. I'm sorry because she has to fight Amanda who has been in the corner sulking since she lost to Rebekah.

After I roll out of the ring, Josh is there to greet me. He kisses me, trying to squeeze as close as he can to me. I laugh, even though the situation isn't funny. "Let's never become sumo wrestlers," I say, needing to be closer to him. He steps back so the air in our suits adjusts. Either way he's not as close as he was and it's all due to my big mouth talking about the future.

CHAPTER
twenty-three

Joshua

I didn't mean to move away from her, but when I inhaled at the thought that she still wants a future, I inadvertently moved. From looking into Joey's eyes, she's already thinking that she's messed up. I glance around to see who's watching us and of course, Bronx is. He knows something's up and I hate that he's so intuitive. I want to tell her how I feel, but not right now. Not outside during this game where everyone can hear us. It has to be done in private.

I try to smile, to give Joey a sign that everything will be okay, but I'm not sure she understands my feeble attempt. She turns and watches as Bronx and Cole climb into the ring, preparing to battle it out. If we weren't vying for prizes, or votes, this game would be a blast with friends. I can see why this is so popular. It's something I'm going to have to do with Rob once I'm out of here.

Millie stands next to us, and her and Joey pound on the mat and cheer for Cole. It makes me wonder what Bronx thinks. Sure, he's a novelty, but that wears off soon. This morning I read too much into a situation because I was angry at how I acted with Joey. My jealousy issues are something I'm going to have to work on because the last thing I want to do is scare Joey away with my caveman attitude. She's free to do as she pleases, especially when we're out of the house. I don't want her to think that she has to be at my beck and call. Although, my schedule will dictate when we can and can't see each other. I just want us to have a honeymoon first. That is, if she'll even give me a chance.

Before I know it, Cole is sliding out from under the rope with a dejected look on his face.

"What happened?" I drifted off into a futuristic daydream and didn't even support my friend.

"My feet got tangled, and he used it to his advantage."

"Bastard," I mutter barely under my breath.

Cole shrugs. "I would've done the same thing."

I nod in agreement because I would've done it as well. In this game, you take every opportunity that arises regardless of the outcome. We're here for ourselves and our spouses and no one else.

Patrick announces that round three will be Millie vs. Amanda and Gary vs. Cole. Cole sighs heavily and falls to the ground.

"I need a break," he says, panting. The heat, coupled with the amount of plastic we're wearing, is exhausting. With round three match-ups announced that means I'm getting my moment with Bronx very soon.

Millie comes out victorious and tackles an already on the ground Cole. I look away from the moment that they're sharing. From what he tells me, once our obligations to the show are over he's whisking her away to a cottage his grandmother owns in the mountains of Oregon. The cottage is off the grid and they're going to really get to know each other.

I'm not sure what Joey and I are going to do, but we

won't have much time unless she wants to come with me on location. A week after our obligations to the show end, I start shooting a new movie down in Alabama and while 'Bama may not be a destination honeymoon, when I'm not working, her and I can explore the south together. I tell myself if I keep thinking we have a future, there's no way she'll tell me no when the show's over.

Of course, I'm just assuming that she'll even want to come. If I don't step up and tell her how I feel, it'll be too late. For all I know, I've scared her away from any thoughts at a future together.

Rebekah and Joey are up next to start round four and it takes a whole twenty seconds until my girl is flat on her back due to some flying ninja kick out of Rebekah.

"And here I thought she was a nice girl," I say as I pull Joey out of the ring.

"Did you see that? It's like she turned into some freaky ass bird and came flying at me." Joey's whining, but I don't care. If I saw whatever that was coming at me, I'd probably wet myself.

"It's okay," I tell her, pushing her hair out of her face.

"Can you help me out of this?" She stands, turning her back toward me. I want to help her out of her suit, but she has one more battle. I yank on the Velcro and let some cooler air in there.

"You have at least one more battle," I announce and see her body physically sigh.

"I never want to do this again," she states and I agree with her.

"But you want to try the oil, right?" Bronx asks from inside the ring. I hear my name being called and quickly put Joey's costume back together.

"There are some things you shouldn't say to another man's wife." I maneuver into the ring and stand chest to chest with him. I want to bump him, but it's harder than it looks.

He laughs and holds his hands up. I hate him.

The bell rings and I stand here with my hands on my oversized sumo thong. I can hear Joey in the background yelling at me to move, but I don't. I'm trying to save my energy. If Bronx wants to run around like a freak on 'roids, I'm going to let him. In my mind, I'm stronger than he is. I've had months of doing nothing but working out and eating the healthy and delicious food my Joey has made for me. I'm not even going to pretend that the cake she makes adds any pounds.

Bronx doesn't realize that I'm baiting him. This time I'm in control of what goes on in our lives. He can't sweet talk or screw someone to get him a victory. When he lunges at me, I sidestep. As long as Joey's in the competition I'm not willing to lose, but if I'm afforded an opportunity to make him work his ass off for the next three minutes I'm going to take it.

He stumbles over his feet, hitting the ropes first. I almost feel sorry for him and should put him out of misery, but after the way he's been acting I sorta like this game. He's no match for me in this ring. Or maybe he is and I'm the one he's toying with. It doesn't matter because it ends now. If he loses here, he has another round. I get to rest before I have to face him again. Suddenly, I'm Team Gary.

"Let's go, babe," Joey yells, giving me enough of a push to just finish this off. I rush Bronx and tackle him against the ropes. He loses his balance, falling backward and out of the ring, instant disqualification. I'm on to the final round and he has to battle it out with Gary, who doesn't seem too upset that his wife is out of the competition. If Joey were out, I wouldn't even be in the ring. There isn't a date that could be offered that I'd want if I couldn't share it with her.

I start to climb out to my three cheerleaders, Joey, Millie, and Cole, but stop short and take in the scene before me. Joey and I are in a stiff competition with Cole and Millie, and yet we're friends. I have no doubt we'll be hanging out once this show is over and I finally pull my head out of my ass.

"Round four," Patrick says. "Millie and Joey will go first, followed by Gary and Bronx."

Cole and I heave the women into the ring. They've already had to fight once, but as luck would have it, they're at it again. I know Joey is tired—we all are—but her tiny frame is having a hard time keeping the weight of suit up. I can tell by her posture that she's sagging a bit.

Joey falls, letting Millie tackle her. The match is over before it even started and I know Joey did that so she can be done. As soon as she's out of the ring, I'm helping her take her suit off. I still have another battle, although I intend to lose. I just hope its Gary that I'm losing to and not Bronx. I'm not sure I could stomach that defeat.

"I'm so tired," she says, falling into useless arms.

"I know. It's done now. You can sit and watch."

"I really need a nap."

A nap is just what we need and a shower. If we can't have the master suite, the shower will have to do. I need her, especially after this crap with Bronx.

"As soon as we're done, we'll take one." I hope I'm not overstepping by inviting myself. Alone time with her is worth it even if it means I'm watching her sleep from my side of the bed.

Gary and Bronx are up next and I try to hold Joey as we watch. Losing is even more appealing now because it gets me out of the fat suit quicker.

"You know, I think I've lost all that weight I've put on from eating your cake."

"I never said you had to eat my cake," she retorts.

I lean toward her so she's making eye contact with me. "I want to eat your cake." I hope she gets the hidden meaning in my words. I know they're stupid, but I'm trying. I've been wasting far too much time and need to put myself out there.

Joey's expression is hard to read and I chalk that up to

213

her not expecting me to say something like that. I turn back and watch the match, surprised to see that Gary is on top of Bronx and Patrick is already counting. It's as if time stands still while we wait for Patrick to announce that Gary is the winner. And when he does, Gary is jumping up and down while the rest of us clap for him.

Now that Joey is out of her suit, I can reach her a bit easier. I kiss her on the head and climb back into the ring for the sixth and final round. Gary meets me in the middle and leans into me.

"Can you let me win?"

"Why?" His question shocks me even though I have no intentions of winning this match, but I want to know why.

He's acting coy. A trait I haven't seen in him since the show started. "I'd like to spend some time with Rebekah. We know each other." He looks around and I'm not sure why. He has to know the camera is catching everything he's saying and dubbing it for the viewers at home. He's just sealed his and Amanda's fate at coming in last. I say last because Bronx's fans will be heavy supporters of him, regardless.

I don't give Gary an answer as I step away from him. If he wants this, he's going to have to fight for it. The bell rings and he comes at me like a thundering bull. If we were cartoon characters, his face would be red and steam would be billowing out of his nostrils. My reaction time is slow, and he slams me into the ropes. I'm thankful that the sumo suit takes most of the brunt force and allows me to bounce toward him. We grapple in the middle of the ring and it dawns on me that I've never asked whether he played sports in high school.

Joey and Millie start the countdown from ten seconds. It's now or never. I move toward him, tripping over my own feet. I put on my best Oscar face as I fall to the mat, letting my arms flail. When Gary jumps on me, I groan and struggle to push him off me. I even whine a little for effect. I could fight him off, but who am I to stand in way of true love, or whatever connection he has with Rebekah. Bronx, however, might have a different idea and I'm sure Amanda will lose her shit.

Gary whispers thank you before he stands, setting me free. As soon as I'm out, Joey is there to help me out of my suit.

"You can't be serious," Amanda yells as she rushes to the mat. "If you go on the date with her," she points at Rebekah, "you and I are done."

Gary's head turns as if it's on a swivel, looking from Amanda to Rebekah. "It's just a game," Gary remarks, but Amanda isn't buying it. She must know something, or she's insanely jealous. Although, with the way Rebekah is around the girls, I'm not sure what she'd be jealous of.

"I mean it, Gary," Amanda says, storming off.

"What was that?" she asks as her cold hands cool my overheated skin.

"I'll tell you during nap time," I reply as I wink at her.

She stops, and looks me in the eyes. The smile is faint, but it's there, creeping along her lips. Joey's cheeks flush and I want to jump up and down with excitement that I finally said something that is tearing down the wall around her heart.

I follow Joey to the side of the ring and start chanting for Millie. Cole joins, encouraging his wife to beat Rebekah. I find it odd and elbow him, giving him a questioningly look.

"If she wins, I'm assuming the fans would still vote for us."

I nod in agreement with his thinking. At least he's looking at this from a positive viewpoint.

But the match is over before we know it, with Millie on her back and Rebekah sitting on top of her.

"That woman is deadly," Joey says, earning a glare from Rebekah. "See what I'm saying!"

"Congratulations, Gary and Rebekah," Patrick says

enthusiastically through the loud speaker. We all clap, mostly thankful that this beast of a show is over.

"Get some rest, newlyweds. Master suite competition begins at midnight."

Gary and Amanda start arguing before any of us can really comprehend that in a few short hours we'll be back to competing. The thought of sleeping in the master suite tonight does excite me, though, and I start to mentally make plans for Joey and I in the tub.

I grab Joey's hand and drag her through the house and into our room, pulling the sliding door behind us.

"Joey, I—"

She holds up her hand, stopping me before I can tell her how I feel. "I want to finish what I was telling you earlier. Last night I read for a little bit because I wasn't feeling very well."

"You slept with sweatpants on," I blurt out, having lost my filter.

She starts to laugh, but covers her mouth. Joey looks at me with a straight face. "Because Rebekah gave this Holy Roller speech about the amount of skin she was seeing already so I put them on, hoping she'd shut up. When I came to bed, I was so tired I just lied down. I didn't mean to fall asleep."

"So you're not mad at me?" I need to know because all afternoon I've been worried that I've screwed up any chance of us being a couple outside the show.

"You're cute, you know that?" she says, leaning up on her tippy toes to meet my lips.

"Wanna make out or sleep?"

"Shower?" she questions.

"They taken, we have to wait our turn, so back to my original question. Wanna make out or sleep?" Please say make out because making out can and will definitely lead to touching and I want to touch her.

"Oh, I'm all for a bit of tonsil hockey."

I thank the heavens above when she jumps into my arms. I hold her for a moment before I let my lips do all the work. It's only a matter of seconds before I'm aroused. I maneuver us under the comforter, cloaking in a little bit of dark. As I lay her down and her hair fans out over the comforter, I know that in this moment that yes, she's definitely worth it.

I just have to find the words to tell her, and make her believe it's me Joshua Michael Wilson who is falling for her and not Joshua Freaking Wilson, the guy on her hall pass list.

CHAPTER
twenty-four

Joey

Waking up in Josh's arms, his legs tangled in mine, is the best feeling ever, except I need a shower. Waking up to the sound of Linda telling us we have ten minutes until competition is not my cup of tea, especially since we fell asleep and missed our chance to wash the grim off from earlier. It's 11:50 p.m. and I feel like I can conquer anything. Hopefully, this holds true as we have the master suite competition in a few minutes. Why it has to start at midnight is beyond me. I'm tired, happy to be with Josh, and could sleep throughout the night without any problems.

Right now, I feel like we've turned a corner in our relationship. I want to be brave and sit him down—discuss what happens after the show—but I'm afraid. I'm so terrified to see the look in his eyes when he tells me nothing has changed and that he'll still be pursuing the annulment. Only it won't be because we hadn't consummated our relationship. I don't think that excuse can even hold up. Neither of us was intoxicated or mentally unstable. I could say I was coerced, but one look at my bedroom would prove me a fool. I think Josh is out of luck. If he wants out, it'll be a divorce.

One I'd give him if he asked because I've known since day one it'd happen.

Josh stirs in my arms, pulling me closer to his naked body. After the sumo competition we came in here to talk, which lead to kissing, which lead to getting under the covers. From there fingers worked the strings of my bikini and somehow toes were able to shimmy down his shorts. Sadly, for the freaks watching the twenty-four feed we didn't have sex on camera. We did, however, fool around. Josh and I are getting to know each other. We're just doing it a bit backwards.

"We have about five minutes," I say as I snuggle into his chest. Right here is where I want to be. I could die here in his arms and be happy.

"These producers are freaking evil. After the luxury comp from hell, why can't they let us sleep?"

I shrug in his arms, knowing that he's really not looking for an answer, he's just complaining. On the inside, I'm complaining, too.

"Two minutes, newlyweds."

"Linda's so annoying," I mumble as I sit up, careful to hold the sheets to my body. The last thing I want is for my tatas to be all over social media. Josh slips his T-shirt over my head before getting out of bed. As soon as his back is to me, I pull his shirt to my nose and breathe in deeply. His scent is something I'm never going to forget.

Getting out of bed, I rush to get dressed so we can meet everyone for the competition. With my hair piled in a messy bun and Josh sporting a ball cap we walk out together, ready for this midnight competition.

"I really hope this doesn't involve water."

Josh pulls the top of his shirt open and looks down. "Ah, you put a bra on. That means no wet T-shirt contest for you."

I slap him and walk away to join Millie at the kitchen

island. After pouring myself a cup of coffee, I join her in our zombiefied movements as we suck down the much needed caffeine jolt.

"Newlyweds, please go to the backyard."

Screw off, Linda.

There's a loud audible sigh from each of us as the black curtain lifts and bright lights light up the backyard. We line up and wait for the doom that awaits us.

Bronx is the first one at the door, sliding it open for us to step out. Each of us mutters something unintelligible as we take in what's before us. The backyard has been converted to a neighborhood. There are four houses, each a different style and each with our last names on.

"Good morning, this is your domestication challenge," Patrick says over the loud speaker. It's nice to know he has to be up for this as well. "For the past few months, you've had it easy and real life is anything but. For the next few days you'll be competing in the most grueling competition *Married Blind* has ever done. This is where you'll live and sleep until one last couple is left standing. Each couple has different scenarios and your only competition is yourself.

"You will follow each challenge until you give up. If you want to call defeat, you'll both be required to press the red button in the center of the yard. Newlyweds, please go to your respective houses and get to know your home. Your challenges will be timed."

Josh takes me by the hand and leads us to what's going to be our home for this challenge. The outside is white with blue shutters and a white picket fence. Even the mailbox says Wilson. Josh opens the door, turns around, and scoops me into his arms.

"I have to carry you over the threshold."

On the inside, I'm swooning and dying at little at how freaking sweet he is. On the outside, I'm rolling my eyes and enjoying being carried. I wish it were real though.

Josh sets me down, saying, "Whoa," as he takes in the house. It's small, but definitely a home. We enter in through a small foyer with a living room right in front of us. One of the loveseats from the main living room is in here, something I didn't even notice was missing when I woke up. There's a small staircase and a hallway that I'm assuming will lead to the kitchen and hopefully a bathroom.

"Well, we should get to know the house, right?" I say as I start to walk down the hall. There's a kitchen with one small counter, a tiny fridge, and a two-burner oven. For seating, there are two barstools pushed under a small counter lip. Josh stands behind me as I open the cabinets. We have two of everything as far as dishes go, but only one frying and saucepan.

"I think when they did our house they forgot about your career."

"You ain't shitting. I'm almost afraid to see what's upstairs."

Hopefully a bathroom since there isn't one downstairs. I follow Josh as he climbs up, having to duck until the staircase opens up. The bathroom has a single shower with no tub and two bedrooms off the side. The "master" bedroom is small with a queen size mattress and box spring leaving barely enough room to get by.

"My apartment is bigger than this."

My response wants to be, "Can't wait to see it," but I know that's never going to happen so I just nod like I already know what it looks like. The apartment Tony and I had leased for after our wedding was bigger than this.

We move down the hall to the second bedroom, but find the door locked. "Great, our house is haunted," I say, causing him to laugh.

The doorbell rings and even though this is a show, we're both excited and go rushing down the steps. Josh opens the door as I peer over his shoulder. There's a big box with a letter taped to the front. He pulls the letter off and reads it.

"Congratulations, Joshua and Joey. Inside, you'll find your lifestyle and job details. Welcome to reality."

Josh and I look at each other questioningly before he picks the box up and carries it inside. We tear it open like its Christmas until we see what's inside.

"What the—"

"Fuck?" Josh says, finishing my sentence because in the box is not only a baby, but a fat suit … a pregnant fat suit.

"You've got to be kidding me."

"Babe, I'm saying this now so you can never hold it against me. I'm sorry."

I glare at him. This is worse than having a flour baby with Keith "the stink" Finkly in high school.

"Joshua and Joey, congratulations on the recent birth of your daughter. One of your first challenges is giving her name. Congratulations are also in order for the announcement that you're expecting twins."

My blood boils as he reads this letter out loud.

"Joshua, you're an accountant. During the day, you'll be working while Joey maintains the house." He pauses and looks at me. "How am I supposed to go to work?"

I shrug, still focusing on yet another fat suit that I have to wear.

"Multiple times a day, you'll be faced with challenges. Remember, at any time you feel you can't compete, press the red button outside and your challenge will be over."

Joshua puts the paper down and picks up the baby doll. It moves, scaring the shit out of him. "This is the most messed up shit ever."

"If it poops, not it." I childishly put my index finger on the tip of my nose and stick my tongue out at him.

There's a buzzer that sounds in the distance and Linda follows telling us that our challenge begins now. I pull out the fat suit and stare at it. It feels like silicon, but with large boobs and a bulging belly. I slide his shirt off and undo my bra. I know he's staring, but I don't care. I shimmy into the suit and immediately hate it even though it fits perfectly to my body. Josh chuckles and holds the baby up in front of him, shielding himself so I can't hit him.

"I hate you."

"I know, but you're so sexy." He steps over and gives me a kiss, causing my heart to skip. He picks up my bra and helps me put it on before handing me his shirt.

"I hope they have more clothes for me because anything I own isn't going to fit."

"I probably have to buy you clothes with my fake accounting job. Don't they know I pay someone to manage my money?"

"I don't think they care," I say as the baby doll giggles and starts peeing down his arm.

His eyes go wide. "Did she just pee?"

I nod, covering my mouth. "I suppose we ought to put a diaper on her."

"Do you know how to do that?"

"Yes, I babysat when I was a teenager." I take the doll from him and place her on the loveseat, getting a diaper on her, plus some clothes. It's only seconds later that she lets out a wail. This isn't going to be fun and games.

"Shit, what do we do?"

"Feed her," I say, as I try to get up. The weight from my fake belly holds me down and I have to slide to my knees in order to stand. I hand Josh the doll and rummage through the box and see a few of the things that we need, hoping the rest are in the kitchen, although I didn't see them when we looked. "Bounce her," I tell him, as I pass with her bottle and formula in my hand.

I'm surprised the water runs, but I have a feeling that anything can happen in Hollywood if you're willing to put your mind into it. I run the water until its warm and fill her bottle, adding the powder food before putting the top on and shaking, and give Josh a towel to clean himself up with.

I take her from Josh and cradle her in my arms, holding the bottle for her. The sucking sound with lip movement on this doll is far too realistic for my liking. Whoever created her has created a freaking robot. Robots will take over the world if we're not careful.

"What do we do now?" he asks.

"Um … name her, I guess? I'm not really sure."

"Right," he mutters, running his hand over his ball cap. He walks out of the kitchen without another word while I pretend to care about the baby in my arms. I don't know how long this challenge is supposed to last, but I'm already over it.

I walk through the house and into the living room, expecting to find Josh. Sitting down, I stare at this anatomically correct doll and swear it's made to look like the both of us. However, I know it's not possible and I'm just lacking sleep.

"Her room is behind that door we couldn't open. I took a shot and tried the knob one more time and it opened. There's a crib and some other things in there, but I don't know what they are. I'm dad dumb, sorry."

"You don't have to be sorry. This isn't exactly something we had to discuss." I'm sure Millie and Cole did, though. Josh and I are like the gallon of milk that you forgot about that expired yesterday.

"I know names are supposed to mean something, but honestly there isn't anyone that I'm close to that I'd want to call even a doll."

"Is there a name you like?" I ask.

He shakes his head. "Not gonna lie, I never thought about having kids."

"Right … so um, how about something generic like Heather or Apple?"

"Apple?"

Shrugging, I remove the bottle and start to burp the baby. If she's already peed on Josh, I'm sure she pukes.

"This is really hard."

I roll my eyes. "It's not, Josh. You just pick a name and call the doll by that name. How about Jennifer."

"Okay."

"Okay."

The doorbell rings again and I chose to stay sitting on the couch. Even though I'm not pregnant, I feel way overweight and I don't want to move. Josh comes in with the letter in his hand.

"I think that this show hates us."

"Why?"

"Because we're in debt, which is so far from real life it's not even funny, but here we are in financial ruins and I work a job where I barely make enough money to cover our bills. We have one kid and two on the way." Josh covers his face and groans.

"It's just a game, Josh. They're trying to stress you out. If we don't want to play, we just go outside and press that button and we're back in the house."

He shakes his head and comes over to kneel in front of me. "Do you want to quit?"

Don't get me wrong, being out of this suit would be nice, but it's a game and we're here to win. "No, we want to win, right?"

He nods and kisses my knee, letting his lips linger for a moment. "My work comp begins in a couple of hours. We should get some sleep." He helps me stand and waits until I pick up the baby, aka Jennifer. Josh follows me upstairs and into her room. It's decorated in baby animal theme and it gives me pause wondering if I'll ever have the opportunity to decorate a nursery.

I set the baby in her crib and pray that she sleeps through the night. Knowing our luck, the answer is no. Josh waits for me at the door and somehow knows to keep it slightly open. We all but collapse onto the bed in our room and I quickly realize that he and I can only spoon. Except it's hot and I don't want him to touch me right now.

If this is supposed to be a glimpse into our future, I'm not sure I'm ready for it. Part of me is relived that Josh and I never have to face this and being fake prego and already parents is putting a damper on how we sleep. I look at him, passed out cold and a mile away from me. He looks like he doesn't have a care in the world, and I suppose that's true, he doesn't. This is all game play and not meant to be real, but what if you want it to be real?

Rubbing my hand over the protruding belly suit, I can't help picturing what it'd be like to be carrying his child or to have our daughter sleeping in the next room, a child that looks like a combination of the both us and who depends on us to nurture him or her. That's where this show fails in epic proportions. Not only do they mock the meaning of marriage, but now they're adding children to the mix. I'm not sure I want to win, or even continue to participate, but I will because the money is important to Josh. He has plans to do some good in his community and who am I to try and stop him?

All too soon a buzzer goes off and Josh springs to life, confused and disoriented. I want to laugh, but the fact that I'm so tired, hot, and haven't slept because I've been worrying about a future that I don't have stops me.

"What's that noise?"

"My guess, it's time to start the day." I shrug, keeping my eyes on him. He hasn't looked at me once and in the back of my head I know he's tired, but I'm pregnant with his twins and he should look at me.

"It's just a game," I mutter to myself as I try to sit up. Whatever I did to deserve purgatory in fat suits, I'm sorry. I'll scrub bathroom floors for the rest of my life if I never have to wear one again after this competition.

"What time is it?"

I shake my head. "No idea. My watch is inside the house." That's a lie. I don't wear one. I'm a strict look-at-my-cell-phone-type-of-girl.

Josh slides out of bed and pads to the bathroom. Everything in this house is so close together I can hear everything, but shockingly can't hear our neighbors. I wonder about Millie, Amanda, and also Rebekah. *What's their life like right now? Will I get to see them?*

"I guess I go to work now."

"All right," I say as I stand and walk over to him. What do we do now? I have no idea, but do know our lives would not be like this. "If we were outside this house, this game, what would be happening right now?"

Josh sighs and takes my hands in his. "I've thought a lot about what life on the outside could be like for us and this isn't it. I don't know if this is meant to scare us or what, but we've been in here for hours and I already hate it. I don't hate the fact that you're pregnant or we have a kid, but the fact that this isn't even close to what our reality would be. Am I rich, hell no, but I earn enough money to afford something better."

"Josh, what are you saying?"

He looks into my eyes and smiles. "I'm hoping you want to give us a chance when we get out of here. I know I don't deserve it, but I want to see where we can go with this. I still don't like the idea of being married and I'm not saying we need to divorce, but win or lose, I'm hoping for a chance."

CHAPTER
twenty-five

Joshua

"Someone freaking pinch me."

That's what Joey's response is to my heartfelt-lay-it-on-the-line-emotional-dump. She wants to be pinched and who am I to deny her? I grab a bit of her skin between my thumb and forefinger and squeeze. Her mouth drops open before the wailing ow is emitted. Joey slaps my hand away and glares at me.

"What was that for?"

"You said to pinch you, so I did."

"Yeah but—"

I take her face into my hands and hold her gaze with mine. "No buts, Joey. I know you're freaking out because of the way I acted and the things I've said, but this is me putting it out there for you and for us. I think you and I have a connection and I want to explore it. I don't know where it's going to go, and we may hate each other when we get out of this house, but the thought of never seeing you again, or having to wait a year to see you at the reunion show doesn't sit well with me."

"Your day is starting now." Linda's disembodied voice echoes through our cult compound and I find myself asking if this is worth it or do Joey and I just ditch out. I can't do that to Joey, though. Who knows if we're going to make it, and if we don't it'd be nice for her to have a nest egg.

Still holding her face in my hands, I bring her forward as far as I can to kiss her. I'm trying not to let the fact that she looks pregnant scare the shit out of me, but it's definitely plaguing my mind right now. I just have to keep reminding myself that it's fake. I don't know if I'm ready to see Joey with a child, but I also know I'm not ready for her to leave me.

"Newlyweds to the courtyard," Linda says, breaking my connection with Joey.

"How many days until this is show over?"

I laugh, but mentally count the days in my head. "Not soon enough," I tell her as I take her hand in mine and walk us down the stairs. As soon as we're outside, I can't help but look at everyone.

Joey is the only pregnant one. Gary is holding a baby in his arms, which reminds me about the one we left upstairs.

"Shit, the baby," I say as I run back into the house and take the steps two at a time. Parents of the freaking year right here! I throw the door open in dramatic fashion and rush to the crib, scooping her up. I'm sure she needs to be changed, but I don't know how to do that. I don't think we're vying for points right now so this is as good as it's going to get.

When I walk back outside, I hear gasps. Oh yeah, I knocked the virtual Joey up good and proper. In real life, it's not happening anytime soon. If we can make a go of it, I want to enjoy her and build a life before we even think about having little humans. I also need to be confident in my ability to be a father before I even consider it.

"Newlyweds, each of you have been given a different life to lead. While you won't be able to go to work, you will receive a salary to which you need to budget your expenses with. Houses have to be cleaned, children taken care of …" Patrick laughs as if this is some sort of joke. I'm sure it is to him, but not to the rest of us. This challenge could last weeks if he's not careful. Viewers will get bored and forget we're even on.

"Each time the buzzer goes off, check your mailbox. I'll be back to check with you later."

"I'm a stay at home dad," Gary yells, earning a righteous glare from Amanda.

"Can't imagine that went over well," I mumble to Joey who hides her snicker.

Cole and Millie walk over to us. Cole is barely able to contain his laughter as he points to Jennifer. Millie elbows him and takes the doll from me.

"What, never seen a man hold a doll before?"

"Just didn't expect to see you holding one and for her to be pregnant," Cole says. How he got so lucky in the lack of kids department irritates me. Millie and he have been blissful this entire time. They need some drama.

"Oh yeah, being in a fat suit again is right up my alley."

I pull Joey to me hoping to take some of the pressure off her back. The suit is heavy and I know it's a burden for her to wear it.

Overhead dark clouds roll in and it starts to rain. A rarity in California, but likely needed. Everyone starts to scatter, except for Joey. She stands there with her head back, letting the rain pepper her skin. She's beautiful in every way possible. I can't believe I was so stupid to tell her that we couldn't be together.

I tilt her head up and capture her lips with mine. Her fingers push through my damp hair pulling slightly. My hand cups her face as our tongues dance. This kiss isn't for game play or because we're on national television. It's because she's beautiful and deserves to be kissed. It's because I want to kiss her like there's no tomorrow.

The buzzer sounds and the telltale click from doors opening play in the background. Mailboxes open and close, but I don't stop. I can't pull away from her. I know, in this moment, that I've made the right decision. Being with Joey is going to be the easiest thing I've ever done.

When I pull away, her eyes are still closed and raindrops rest on her eyelashes. I want a camera to capture this moment and wish we were anywhere but here. I hate saying this, but I love the thought of the paparazzi taking pictures of us so I can keep them on my phone. The first thing we're doing once we're out of here is taking a damn selfie, and yes I'll be posting it on social media.

"Josh, please pick up your mail," Linda interrupts us once again. Sighing, I kiss Joey again, but only briefly. I'm going to have to talk to her about foregoing this competition because right now I'd rather be sitting inside the house getting to know her even better.

Pulling the mailbox open, I retrieve the letter. I realize that this is the game of Life, and the only thing missing are the cars that we need to move around the game board.

"We have a leak and a missing child," I tell Joey. Her eyes go wide and her hand covers her mouth.

"Shit, who has the baby?"

"Millie," I reply, as Joey turns toward their house. I go into the house and look for the leak. Nothing on the first floor indicates running water, and climbing the stairs I dread where a leak could be. The bathroom and our bedroom show no signs of water, leaving only the baby's room. When I open the door, I see the rain from outside pelting down onto the crib.

"You've got to be kidding me. This is exactly why I'll never own a home."

I can't call a contractor, because according to this game I wouldn't be able to afford it. So I move the crib out of the way to at least save that stuff.

"Wow," she exclaims from behind me.

"I know." I sigh. "What are we supposed to do?"

"I think use our friends. Cole is a contractor."

"Do you want to quit?" I ask her. "I don't care about winning right now. This won't be our life."

She looks from me to the doll in her hands to the bulging belly. Her nod is slow, but it's there. I never thought I'd quit any game in my life, but this one has to stop. I barrel down the steps and out the door to find Gary, Cole, and Bronx all heading to the buzzer. I step back in as coyly as I can and whisper for Joey to come downstairs.

"Everyone hates this game," I say into her ear. "The guys are out there right now pressing the button. Let's wait five minutes."

Sure enough the buzzer sounds three times and Patrick is on the loud speaker proclaiming us the winners. I have a distinct feeling this game did not go as they thought. Their idea to beat us down and cause situations that aren't necessarily going to exist doesn't make much sense.

I help Joey out of the fat suit, which is a little harder than helping her put on it. I do my best to shield her from the cameras. I really don't want anyone looking at her body other than me.

"I'm so happy to be out of that thing."

"I have to say I like this Joey much better. The other was miserable, and it hadn't even been twenty-four hours yet. Imagine if it were the real thing."

As soon as the words are out of my mouth I want to take them back. She visibly freezes and avoids eye contact. "Are you ready?"

"Um, yeah," I say as I walk in front of her. Foot in mouth should be my new name.

When we step outside happy, but exhausted friends greet us. Even Bronx offers us a congratulatory pat on the back. This challenge was hell. I don't look back at the pretend home that could've been my realistic doom as I enter the house. None of our furniture is back, but I don't care. I'm in need of a shower, or a bath. A nice long bath with my wife sounds pretty amazing right now.

Bringing my hand out of the warm water, I let my finger dangle over her chest. The water trickles down, beading on her skin. Joey's head rests on my shoulder and her legs are locked under mine. This is one of the most intimate moments of my life and it's happening during a TV show. The rest of our time here can't go fast enough. At this point, it doesn't matter if Joey and I win, I just want to get her alone. I want to be free to explore her body without having to be in the shower or winning a competition. I want to hold her without being interrupted.

First things first, as soon as I see Jason, I'm telling him to tear up the annulment papers. I hope he and Matt won't be waiting for me, but if either of them is, they need to know that Joey isn't going anywhere. Jason is going to pop an artery. He's all about pre-nups, clauses, and amendments. Even if Joey leaves me six months from now, I'll give her anything she asks for. She's with me because of me, not my checkbook.

"I'm filming a movie in Alabama a week after the tour is over."

Joey adjusts slightly, water sloshing around. "You'd think with me being your number one fan, I would know that. I'm off my game."

I wrap my arms around her, pulling her closer. "I'm thinking that you could head up my fan club. As president, I'd offer you some fringe benefits." That was corny, but didn't sound so bad when I was running those words through my head.

She turns in my arms, her breasts on full display and begging for me to touch them. I hold back though because she has a serious look on her face.

"You don't know anything about me."

Her statement confuses me. She's right. I don't. "You know what, you're right. We've spent all this time together and I haven't asked you the important questions. You know everything about me, so why don't we change this tiny tidbit?"

"Tiny?"

I lean forward and slide her over my legs so she's straddling me. "I say tiny because nothing you tell me now can change the way I feel about you. I know the important things, like what happened with Tony. One thing I don't know about you is where you're from or when your birthday is."

"Okay, well I'm from Springcreek, Oregon and my birthday is September eighth."

"Hmm," I say, moving her wet hair behind her shoulder. "So we could be on our honeymoon and celebrating your birthday, huh?"

"Honeymoon?"

Pulling her forward, our lips meet as if they need to touch. The lukewarm water moves around us. Joey shivers and as much as I'd like to think it's from my awesome make out skills, it's because we're cold.

"Do you want to go to bed?" I ask as my lips kiss the flesh behind her ear, trailing my tongue down her neck.

She nods and in a perfect world I can stand and hold her to me, but I can't. I tap her leg and she stands before me, naked and beautiful. I've been waiting for weeks to be in this room with her and now that I have her behind a closed door with no cameras I can finally be with her. I know it won't be the same as when we're together on our honeymoon.

Joey walks to the bed, mesmerizing me with the sway of

her ass. I can't watch as she crawls over the comforter. I think my heart stops when she looks at me with bedroom eyes.

"Tell me how things will be when the shows over," she says as I crawl over the top of her. I kiss a trail starting at her ankle until I've reached her lips.

"We're going to go somewhere warm and private. I want to swim in the ocean with you. I want to make love to you under the stars and I want to rub lotion all over your body. We have a week before I have to go to work." I pause and look at her. "Will you go to Alabama with me?"

"Under one condition," she says.

I search her eyes for any sign that she's about to give me a major ultimatum. I see nothing but love and admiration, both feelings that I intend to shower her with once we're out of his house.

"What's that?" I hedge, preparing for the worst.

"We visit the water tower and the beach from *Sweet Home Alabama*?"

I sit up on my hands slightly, unwilling to really disengage from her. "Do you like that movie?"

"It's my favorite."

"Of course," I tell her without hesitation. I'll do whatever she wants as long as she's there waiting for me at the end of my shoots.

"Excellent," I say as I settle myself between her legs. Everything about her is perfect and the fact that she's so willing to come on location with me makes me happy. In a few short weeks, all of this will be over and we can start our lives. I rub my arousal against her, gauging her reaction. Joey flexes her hips, showing me that she's ready.

"Condom," Joey whispers, reminding me that I need to be responsible.

I reach for the bowl and grab the first one I see and tear open the package without looking at the color. If it's blue, I may have flashbacks of it sticking to my leg. After I'm fully sheathed, I push in and her eyes close.

"Look at me," I ask as my fingers caress her cheek. When she does, her eyes are lit with desire. We move together in unison, our bodies creating the needed friction we've been waiting for. Joey locks her ankles behind my back, giving me less space to move. Everything is tighter, deeper this way. Her hips rock into me while her heels push down on my back urging me to go faster. I bite down on her nipple and her back arches, showing me that she loves what I'm doing.

"Joshua …"

"God, Joey, hearing you say my name …"

She whimpers and starts moving faster. I need to learn her body. I have to know the signs so I can make her feel amazing. My hand slides down between our bodies, giving her the pressure she's looking for. I groan when her walls clench and lose control.

I fall on her, out of breath and sweaty. Rolling slightly to the side, I pull her to me, unwilling to let her go. She nestles in my arms; her fingers dance over my skin until her lips take their place. She's going to drive me crazy, but somehow I think that's her intention. When she pushes me down and climbs on top of me, I have no choice but to submit. With Joey straddling me, all sense is gone.

I'm way overboard and there's no saving me now.

CHAPTER
twenty-six

Joey

The day is finally here. I should be packing or making arrangements to meet Millie for lunch in a couple of weeks, but I'm not. I'm freaking out. I'm hiding in the shade under the pretenses that I don't feel well and need to be left alone. Tonight, Joshua and I will be alone together for the first time. I don't count our time in the master suite because people were still in the house, lingering and always making stupid snide comments about what happens behind the closed and tightly locked door. No, later tonight it'll just be him and I without any interruptions and I'm freaking the hell out. I know it's not our first time, but it feels like it.

Everyone is doing their own thing today. Josh is doing laundry and packing. Amanda is sunbathing and avoiding Gary. I don't think they're going to make it. Gary is pretty smitten with Rebekah, but neither of them has said how they know each other. Bronx insists that his marriage is legit and they're in love. Rebekah does dote on Bronx, which is sort of sickening, but who am I to judge? I think my husband walks on water. Cole and Millie are freaking out about what tomorrow brings and where will they live. They both have good jobs that neither is willing to give up. They're both banking on winning tonight. Part of me thinks they will, but I think it'll come down to Josh and Bronx. Their fanbases will be voting in droves and Cole and Millie can't compete with those fangirls. I can't either, but I'm going to try.

Bronx walks outside and starts to stretch. I shouldn't be looking him. He's beautiful, fit, and stupidly gorgeous. He didn't always look like this, though. The Bronx I knew was a bit on the scrawny side, and often times shy. When he said he was dropping out to pursue acting I thought he had fallen and hit his head, but he was determined and it's paid off. Even behind my sunglasses he knows I'm watching him as he wiggles his fingers at me in a dumb wave. I could pretend I didn't see him, but it's too late for that since he's walking over this way. I could act like I'm sleeping, but knowing Bronx he'll just wake me up.

He sits down next to me and sighs. I should ignore him, but he's my friend. I do like him as such even though he tells me I'm making a mistake with Josh. Maybe he's just looking out for me, or maybe he's the blinking neon sign that is telling me to run and run fast. Thing is, I'm in love with Josh. It's not the stupid celebrity crush type of love where I'm falling to my feet and crying my eyes out when he walks by type, but the type where my heart aches when he's not near me and my skin tingles when he caresses me. It's the type of love where my breathing hitches when he walks into a room and my heart stops when he says my name. I have to trust that he feels the same way or he wouldn't want to try anything after the show.

"What are your plans for after the show?"

"The press tour, or don't you have to participate because you came in late?"

Bronx doesn't answer and I can't be bothered to press

him for more. This is his avoidance tactic, and it makes me wonder if he's in this game to win, or if he was a diversion sent in. I wouldn't put it past the producers to do something like this.

"I meant when everything is done. You know, when you're no longer obligated to Josh."

It's times like this when I wish I could get up and leave. Even after the show is over, I won't be able to escape. The show is in charge of everything from where I stay to when I eat and what I wear. The only benefit is that I don't have to pay for any of it and I get a new wardrobe.

"I'm not sure. We haven't discussed anything in detail." I chance a glance in Bronx's direction. He's spread out on the grass with his arms behind his head, eyes closed.

"And what are you going to do when Jules is waiting for him?"

I roll my eyes and turn away from him. "What makes you think she will be?"

Bronx tugs on my shoulder, turning me toward him. He lifts my sunglasses away from my face, forcing me to look at him.

"Joey, I'm not trying to hurt you. I just want you to protect yourself. When the show is over, he'll go back to her. They're like magnets. I would know because at one point I really liked Jules, but even when she was with me, she was with him. It sucked because being in the middle of the Wilson Maxwell drama isn't anything to write home about.

"I fell for that girl, so I know what he's thinking. I tried my hardest to be what she wanted, but it was never enough. Even their public break-up wasn't everything the media made it out to be. She didn't cheat on him, but the pictures of us in public were enough for him to end it. She and I gave it try, but she couldn't stay away and neither could he. This time isn't going to be any different.

"Jules Maxwell will be here tonight, waiting for him. His

lawyer will be waiting for you. I just want you prepared."

"We're married," I mutter, unable to find my voice. I bite the inside of my cheek to keep the tears at bay. I will not cry over Josh, definitely not on national television.

"Yeah, and so are Rebekah and I, but that doesn't mean she doesn't have feelings for Gary. Hell, once again I'm in the middle and will have to make a decision. She knows him from church and they're far more connected than her and I. I'm turning a blind eye for true happiness and all that other crap you women want. It sucks knowing your wife is in love with another man and it really hurts knowing you came onto a reality show only to have that man thrown in your face."

"I don't think Josh is like that, Bronx. We've talked about tomorrow and even when Jules had a video message for Josh, he was repulsed."

"It's acting," he says very nonchalantly.

"And what if you're acting now?" I ask as I sit up, officially pissed off. "What if you're bullshitting me so I make some rash decision? Maybe you want me to walk away from Josh so I can be with you? I thought we were friends, Bronx?"

"We are," he says, matching my position. "If I didn't care about you, I wouldn't be telling you this. Jesus, Joey, just watch yourself because the last thing I want is to see you hurt."

I shake my head, sliding my sunglasses back on. I don't want him to see me anymore and I can't really look at him without wanting to choke the life out of him. "How do you know she'll be here?"

"She told me."

I nod and stand up, leaving him as he calls my name. Amanda says my name as well, but I ignore her. No sooner do I step in the house is my name called for the confession room. I pause at the door and take a deep breath. What just happened outside will not carry over to this video feed.

Sitting down, I slide my sunglasses to the top of my head

and wink at the camera. Game face is on and I'm ready.

"It's your last day, Joey."

My smile is big and cheesy. "I know. I'm thrilled to start my life with Joshua." Because yes, he and I will have a life, regardless of what Bronx says.

"Are you happy you came on the show?"

"I am," I tell the viewers. "I've met some great people and have developed lasting friendships. The food was good; competitions were a little stressful, but enjoyable."

"What will you miss the least?"

I laugh because the list is long. I pretend to think even though I already know the answers. "The cameras," I say truthfully. "I won't miss them at all."

"And the most?"

"Ah, I think the lack of responsibility. It's sort of like being on vacation."

"Thank you, Joey. We'll see you at the finale."

The bathroom is a cloud of perfume and hairspray. We each did each other's hair and make-up, except Amanda had to add a bit extra to hers. We don't care because in a few short minutes we'll be out of here.

All of our bags are now out of the house. When our names are announced we'll walk out as a couple with no worries, except for the ones plaguing me about Josh. I didn't ask him about Jules because I don't want to know. I'm going to trust my husband and the things he's been telling me. That's what a good wife does. She puts her faith in the man she married, regardless of the circumstances. Bronx may not care about Rebekah flirting with Gary, but I won't tolerate Jules doing the same with Josh.

When I come out of the bathroom, I pause and take a mental picture. The guys are together one last time, sharing a beer. I'd like a shot of something to calm my nerves, but I don't think that's wise. I'll just lean on Joshua for support and guidance. He's a pro at handling these types of things.

Josh catches me staring and flashes me his killer smile, the one that makes me weak in the knees and makes my stomach turn inside out. He gives me butterflies. It's a feeling that I hope never goes away. When he stands, my heart beats a little faster and my palms start to sweat. I've seen this man in all his glory and still I'm imagining what he looks likes under this black button down shirt and black slacks.

The way he walks toward me has me rubbing my thighs together. When he reaches me, his fingers glide up my arm until his hand is cupping my cheek. Joshua cradles my face in his hand as he leans in giving me a taste of the beer that still lingers on his lips.

"Only a few more hours," he whispers against my lips, effectively rendering me useless. How Bronx can say he's going to leave me for Jules I'll never understand. If he didn't want me, he wouldn't be like this. We had boundaries before. Guidelines were set. He crossed them first. He took the walls down when I insisted on keeping mine up. He's not a Hollywood playboy, jumping from bed to bed like Bronx. I feel stupid for even giving Bronx's suggestions merit.

The doorbell sounds, and that's our cue to get ready. We'll be announced one by one until all four couples are in front of the live studio audience. I have no doubt my parents will be out there waiting. My mom isn't going to pass up a chance to meet Josh.

He takes my hand and pulls me into his side, guiding us behind Cole and Millie. Amanda and Gary are going first with Bronx and Rebekah going last behind us. Maybe this is way we got married, just none of us knew. At least we aren't walking out in blindfolds this time.

The cheers are loud when Gary and Amanda walk out and even louder when Cole and Millie take the stage.

"Don't be nervous," he says as he squeezes my hand. He knows how I'm feeling. I look over my shoulder at Bronx. He winks at me, earning a righteous eye roll.

"Joshua and Joey Wilson," Patrick Jonas says our name and hearing it makes my heart pound in my ears. Josh kisses my hand before walking out to the waiting crowd. As soon as we're away from the door, he has our hands raised in some type of victory cheer and the audience is on their feet. Maybe we stand a chance at winning after all.

I spot my parents and wave. My dad blows me a kiss and my mom fans herself. It's a good thing there will be some distance between us or my mother might land us on one of those talk shows because she's stolen my famous husband and wants us to live all together as one big happy family.

As soon as Bronx is out, Patrick Jonas is center stage recapping touching and embarrassing moments. I'm not paying attention because I'm searching the crowd for Jules Maxwell. If she's here, I want to be prepared.

"Now the moment we've all been waiting for." Josh squeezes my thigh. His hand has been resting there since we sat down, making me want to kick Bronx for being such an ass. "Coming in fourth place … Gary and Amanda Williams."

Everyone claps, but Amanda looks dejected. Patrick doesn't waste any time and opens the next envelope. I want to see his face, but can't because he's facing the crowd. His expression would give everything away.

"Coming in third … Bronx and Rebekah Taylor."

The dramatic pauses are killing me. Each time he stops talking, I feel like my heart is about to beat right out of my skin.

Bronx and Rebekah wave to the crowd as I glare at him. I'm sending him telepathic messages to turn around and look at me so I can rub it in his face that Josh and I still have a chance, but he never does.

"Now for our winners," Patrick says as the audience

grows impatient.

"Wait," I whisper to Josh, "doesn't he announce second?"

He shakes his head. "No point. They like focusing on the winners."

"That's stupid."

"The winners of *Married Blind* Season three are ... Cole and Millie Brooks!"

My mouth drops open as confetti and balloons fall from the ceiling. I'm stunned and at a loss for words. I thought for sure Josh's fans would've secured us a victory and maybe that is where we went wrong. We didn't compete hard enough. Josh tugs my hand and walks us over to our friends where we try to congratulate them. They're happy, and I should be happy for them, but I wanted to win. I thought we were going to win.

When the cameras stop rolling, we're ushered off stage and sent in different directions. We're told that if we have family in the audience, they'll be brought back to us. Cole and Millie are taken away before I can truly congratulate them. Josh and I are instructed to wait in another room, where we'll be given our press tour assignments. Before we can even step into the room, before we can finally be alone without a viewing audience, his name is yelled, and it's a sound that I have to get used to.

"Matt, what are you doing here?" Josh hugs the man in front of us, letting go of my hand in the process.

"Business as always, I have contracts that need to be signed."

"Okay, give me a minute." He turns to me. "I'll be right back. He's my agent and I want to get everything signed before we leave." He kisses me quickly, leaving me alone in the doorway. He enters a room just two doors down, tempting me to follow him.

"Hi, you're Joey, right?"

"I am." The man in front of me looks to be early forties

and very distinguished.

"Jason MacNicholl, Josh's lawyer." He grabs my hand, giving me no other alternative but to shake his. A sense of dread has washed over me and I'm finding it hard to smile. Just then the clank of heels catches my attention, turning just in time to see none other than Jules Maxwell enter the room where Josh is.

"Um …"

"I wouldn't," Jason says as holds out some papers. "I just need your signature and everything will be taken care."

"What?" my voice breaks.

"Your annulment, Josh has already signed."

I look down the hall and back at Jason. Laughter bellows from that room. It's Josh's and someone's I'd recognize anywhere. Bronx was right. And just as if he knew I'd be thinking about him, he appears. His face is sullen, his eyes are sad.

"Need a ride?" Bronx asks.

"Please sign here, Miss Mitchell."

Mitchell, not Wilson. I was told I'd be Wilson. Bronx takes my hand in his and gives it a squeeze.

"He lied."

"I'm sorry, Joey."

I take the pen from Jason and scribble my name, dropping it on the paper when I'm done. I don't wait for Josh or my parents, but follow Bronx out and into a waiting car. I want to think my friend is whisking me away, but the truth of the matter is, we all end up at the same hotel. I have to find a way to get out of my room with Josh. I don't want to share with him, but I can't share with Bronx. Something has to give.

CHAPTER
twenty-seven

Joshua

I thought the last person I'd want to see today would be Matt, but that all changed when Jules walked into the room and jumped into my arms. I had no choice but to catch her. When I could finally get out of her vice grip, Matt had a smug look on his face.

"Surprise!" they both say, much to my dismay. Since when is my agent in cahoots with my ex? Since when do they even speak to each other?

"That's an understatement," I tell them in a stern voice. I'm not happy that she's here. Matt, I can understand, we have contracts to sign, but there's no reason for Jules to be here.

"Let me sign the papers so I can get back to Joey."

"Why?" Jules asks in her stupid whiny voice. She juts out her lip and bats her eyelashes. That shit may have worked years ago, but not anymore.

"What do you mean why? She's my wife."

Jules bats away my comment as if it doesn't mean anything. "It was just a game. Your marriage is over. We can just put this silly thing behind us and move on. You've got whatever it is out of your system."

I look at her confusingly. "What are you talking about? My marriage isn't over nor do I plan on it being that way. This wasn't some ploy to get attention from you. I came on the show because I wanted to."

"You were forced to," she spits out.

"Can we sign the papers so I can get back to Joey?" I say, ignoring Jules.

Matt hands me the contract that will send Joey and I to Alabama once the press tour is over for the next three months. I look it over and everything seems to be the same canned language as my last one. This movie is an adaptation to a New York Times Best Selling novel by some guy who writes about romance. His movies are all chick flicks and guaranteed to have them in droves. I'll have my shirt off a lot so it's a good thing I worked out for the past three months.

"Who's my co-star?" I ask before I sign my contract. When I don't get an answer from Matt, I turn and look at him.

"Well, Joshie, it's me!"

"Are you freaking kidding me?" I run my fingers through my hand in frustration.

Matt shrugs. He knows that I don't want to work with Jules, ever. We did it once, and it was the worst experience of my life. She's a diva and I can't stand it; that kind of behavior annoys the shit out of me. Jules whined about everything, right down to the type of glass her bottled water was served in. Her agent was on set the entire shoot and barked orders about everything. Thing is, as much as I hated filming with her, she wasn't like this at home. After that movie, I vowed to never work with her again.

"I don't like this, Matt." I don't care if Jules is in the room. She knows I don't want to work with her.

"Joshie, it'll be great. We'll get to reconnect." Jules runs her hand down the front of my shirt. I grab her wrist and push her away.

"Stop calling me that and we're not reconnecting on any level, Jules. I'm married and I plan to stay married." I step away from her and hand Matt my unsigned contract. "Do something about my co-star or I'm not filming. My wife will have a problem with this." I slap the contact against his chest and walk out.

When I get to the room that's been assigned to Joey and I, all I find is Jason. He's sitting there talking on his phone. He holds up his finger, telling me that he'll be a minute. I start to pace in and out of the room, waiting for Joey to come back. She should be waiting in here with her parents, but there's no sign of her or them. There's not even an empty water bottle to show they've at least taken advantage of the craft services.

"Josh," Jason says from behind me. When I turn around he's smiling and holding up some papers, causing my heart to stop and my throat to swell. I have a pretty decent idea of what's in his hands. "It's all taken care of." He hands me the papers that effectively end my relationship with Joey whether I like it or not.

I don't want to look at the papers in my hands. I don't even want to pretend that I know what they mean. I signed these ninety plus days ago, long before I knew Joey.

"If you're okay with them, I'll file them tomorrow at the court house." I want to ask him if they're still valid since Joey and I had sex and the papers are for an annulment, but I don't want to divulge that information to him right now.

"I'll file them. I have to go down there tomorrow anyway," I tell him. I don't have a clue where the courthouse is, but that doesn't matter. I have no intention of filing them. "Do you know where Joey is? I need to talk to her."

Jason chuckles and I find myself imagining my fist hitting his face repeatedly. There's nothing funny about this mess. I told Joey we'd try and see where things could go with us after the show was over. I made love to her. I planned to spend many days with her until she grew sick of me. We may have married with blindfolds on, but I knew from the moment I kissed her that she was something special.

"She left with Bronx Taylor."

I nod, biting my lip to keep the barrage of curse words from coming out of my mouth. Most importantly, it's keeping me from telling Jason he's fired. Someone is going to pay for this. I take one last look at Jason and walk away with my annulment or divorce papers—I don't even know what to call them—in my hand. I have no idea where her parents are staying or what they look like, but I know where I can find her, at least I hope so.

If I have to spend the night begging Joey to give me a chance, I will. She needs to understand it was an unfortunate incident that my lawyer showed up, likely encouraged to be there by Jules and Matt. Even before I came on the show, I didn't ask him to be at the finale, and for him to show up out of the blue pisses me off. I'm aware he's under the impression that I wanted an annulment, but not before the press tour and I would've never done anything to embarrass Joey either.

This is something Joey should have never experienced.

My name is called from behind, but I ignore whoever it is. Producers, agents, and the media are waiting for interviews. They're expected of me, but without my wife with me, I have nothing to say. Besides, how do I answer the question of where she is? I can't and I don't want to lie.

I push the heavy gray door open and take a deep breath as soon as I step out. Even though we had access to the outside, the walls are no longer closing us in. The normal black Town Cars are lining the studio lot and each car has our names on the door. They want to parade us around while we drive the streets of Hollywood until we're in front of the hotel. The show's creators want the publicity, but I find this to be nothing more than a media circus.

A quick glance at the cars tells me Bronx and Rebekah's is missing. I'm going to tell myself that Rebekah is in the car and they're giving Joey a ride because that is what nice people do. It doesn't matter if Bronx and I hate each other; he's being a nice guy.

"Hello, Mr. Wilson." The driver moves to open my door.

"Can you tell me where you're taking me?"

"The Sunset Tower, sir," he says much to my surprise. The show isn't sparing any expense. They want us happy with luxurious accommodations before they send us traveling across the country.

"My wife … do you happen to know if she's there? We got separated."

"No, sir."

"Thanks." I slide in and he shuts the door. In front of me, in the center console is a bottle of champagne chilling in ice with two flutes and a tray of strawberries. It's the perfect celebratory dessert for a couple who should be starting their honeymoon, or making out in the back of the Town Car with its tinted windows. Except I'm back here by myself with my mind wondering what the fuck just happened. When I left her, I told her I'd be right back. What could Jason have said to her to make her believe that I wanted a divorce? I told her we'd try, and after everything that happened in the house, I'd like to think she'd believe me over some lawyer she just met.

I guess I was wrong.

The car pulls up to the sidewalk and the flash of lights start immediately. The paparazzi don't care who is in the car, they're snapping away so they don't miss anything. I can't get out of this car without Joey by my side. The headlines will be scandalous and more fuel for Jules. The last thing I need is for Jules to think she even has a chance.

I push the lever to lower the privacy glass in between the driver and me. He looks at me through the rearview mirror, knowing something is wrong. "Excuse me, but is there a different place you could drop me off?"

"Yes, sir. I could take you to the employee entrance or the loading dock."

"The loading dock will be perfect, thank you." The employee entrance is ideal, but a keycard is likely needed, or someone would need to open the door and I'd really like to enter the building with as little fanfare as possible. Although, I do need to stop at the front desk and get a key since my wife has decided to race me to the hotel.

Non-authorized vehicles aren't allowed in the loading dock area, but this driver doesn't care. I get the feeling that he's done this a time or two by the way he's speeding through the gate. As soon as he stops, I throw the door open, offer him a quick thanks, and get out. He's gone before I can even shut the door, tearing out of the parking lot like a bat out of hell.

There's a man sitting on the dock, smoking. I wave and act as nonchalantly as possible as I climb the steps. I need to make it seem like I've done this hundreds of times. I'm also willing to bet I'm not the only actor to come in through this door either. It seems like the perfect way to hide from the media.

"Hope she's worth it," he says, stubbing out his cigarette.

"She is." He doesn't need to know I'm going to meet my wife just that she's worth it. She's worth the heartache and anxiousness I'm feeling right now, too.

The loading dock leads through the kitchen. I wave as I walk by even though I'm met with odd stares. As long as I stay away from the guys with knives I should be okay. When I enter the dining area, the clank of silverware against china is noticeable. There are a few gasps and cell phones are being reached for. I'm on a mission, though, and time is of the essence so stopping and posing for pictures aren't an option.

I reach the front desk and give the clerk my name. He smiles, presses the keys on his keyboard, and hands me a card with a packet, which I can only assume is the information for the press tour ... at least I hope it is because I haven't got a clue about what's going on tomorrow. My room number is written on a sticky note to keep my privacy intact.

The elevator ride is painstakingly slow and I feel like when we reach each floor, the car pauses for effect. I know it's not the case, but I'm in a hurry and want to start damage control. I breathe a sigh of relief when my floor illuminates and the doors slide open. The moment I step out into the hallway, my heart beats faster and my palms sweat. I don't know if it's from the anticipation of seeing her, and knowing the cameras are gone, or if it's from fear that a lamp will be thrown at my head once the door opens. Either way, I'm willing to find out.

Sliding the keycard in, I wait for the telltale sign of a click before pushing the handle down. I step into the room; it's a small suite, but still luxurious. Even from standing at the door I can tell we have a nice view, but it'll be all for naught if she's not speaking to me.

"Joey," I call out as I walk through the room. Nothing is out of place and it looks like she isn't even here. When I step into the bedroom, my suitcase sits next to the bed, but the other side is empty, leaving me confused. I should call Bronx and ask him, but that would require me to call my agent or Jules to get his number and neither is going to happen right now.

I move around the room and can tell she's been here since the side of the bed where her luggage should be has been sat on. Walking into the bathroom, I flick the light and find a note taped to the mirror.

I'll be staying with my parents

No signed name. No phone number on how to reach her. No hotel information. I've got nothing until tomorrow when we meet with producers to get our schedule.

252

CHAPTER
twenty-eight

Joey

When I look in the mirror, I expect to see a different woman, one that is married to her celebrity crush. Instead, I see a woman who has been through hell and hasn't quite made it back. Joshua had given me hope, but that hope quickly turned to fear in the blink of an eye. I'm back to being the woman who got lucky enough to land a heartthrob, yet couldn't keep him.

Riding to the hotel with Bronx would've been awkward if Rebekah hadn't been in the car. The problem is, I felt like a third wheel. And not just any type of third wheel—the kind that gets dumped on a double date and has to go home with her girlfriend and her date. The Town Car was ready for a couple and I felt like an invader.

When the car reached the hotel, there were so many paparazzi waiting and they immediately started taking pictures and it scared me. Bronx was nice enough to ask the driver to drive around to the side and drop me off. He said there'd be a less likely chance that I'd be recognized without

Josh holding my hand. I smiled softly, but on the inside I was breaking down. He'll never know how hurtful his words were even though he was protecting me.

In little under an hour I have to see Josh. I have to sit next to him and figure out a way not to be cornered by him. Yesterday, I was able to convince the producers that Josh and I were going to have a real ceremony and we decided that we'd sleep in separate rooms until then. They came up with the idea of keeping us separate until the final press tour stop, surprising even me with that one. That was the easy part. I would have thought that they'd want to keep us together and monopolize on the 'celeb finds true love on the show' angle. The hard part was actually leaving the beautiful room that was meant for me. The room they've now given me isn't nearly as nice, but it's time away from Josh and I need that right now.

I apply my make-up in slow strokes, making sure that the bags under my eyes are covered sufficiently. Sleep did not come for me last night. Josh was on my mind, and I was curious if he had even come to the hotel, and if he did, did he bring Jules with him once he realized I was gone? As hard as I tried to think that he wouldn't do something like that, every time I'd close my eyes, her face popped into my thoughts, keeping me wide awake.

I stand back and look at myself in the mirror. I've lost weight. I need to eat a damn steak or something to put some meat on my bones. I'm thankful this press tour is over in two weeks so I can get on with my life. I don't know what I'm going to do, but moving is an option. I need to go where people don't know me and I can blend in. Small town living isn't going to cut it because I don't want people to feel sorry for me. No one needs to feel sorry for me because for ninety-days I was Mrs. Joshua Wilson.

The conference room we're meeting in is small. There are large packets sitting on the tables, each with our names typed on them. I sit down and open mine, dropping my plane tickets, hotel reservations, and car information all over the table. As I look through, I see that I'm going to New York and doing all the major morning shows and New York night talk shows. My fangirl moments are all going to be met in this year.

I try not to look when the chair next to me is pulled out. I also tell myself to stop breathing because a freshly showered Josh with cologne is to die for. He leans in and I scoot to the side.

"We need to talk."

Worst. Line. Ever.

Who the hell taught these men to open with this line? There's no "we" in this equation. He's going to say some shit and I'm not going to have a say in anything. This is a one sided divorce and I don't have a leg to stand on.

"Good morning. First let me start off by saying thank you for another successful season of *Married Blind*. The ratings were through the roof and we have you to thank for that."

The man at podium acts as if we're supposed to know who he is, and maybe everyone does except for me. He continues to talk about ratings and some logistics that have me zoning out. I'm eager to get on with the press tour and lie my ass off about how great the show is. I know there will be questions about Josh, but I just spent the past three months on a reality show, I'm sure I can make something up.

"As you can see, Gary and Amanda have opted not to join us. In fact, they filed annulment papers last night after the show. That information will be made public at a later date. Please do not answer any questions about them, aside from 'they're great'. Gary and Amanda are free to give their own press releases when the time is right for them.

"Everything you need is in the packet in front of you. You'll be traveling with a personal assistant. This person will be your best friend, right-hand man, or whatever else you want to call them. They have my contact information if needed. They'll also make sure you're on time for all your interviews. If you need anything tell your PA, it's their job to make this as easy as possible for you. We'll see you in two weeks for the season premiere of the *Helen* show."

The moment he's out of the room, everyone opens their packets and empties the contents onto the table. I know we're all heading to the same places, just on different days so the chances that I'll see any of them are slim and that's how I want it. The only person I'm willing to travel with is Bronx. I know him, he knows me and he knows the situation with Josh. Bronx won't ask questions or make me feel like I'm less of a human because of what happened. I don't even have a problem with Rebekah. I'd probably welcome the friendship.

Josh snatches my packet off the table and walks out of the room. I have no choice but to follow. He storms down the hall like a petulant child, ignoring my footfalls behind him. I get the bright idea of kicking his foot with this next step but think differently when I see people walking toward us. As they pass, they whisper his name, unsure if it's actually him or just a lookalike. I could scream his name and have them return for autographs and pictures, giving me a chance to steal my packet back, but I don't.

I follow him into another conference room. It's larger than the other, giving him more room to pace. He's like an old man with the packets tucked up under his arm and his fingers massaging his temples.

"I need my packet. My flight leaves soon."

He looks at me as if I've said something in another language. "What flight? I'm sure we're doing the media circuit here."

I slowly shake my head and pull my information out from under his arm. "I'm not. I'm heading to New York. You're staying here."

"What are you talking about?" He looks confused and

rightly so.

"The producers needed to separate a few of us because of Amanda and Gary, and I volunteered."

"Joey, we need—"

I don't give him a chance to respond before I'm walking out the door and back down the hall. When I hear the door bust open, I quickly step into an alcove and wait, praying that he walks the other way. He calls my name, but his voice is distant, assuring me I'm in the clear.

When I get to my room, my personal assistant is sitting in the chair typing away on her phone. She looks up and smiles before pocketing her phone.

"Hi, I'm Lou," she says as she stands to shake my hand. She's average height with long black hair pulled tight into a ponytail. "I took the liberty of packing your suitcase and the car is ready for us."

"Great ... oh by the way, I'm Joey."

"Is that short for anything? My name is Louise, but I don't look like a Louise, so I'm Lou."

I like her already. "It's long for Joe," I say with a smile. She laughs at my joke, making her my best friend without even trying.

Lou grabs my suitcase and hers and figures out a way to get out the door without any help. "I can carry my bag," I tell her, which really isn't carrying, but pulling behind me.

"No worries, I've got it."

I shrug and follow her to the elevator, praying that Josh isn't on it, or waiting in the lobby for me. I shouldn't have told him that my flight was leaving soon, but it was the only way to get him to ease up on the death grip he was holding.

When we get to the lobby, she rushes us right out. Even if Josh was waiting, I don't think he would've seen me. Lou is barking orders at the driver as soon as we reach the car. She talks a mile a minute, but the driver seems to understand and wastes no time taking care of our luggage and getting us on the road.

When I flew into Los Angeles, I never looked at the sights. I didn't want to be here and now that we're driving along the freeway, I think I want to visit. I'd love to take in all that Hollywood has to offer and do a tour to see where Hugh Hefner lives and catch a show at the Hollywood Bowl. I suppose if Josh and I would've won, I'd be able to do just that. Maybe LA is where I need to move to. It's big enough that I'd get lost, but I'd need a guarantee that I'd never see Josh and I don't know if anyone can say that.

Celebrity status is something to relish. Instead of waiting in the terminal with the other travelers, we get to wait in the lounge. I immediately spot a few actors and quickly hide my inner fan-girl. I don't want to embarrass Lou by jumping up and down. Sightings like this shouldn't even bother me considering I'm friends with Bronx. He's famous, and hell, as far as everyone knows I'm married to Joshua Wilson. Maybe that's why I'm in this room … I'm an actor's wife. Might as well run with it while I can.

When boarding is called for first class, Lou tells me "that's us". Lou and I walk side by side. She's carrying a laptop bag and pulling both our suitcases behind her. I have my purse. I feel empty handed and useless.

"Please, let me take this." I put my hand on my bag and give it a slight tug. "I get that you're supposed to do stuff for me, but your hands are full. I can do this."

Lou looks around, as if someone is watching, and finally lets go of the handle. I feel better knowing she's no longer overexerting herself on my behalf.

"Would you like window or aisle?" she asks when we walk onto the plane.

"I'm fine with the window." I'll be able to look out and take in everything I missed when I landed here the first time.

Lou sets her laptop bag down and puts our luggage in the overhead bins. She signals to the seat and I slide in. No sooner do we sit, does the flight attendant appear to take our drink orders. I order a cocktail, while Lou orders a soda.

"I'm going to confirm your appearances." She takes out her laptop and quickly goes to work. We aren't even off the ground yet and she's busy. Once I have my drink, I suck it down. Leaning my head back I close my eyes, and all I can see is Josh standing there with his eyes locked on mine, asking why I'm flying and he's not.

CHAPTER
twenty-nine

Joshua

Watching Joey run away from me sends a sharp pain right into my heart. I thought I knew heartache before, when I was with Jules, but it was nothing like this. My chest burns while my heart beats a bit slower, making time stand still. This feeling is new to me and I can honestly say I don't like it. I like how I feel when she's in the room: comforted, peaceful, and loved. I know she loves me, even though she tries to hide it and I know that my attorney, Jason, has hurt her. It's not just Jason, but her ex as well. Hell, even *I* hurt her while we were in the house. Fixing the situation is going to take some ingenious planning. Its times like this when I wish I had a sister, or a mother who gave a shit. I need some womanly advice.

It occurs to me that Joey mentioned flights and I assumed we'd be staying in LA. I dig through my packet and only see information on car services. The itinerary tells me what time the car will be at my apartment to pick me up. This doesn't make sense. Joey clearly mentioned flights, yet I'm staying in

California.

"You've got to be kidding me," I mutter under my breath. I have to know why they allowed Joey and me to be separated. I'm not buying this bullshit about Amanda and Gary. They've never done this in the past, so why now? Sadly, I wouldn't put it past my I'm-starting-to-think-he's-a-slime-ball agent, Matt, to have arranged this, and the more I think about him being with Jules, the more I'm starting to wonder if something is going on there. He wouldn't be the first Hollywood agent to screw off his client, or screw his client.

I pull out my cell phone and call Matt. He'll have Barry's number. I know there's a PA waiting for me, somewhere, but this is important. I have to know why they would send Joey someplace without me. I'm her husband, damn it. We're supposed to be a team, a united front and an example that, it doesn't matter who you are, love is out there. I don't know where my last thought came from, but I like it and need to make sure Joey fully grasps that I don't want this divorce.

"Matt, I need Barry's number," I tell him as soon as he picks up. There's no need for pleasantries, he knows who's calling.

"Why, what's up?" he asks. Normally I'd have no problem telling him what my issues are, but right now I don't trust him. He doesn't need to know that Joey isn't with me.

"Nothing I can't take care of with a quick phone call." I turn on the confidence factor and pray that Matt buys it. I don't want his help, not with this. Matt is the perpetual bachelor and sees wives only as a trophy or a cover, neither of which Joey is to me. He hems and haws, makes a few unintelligible sounds before finally rattling off the name and number of one of the producers. I mutter a quick 'thanks' and hang up and recall the number from memory.

On the third ring I hear, "Yo, this is Barry." I pause wondering, if this is his voicemail, but the voices in the background finally register causing me to clear my throat.

"Barry, hi, this is Joshua Wilson. I'm wondering if you could tell me where my wife went? She was frantic after our meeting telling me that she had a flight to catch, but both of us are confused as to why I'm not flying with her." The lie falls easily from my lips. Joey wasn't frantic because I wasn't going with her, it's because she was trying to get away from me. She was doing everything she could to avoid the elephant in the room.

"Hey, Josh. Yeah, man, yesterday after the show your attorney called to tell us you had filed for a divorce and so when she asked for a separate room, we had to come up with a contingency plan to keep this out of the press for a bit. You guys were a fan favorite and we need to keep up appearances until the press tour is over. What you guys do after that is your own business, but you're technically obligated to *Married Blind* until the media junkets are done."

I stand in the hallway with people walking by me. My head is down so I can't tell if they recognize me or not, and right now I don't care because the words "your attorney called" are being repeated over and over again while I try to determine if I heard Barry correctly. Unfortunately, I did, but for the life of me I can't understand why Jason would call them. I took the papers with me. They're in my room right now and heading nowhere near the courthouse to be filed.

"I'm sorry, Barry, my attorney misspoke."

"Glad to hear it, but uh … hang on one sec."

He pulls his phone away from his ear and covers it. The voices in the background are muffled and I hear some clapping.

"So listen, if you're interested we'd like you to make sure all the viewers know how much you love Joey …"

I stop listening when he says 'love'. I'm trying not to think about being in love with her. It's not that I don't want to be. It's that I don't know how to love her without being a soul-sucking-piece-of-shit like my father. I watched him destroy my mother, and every consecutive woman after her. The examples given to me aren't exactly ones I should follow.

"So what do you think?"

I pinch the bridge of my nose. "I'm sorry, what? Can you repeat what you said?"

"Yeah, we want you to declare your love for Joey on national television. Really do it up. Talk about how great it is to be married to her, all the mushy shit you do in the movies."

"Um …"

"It's great, right?" I swear I hear him clap his hands in the background, but I can't be sure. Everything coming out of his mouth is muffled.

"Um …" seems to be the only coherent word I can produce at the moment. I look up and notice people milling around. In the corner, there's a guy in a black coat. He's looking around as if he's waiting to get caught. I know the minute I look away from him, he'll be taking my picture or pulling out the recording device he's hiding in his hand.

"I sense hesitation?"

"No, not at all just … indifference," I tell him. I'd like to believe that if Joey and I were in a room together, I'd tell her that I was falling in love with her, or completely fallen. Thing is, I don't know what it's supposed to feel like—to be in love. If it's this ache I'm feeling, or emptiness, knowing I'm not going to see her for a few days, I must be in love. But to publicly declare it on national television without telling her first just seems wrong.

"Do you love her?"

And there's the million-dollar question. *Do I love her?*

"I'll do it, but on one condition."

"What's that?" Barry asks.

"You give me her number. We didn't have an opportunity to exchange numbers after the show was over."

Barry does what I ask and texts her number. Now I can at least talk to her and make sure she doesn't forget me.

263

The sun has barely risen when the Town Car arrives at my apartment. Last night, Rob wanted to talk like a schoolgirl about the show, Jules, and Joey. All I wanted to do was sleep, or lie in bed and stare at the ceiling and wonder what Joey was doing in New York. Was she out on the town? Did her and her PA go to a Broadway show? Did her PA take her to Times Square so she could people watch? And what about *Junior's* for cheesecake? These are all things I would've done with Joey to show her what else is out there in the world.

Yesterday, after I hung up with Barry, I called Jason and fired him. It was short, sweet, and to the point. 'Your services are no longer needed. Thank you for the work you've done for me, but from this point forward we're no longer associates.' To say he was pissed would be an understatement. He went on and on about how he's only protecting me from the gold-digging whore that Joey is. As soon as he said that, I knew I had made the right decision. I know I don't know Joey outside of the *Married Blind* house, but I do know she's not a gold-digger.

After that phone call ended, I sought out a reporter. I was going to be the first to break the news that I fired Jason. *Joshua Wilson fires long-time Attorney Jason MacNicholl for falsifying documents.* When I saw this piece hit the web, part of me was excited. The other part, not so much because I thought of Jason as a friend and regardless of looking out for my best interests, when your client tells you he doesn't want something you listen.

Rob was gracious enough to give me a rundown of the confession room drama. I didn't really want to hear it from him because I had hoped Joey and I would watch the season together, but Rob couldn't wait to fill me in on how Joey reacted in a few of them. When he didn't see my expression change, he asked the same thing Barry did earlier: Do you love her?

"I think I do."

I say those words over and over as the driver navigates early LA traffic. I'm like the *Little Engine that Could* except my uphill battle is three thousand miles away and has already been on national TV this morning with Bronx and Rebekah. She was so vague when asked about our marriage, making comments about how she really enjoyed the show and that I'm really nice.

Nice? That's how she sees me? I mean, nice is great, but I'm her husband. I want her to tell the world how she felt about me *inside* the house and let me fix the rest. I want her to answer her phone when I call and not send it to voicemail the second she sees a California area code pop up on her phone. I'm banking on the fact that she doesn't know it's me calling and is avoiding any numbers she doesn't recognize. I'm grasping at anything right now that will help me keep my sanity.

As soon as the driver enters the studio lot, the pressure starts to build even though I've done this for what feels like a million times. Questions will be asked about the show, the other couples, and of course Joey. Only this time when her name comes up, I won't be able to help the grin that spreads across my face. Regardless of what's going on, she makes me feel. She makes everything brighter and livelier. I knew from that first kiss we shared that Joey Mitchell was someone special and meant to be in my life.

The PA I've been assigned meets me at the stage door. She starts rambling on about shows, times, meets and greets—all words just going in one ear and out the other. The only show I care about is *Helen*. That's the day where Joey and I will be in the same space, sitting next to each other.

My microphone is put on, my hair fixed, and the obligatory stupid powder spread all over my face during the commercial break. My PA is talking a mile a minute about things I need to be sure to say and cover during my interview with the ladies of *The Chat*. She also encourages me to bat my eyes and turn on my charm, which is easy because these hosts are great to be with.

I walk out on stage during the commercial break and shake hands with the four women sitting around the table, drinking coffee. My spot is at the end, facing the audience. I wave and they scream. A few of the audience members hold up signs professing their love for me. I'm in my element, but not having Joey here with me is upsetting. I wanted her to see me like this—to make sure she can handle it—before we get too far.

"Welcome back to *The Chat*. We are joined by America's heartthrob, Joshua Wilson, who surprised us all by his appearance on the reality TV show, *Married Blind* this season. Welcome, Joshua," Allison Avery says.

"Thank you. It's good to be back here with you beautiful ladies."

One of the other hosts, Beverly Blake, fans herself while the other three blush and Cindy Drew says, "Isn't he to die for?" causing the audience to become louder.

"Tell us, what were you thinking when you signed up for *Married Blind*?" Hayley Gunner asks. She's the focal point of the show and married to one of the network's big wigs.

I smile toward the viewers and tilt my head slightly before looking at the hosts. "Honestly, I signed up so I could help the community center I grew up in to start a rebuilding effort. With the economy the way it's been, funding for centers like this—ones that help the youth stay off the streets—is hard to get. I'm trying to pay back everything that was given to me." It's the same lie I've told a few times to save face from the drunken incident that landed me on the show.

"I sense a but coming," says Beverly Blake.

"I fell in love," I state before I realize the words are

coming out of my mouth.

The ladies gasp, but it's the audience members who catch my attention. I can hear rumbling amongst them and the last thing I need is for Joey to be on the receiving end of bad press from the fans.

"You guys are going to love Joey," I tell them as if I need their approval. "She's very excited to meet you all."

"I have to say, Josh, the chemistry between you and Joey was *hot*!" Allison Avery fans herself. "How much of that was acting?"

"None," I answer matter-of-factly. "From the first kiss, I knew."

"Well there you have it, ladies. Joshua Wilson is officially off the market," Hayley Gunner announces, much to the displeasure of the audience.

As soon as the commercials are rolling, our microphones are shut off. Cindy Drew leans over and asks, "Are you legit married?"

I nod, and start removing my microphone. She shakes her head, tsking while doing so. "I think a lot of your fans were banking on this ending as soon as the show was over. We heard one couple has already filed."

"Sorry to disappoint," I say, as I stand. "But this is the real deal."

The moment I'm off stage, my cell starts to vibrate in my pocket. It's Matt, and as much as I don't want to speak with him, he's my agent, so I take the call.

"Hello."

"You must've lost your mind."

"No, my mind is fully intact. Do you have a new contract for me with a new co-star?"

Matt sighs, sensing that the topic of Joey and my interview is off the table for discussion.

"They want both of you," he says.

I motion for my PA to follow me out the door and into

the waiting car. The driver knows where to go and my PA works on my outfit for the next show.

"Not gonna happen, Matt. I don't want to work with Jules, ever."

"You're really going to throw away a movie deal because of some mail order bride?"

I clutch my phone tightly and grit my teeth. "You listen to me. You work for me, not the other way around. I've already fired Jason. Don't make me fire you as well. Joey is my wife and the shit that Jules pulled while I was on the show was deplorable. Jules and I are done, and I will not work with her. If the producers want me, find another female lead." I hang up without giving him a chance to respond. My PA is staring at me wide-eyed, fear masking her face.

I toss my phone in the empty seat beside me and say, "All right, who's next and what am I wearing?" as calmly as I can without scaring the shit out of her.

CHAPTER
thirty

Joey

"Don't be nervous," Lou says as she grabs my shoulders. Nervous is an understatement. I'm about to go on *The Tonight Show* with Steven Freaking Rogers. Cue inner fangirl screaming moment. Compared to the people he's had on this show, Josh being one of them, I'm nothing. I'm small potatoes. I'm the tiny speck of pepper that lands where you don't need it—the brushed aside piece that lives on the side of your plate until your plate is cleaned and the pepper is gone forever. That's how I feel right now. Tomorrow, no one will remember me as Joey Wilson, instead they'll know me as the desperate girl who went on reality TV to find a husband and got lucky and wound up married Joshua Freaking Wilson for three months.

My life is full of 'freakings'.

I should've said no to this press tour and just gone home. At least in the comfort of my room, I can sit in silence and eat bonbons, not worrying if my butt is getting big. Yet, here I am, in New York City for the first time, appearing on TV.

269

This is different from being in the *Married Blind* house, though. I can't explain it. Even though we were shooting live and the cameras were always on, sitting down in front of a live audience, with people standing outside of the window with their signs, feels so different.

Lou is right, its nerves, but I don't know how to get rid of them. Most of the questions I've faced on the morning shows have been easy: How was the show? What did you like? What's it like being married to Josh? Those types of questions I was prepared for. What I wasn't prepared for was karaoke with Steven. I know he plays games and does sketch comedy with his guests, but I'm just a mundane girl who went on a reality show and married an actor. At the end of the night, I'm still just Joey, a soon-to-be divorcee.

The media junket is a circus. Wake up before the sun—forget about being tired from jet lag and the press parties we're required to attend—and show up at the studio. Lou has picked out a different outfit for each show, even though most are filmed on the same day, and has arranged for my hair and make-up to be done at each venue. The primping, prodding, and the occasional pokes quickly cause tension. I don't know how Josh can put up with this day in and day out. I think I'd start batting hands away and demanding that I do it myself. This is my last appearance. I've been here almost a week and it's time to head back to LA.

Bronx and Rebekah are with Steven now and I'm able to watch from backstage. They're playing his version of the *Newlywed* game and Bronx is struggling to keep his answers PG. Rebekah, of course, is very prim and proper, giggling at just the right moment when Bronx reveals his answers. They make me sick, but in a good way. We'll be going to dinner tonight, along with our PAs, and I'm hoping that I can get to know Rebekah a bit more. Her time was short in the house, with her entering when the season was almost over, and we didn't start off on the right foot.

This part of the show ends and Steven is walking off stage. He high-fives his staff, stops in front of me and takes my hand.

"It's great to meet you, Joey. I'm looking forward to our segment."

Before I can respond, he's whisked away and I'm left standing there like an idiot with my hand still sticking out.

"You'd think you weren't married to a movie star," Lou says as she pushes my stiff hand back down to my side. "Are you going to hurl?"

I shake my head, and swallow. "I'm fine, just shocked that he even knew my name."

Lou rolls her eyes and leads me back to the make-up chair. She pushes me to sit and instructs the make-up girl that I have sweat spots that need to be covered on my face.

"Steven is one of the best in the business. He does his research on his guests so he doesn't have to rely on cue cards. He wants to be personal and make sure you enjoy the interview."

"That's good, right? Or not, because he could bring up my ex and I really don't want to talk about him on TV."

Lou sighs and sits down on the small counter under the mirror. "He won't bring up your ex or anything about your life prior to being on the show. Be careful of how you answer, though, because if you were to answer why you went on the show and you say because you found your ex with your best friend, he could run with that. So be mindful."

"Okay," I reply, trying not to add a list of things to my already frazzled brain.

"Five minutes." A man wearing a slew of headgear walks by yelling at everyone. The make-up artist finishes and Lou takes my hand and leads me to the back of the stage where I will walk on. Another person is waiting and starts adding a microphone to my dress and the belt I'm wearing. For a day I didn't have to wear one, and I already hate it again.

"My next guest scored big on this season's *Married Blind* when she found herself kissing none other than Joshua Wilson. Please welcome Joey Wilson."

I step out, wave at the crowd, and shake Steven's hand again. He asks how I'm doing while the music plays and he waits for me to sit down before he takes his seat.

"Welcome, welcome."

"Thank you. It's so great to be here."

"So what's it like to have your life filmed twenty-four hours a day?"

I take a drink of the water that has been set out for me, stalling so I can craft my answer accordingly. "It's like living under a microscope, and if you're up when everyone is sleeping, you can hear the cameras moving, or following you. That's creepy."

"Are the cameras *everywhere*?" Steven winks, causing me to laugh.

"Except the master suite."

Steven pretends to be shocked, but we both know he knows all about the show. From what we were told, he's a big fan, which is why he brought us all on here. "So let's cut right to the dirty, …you know, since you brought up the master suite. What's it like kissing Josh Wilson? I think all those women want to know." He points to the audience and they start screaming. I can't help but smile. At least they're not slinging insults at me.

I bite my lower lip, contemplating how I should respond. For me, kissing him was magical, earth shattering, and way more than I ever thought it would be. Hell, I dreamt about that moment and for it to come true—there are no words. But no one needs to know that.

"Well I guess that would depend on what time of day you're asking about, Steven." My attempt at being funny is met with resounding laughter. I'm mentally patting myself on the back for being quick on my feet. Truth is I don't care what time of day it is, each kiss is better than the last.

"Did you ever expect to be kissing Josh Wilson?"

"Oh gosh, not in a million years. We're kept pretty much in the dark, pun intended, until after the first kiss. I believe I passed out when I saw him."

"You did. We have the footage."

Lovely, just want I want to be reminded of. I turn and watch the clip and everyone sighs when Josh touches my cheek with his hand. As I watch his lips press against mine, my fingers graze my lips, yearning to feel the burn once again. Last week when I saw Josh, I should've jumped in his arms and kissed him one more time, just so I had a fresh memory of what it felt like to be kissed by him. As soon as I hit the floor, I can hear the laughter of a few people in the audience. Thankfully there are more ahhs being thrown my way.

"I guess he's just that smooth," I say, with a shrug.

Everyone erupts with laughter and cheers. Score one for Joey. I can't help but maintain my perma-grin. Any fear I had about being on this show has been quickly dissolved. Steven is fabulous.

"How in love are you and Josh?"

"Oh I don't know. I guess as in love as any couple that spent the past ninety days together."

"Hmm, I wonder if Josh feels the same way? Let's see what he had to say this morning."

No, let's not because he doesn't feel the same way, but I can't say that. The producers have asked that we keep up the pretenses of being married so that people will believe in the show's magic. This time I turn cautiously in my chair to watch the clip.

Josh's face lights up the screen, bringing tears to my eyes. I miss him already and it's only been a week. I don't know how it's going to be when I'm not seeing him ever again. This heartache is going to be a hard one to get over. Not because he's my celebrity crush, but because I truly fell for the man he is. I love who he is on the inside and had hoped we'd have some type of future together.

He's surrounded by four women I love watching. I even tried getting tickets once, when Josh had a new movie coming out, but to no avail.

"I fell in love," he says before adding, "You guys are going to love Joey. She's very excited to meet you all."

He's in love?

I'm excited to meet everyone?

Wait ... he's in love?

I wipe away tears that have fallen before turning to face Steven and the crowd again. I refuse to believe the words coming out of his mouth. He's an actor. It's part of his job to pretend to be someone he's not, and I wouldn't put it past the producers to have put him up to this. They allowed a video message from Jules to air during our time in the house. Surely, they'd ask him to do this.

"Well there you have it folks, Joshua Wilson says he's in love with Joey."

Everyone claps, but I can't help feeling that they're being forced to do it. As soon as we move into a break, Lou is by my side. She's excited about Josh's proclamation of love. I don't have the heart to tell her that it's fake, that he's being forced to say that. Our love for each other is completely one-sided.

My make-up is fixed and one of the production assistants shows me where to stand for the next segment. I picked two songs earlier, Lady Gaga's "Bad Romance" and Rick Springfield's "Jessie's Girl" for karaoke. I have no idea what Steven has chosen.

Steven joins me on stage, looking fresh and relaxed. I don't know how he does this multiple times a day because right now I'm not sure I can finish one show.

"All right, it's time for karaoke. I'll go first," he says as he takes the mic in his hand and starts moving to the music of "Footloose". He dances out the final scene of the movie, much to the audience's pleasure.

I step up and close my eyes, remembering my practice session in the green room earlier. Once the music starts, I mouth the words to my favorite Gaga song and get the crowd going. They're up on their feet, singing with me. When my song ends, I take a bow and hand the mic over to Steven.

"Wow! I don't know if I can top that, but here it goes."

"You Give Love a Bad Name" kicks off and Steven whips out his air guitar. Everyone starts laughing, even me. I begin playing the air drums, causing Steven to laugh. When he finishes, he gives me a high-five and tells me to knock them dead.

The beat to "Jessie's Girl" starts as I take the mic and dance around stage. The show's band is into it, all playing their own version of air instruments. When I've hit my last fake note, Steven is there clapping and telling everyone to have a safe night. We stand there and wave until the cameraman announces that he's done.

"Thanks for coming on," he says, as he gives me a hug before disappearing behind the curtain.

And just like that my media tour in New York City is over. In two days, I'll see Josh and my life will change forever.

CHAPTER
thirty-one

Joshua

This past week has been long, one of the longest of my life. I know that if I were able to talk to Joey, it would make things go faster, but each call went unanswered and each text unreturned. I'm going with the notion that she didn't bring her phone to New York instead of her ignoring me. I'm trying to think positively.

It's not working.

My wife thinks I want a divorce. When we first met, I did. The idea of marriage frightens me to no end. Joey deserves happiness. I want to be the one who provides it for her, but I have to learn *how*.

I stare out my apartment window. My view is nothing spectacular as my apartment is on the second floor and overlooks the community swimming pool. Palm trees offer shade and ambience, but it's a place I never visit. A few of the college co-eds that live in the building party there often and Rob joins them occasionally, saying they're fun to hang with. He likes the attention. I get enough of it when I'm on set, I don't want it when I come home. Right now the only attention I do want is from Joey, and she's not willing to give it. That means I need to fight for it.

"What time is the car picking you up?" Rob asks.

Glancing at my watch I sigh. "In about twenty minutes." Rob stands next to me, likely looking at the same scene I am: a mom with her two kids, splashing in the pool.

"Are you nervous?"

Putting my hands in my pockets and feeling the smooth edges of the velvet box I picked up yesterday, I shrug. "Not for the show, but I'm nervous about seeing Joey."

"What if she says no?"

Rob and I spent last night drinking and gossiping like two women. Words were slurred and truths told. It's easier to admit that I'm in love with Joey, or falling in love with her. She's easy to love with her quick wit, killer smile, and the way her body was made to fit mine. I've heard that before, the part about a body fitting yours, but didn't believe it until I held Joey in my arms. The beginning of my end was when I kissed her on stage. The way my body responded to her I knew I was a goner. I just refused to admit it.

"I'm scared of what could be. I drove the point home each time we got close in the house that this was over as soon as the show ended, but in the last month something changed. Every time I thought we were on the same page, another curve ball was thrown at us. First it was Jules and her bullshit video. Then Bronx moved in and if that's not enough, they freaking know each other. And then there's Jason. The worst part about Jason is that I had just told her I'd be right back. She won't return my calls or texts. I have no idea what I'm walking into today." I lean against the window, clearly feeling sorry for myself, and let out an exaggerated sigh. "I guess if she says no, I file the paperwork and dissolve the marriage."

The intercom by the door buzzes and Rob goes to answer it. It's my show-appointed PA telling me the car is here.

"Here goes nothing," I mutter, as I grab my sport coat, checking my pockets for everything and opening the door. "Wish me luck."

"You're Joshua Wilson, you don't need luck."

The one thing Rob doesn't know about is Joey is about her fangirl crush. I've kept that to myself for fear he'd say something to piss me off, embarrass Joey when they meet, or tell Jules. I think it's cute and makes for a fantastic story. I love the fact that I'm her number one because I have to admit that she's mine as well.

The drive to the studio lot where *Helen* is filmed is only a few miles from my apartment. The driver takes the side roads, which in LA can cut up to thirty minutes off your travel time. My heart starts racing as soon as we go through the gates. My eyes are searching everywhere for any sign of Joey. The moment the car stops, I'm out and crossing the lot to the nondescript door that is marked only by a stage number.

"Joey," I call out as soon as I step into the hallway. People turn and look at me, offering me strange looks. My PA is running behind me, her heels clicking on the concrete. She's on her phone rambling a mile a minute with her arms flaying about. If she's not careful, she's going to hit someone.

I turn into the greenroom, and it's like a weight has been lifted off me. There she is, in a royal blue dress with her hair in curls. Her back is facing me as she speaks to Millie. Cole comes up to me, standing in my line of sight and grabs my hand.

"It's good to see you."

Dude, I just saw you a few days ago, is what I want to say, but don't. "You too, man."

"I have some news that I need to tell someone before I explode," Cole says, looking a bit agitated.

"Yeah, what's up?"

He pulls me into the corner of the room, but my eyes

never leave Joey. I hate that she hasn't turned around to acknowledge me. I'm her husband; she should at least look at me or turn her head when people walk into the room.

"So what's up, Cole?" I'm not trying to rush him, but damn it if I don't need to go over and see Joey. I need to make sure she's real and not a figment of my imagination.

"My mom doesn't like Mille," he tells me in a hushed tone.

"Oh." I furrow my brows because I'm not sure how to answer him or what advice to offer. The fear is there that Joey's parents won't like me, but they already said in the video feed that they couldn't wait to meet me, so I'm banking on them loving me.

"Right, but the kicker is that she's pregnant."

"Wow, congratulations, man!"

He shakes his head. "What do I do?"

"Um…" I run my hand over my hair, knowing it'll be fixed before we're sent on stage. "Well you're already married, so I guess you decide who moves in with whom and raise your family."

Beads of sweat start to pebble on Cole's forehead and he pulls at his tie. He glances over his shoulder at Millie, who doesn't make eye contact with him.

"Cole, are you a mama's boy?" It's a harsh question and I probably could've phrased it better, but sometimes being blunt is the only way to go.

He looks at me sheepishly and gives me a grin turn grimace.

"Ah shit, man, you gotta cut the cord. You're married and about to have a baby!" I say as quietly as possible. It's times like this when I think my relationship with Joey is perfect. We don't have this drama, now that Jules has been set straight, thank God.

"How?"

"Move far away and start your life with Millie. She's a

fucking knock-out and you guys hit it off from day one. Don't throw that shit away."

I pat him on the shoulder and step away. When I reach Joey, I slide my hand into hers, smile at Millie, and lean down to whisper in Joey's ear, "Can we talk?" She doesn't go rigid like I expect, but doesn't necessarily hold my hand either.

When she turns to face me, I'm dumbstruck by how beautiful she is. Her hair is framing her face perfectly, and her subtle make-up is drawing attention to her light blue eyes. I could get lost there for hours if she didn't find staring creepy.

"You're so beautiful," I murmur as the back of my hand caresses her face. She leans in; the movement is slight, but I feel it. Her eyes close and I can tell she's fighting her heart and mind. I need her to listen to her heart.

"Josh and Cole, you're up." My hand drops the second my name is called. I stare at him with the 'are you fucking serious right now' look.

"I'll be right back," I tell Joey, kissing the tip of her nose before following the assistant to hair and make-up.

As soon as I sit down, my leg starts bouncing. I'm on edge. I'm pissed. I miss Joey. I only need five minutes to pour my heart out before we go out on stage. Why can't someone throw me a damn bone? I'm sick of being in the doghouse.

"Stop moving," the make-up artist says and from experience I need to listen or I may end up looking like a cast member from *The Rocky Horror Picture Show.* I've seen it happen to Rob, it's not pretty.

"Three minutes," the same assistant walks by, yelling into the room.

"You've got to be kidding me," I mumble, earning a dirty look from the make-up artist. "Sorry," I tell her, not wanting to piss her off.

"You're a pro," she says. "Your hair and make-up doesn't take us long."

She's right because with one minute to spare, my flaws are hidden and my hair is looking like I just woke up—pretty much like the hair I came in with.

Cole and I are ushered out; he's still sweating and the make-up artist assigned to him is doing everything she can to keep his face painted. She calls for an ice pack and slips it down his jacket, much to his chagrin. I stifle a laugh and want to pat him on the back, wishing him luck, but feel it's unnecessary.

We're seated in order: Cole and Mille, followed by Joey and myself. At least I can press my leg against Joey's to feel close to her. I change the way I'm sitting so I can put my arm around her and hold her hand with my free one. She doesn't relax into me, but that doesn't stop me from kissing her shoulder.

"Joining us today are the winners and runner-ups from season three of *Married Blind.*" The audience is cued to cheer. I wave and smile, inciting more cheering.

"Welcome," Helen says. We all greet her in return.

"Wow, I've never seen three, even four, such diverse couples on the show before. How was it living in the house with everyone?"

"The guys were horrible at house cleaning," Millie says. "Joey and I were always picking up after them."

"So it was close to real-life?" Helen laughs and the girls nod. "The comps got a little crazy, which one was your favorite?"

"Oh boy," I say, thinking back to the honey and flour comp. It was so messy and hard to move, but Sumo was my favorite. "Definitely Sumo wrestling," I say, with Cole agreeing. "We were able to get a lot of aggressions out without hurting anyone."

"Cole and Millie, you guys seemed to hit it off right away. Did that surprise you?" Millie looks at Cole and smiles. Sadly, he doesn't return the gesture and that's not lost on Millie. I feel bad for the both of them right now. "Cole is great. I knew early on that he was someone special for me."

"And what about you and Josh?" The question is directed at Joey, but I don't give her time to answer.

"I fell in love. Joey is the most beautiful, smart, funny, and down to earth woman I've ever met. She gets me and doesn't let my profession define us. I love her." I take my hand away and place my fingers under her chin to turn her face toward me. "I love you, Joey."

The crowd erupts in a boisterous cheer. Once they've calmed down, I drop down to my knee and pull out the black velvet box that has been sitting in my pocket since last night. I open the lid, earning gasps from the three women closest to me.

"Joey, I know we're already married, but I would really like to do things right. Will you marry me in front of our family and friends? Will you be my partner in all things and marry me … again?"

I gaze into her eyes as her hand covers her mouth. She glances from me to the crowd who are yelling for her to say yes, and some even saying that they'll marry me. I try not to laugh, but I can't help it.

It seems like minutes until words are spoken.

"We'll be back after the commercial break to see what Joey has to say."

CHAPTER
thirty-two

Backstage at the *Helen* show, the producers of *Married Blind* stand there, shocked. They were already dealing with the fallout from Amanda and Gary's relationship and Amanda's lawsuit that had been filed earlier this morning citing fraud; and were preparing a press release for after today's broadcast in light of the Joshua and Joey Wilson fallout that was soon to happen once their divorce hit the newswire.

None of them expected to watch Josh get down on bended knee and propose.

"Can you zoom in on the ring?" Barry asks the cameraman who does as he's asked.

"At least five carats," Barry's assistant says.

"Run a quick promo," Barry barks.

"Sir?"

Barry rolls his eyes at the incompetence. "Clearly we have another show."

"Right, of course, what would you like to call it?"

"Married Blind: Reality," Barry says as if his assistant should've read his mind.

During the commercial break, while the audience waits for Joey to answer, the promo ad runs announcing a fall airing of *Married Blind: Reality*, leaving the viewers at home wondering what on earth it can be about.

Once the assistant has run off, Barry dials his boss and waits patiently for the call to connect. Once it does, he spills on his idea, confident that his boss will say yes. Joshua and Joey Wilson were fan favorites … there was a reason why they didn't win.

acknowledgements

To my crew, as always, thank you for everything that you do to help bring each idea to life. Yvette, Traci, Georgette, Tammy – you guys put up with a lot of harebrained ideas and I appreciate it. Amy, Audrey, Kelli, Tammy and Veronica – you guys work so hard to make sure everyone knows about my stories, thank you. Christine – thank you for pushing me to make the right decision!

The design team: Sarah, as always, you blow me away with each cover you give me. Emily, your crew is amazing and works tirelessly to bring our books some flavor.

To my family – as always I appreciate everything you do.

Love's Second Chance
By LP Dover

Prologue

Korinne

What do you do when you have nothing else to live for? When the world closes in on you and rips your soul apart, leaving you dying and aching on the inside. How does one regain the pieces that have been scattered to the wind?

On the day I lost Carson, my world went gray and dark. The light inside me died when he was taken from me. I remember wiping the tears angrily away from my eyes as I sat there beside him. I wanted to see him clearly, to remember everything about my final moments with the man I had loved, cherished, and called my husband for the past two years. We were building a life together, and now it was going to be lost.

Holding his hand while he lay broken and battered in the hospital bed, I couldn't begin to fathom what my life was going to be like without him. As strong as Carson was, I knew it took all of his strength to even try to hold on. I wanted to take that pain away and keep it as my own. No one should ever have to see the person they love die in front of their eyes. I knew I would never forget the love and adoration in his gaze when he spoke those final words on his last dying breath.

"I love you, Kori," Carson says to me, his breathing raspy and forced, and I know it's agony for him to breathe because of the broken ribs. His face is almost unrecognizable from the damage of the crash, but no matter what, I'll always see the angelic face of my husband in my mind. My heart has broken into a million pieces just looking at him so helpless and visibly in pain. If I could trade places with him to spare him the anguish I would. A million times over I would.

"I love you so much, Carson. You can't leave me, please don't leave me." I choke as a sob escapes my lips. I have to remain strong for him, but how can I when he's facing death and I'm about to lose him. A tear escapes from the corner of his eye, and before I can speak again he grips my hand tightly.

"Shh, don't cry. I need you to promise me …"

I lean over him, desperate to hear what he wants me to promise him. I'll promise him anything if it will keep him here longer. "Promise you what, Carson?" I say quickly, knowing time is running out. The beeping of the machines begins to slow down … slower and slower. Breaking down into tears, I desperately try to cling onto him, to feel the life inside of him before it dies away. How can his time be up when he has so much to live for?

With quivering lips, I kiss him gently, branding the feel of him in my mind so I will always remember. Our final kiss, the last one we will share forever. His eyes flutter open one last time and on his last breath he cries, "Promise me you'll …" But that's as far as he gets. I sit there frozen, stunned into silence, when I see that he's breathing no more.

"Promise you what, Carson?" I scream desperately. I need to know what he was going to say. I take his face in my hands, willing the life back into his body, but his eyes stay locked onto mine as his soul is set free. The machines begin their long and drawn out beeping, signaling the passing of my beloved *husband. I am frozen in place, numb on the outside but in despair on the inside as I stare at the lifeless form of the man I have grown to love and cherish. His body is still, so very still. My tears flow like hot rivers down my cheeks, landing on his bruised face. "I love you. I will always love you," I cry. My lungs feel constricted and the world seems to be closing in around me. I can't breathe, I can't think, and I sure as hell can't believe that my husband is now gone ... forever. How am I going to face the future without him? He's gone ... and from this moment on, so is my heart.*

Just when I thought moving on was possible, that day and the way it felt would come stumbling back in like a plague, consuming me with its pain. Sometimes I wanted to imagine it was all just a bad dream, but then reality would strike and the memories came flooding back of the day Carson died, and of the fear that if I ever decided to love again I'd be doomed to face the same torment. Bearing that kind of pain again was not something I wanted to endure.

Chapter One

Korinne - The Move Back

"Are you sure you want to move back? You know, you can stay here as long as you like." My mother's warm face showed her concern, and if she had her way she would have made me live with her and my father forever. As much as I loved my parents, we all knew that I'd be miserable if I stayed there.

When Carson died, I decided to live with my parents for a while. I needed to get away to try to deal with my grief, but mostly I didn't want to be alone. I had no siblings or close family in Charlotte so I had no other choice except to stay with my parents. For six months I had lived with them at their beautiful home in the historical district of Charleston, SC. I loved it there, but it was time for me to go. After loading the last of my belongings into the trunk of my car, I turned around to face my mother. I had been told I looked just like her, except for the hair color. Mine had always been a golden-blonde, whereas hers has always been a deep, chestnut brown. Also, we both happen to be as stubborn as mules, but my mother never owned up to it.

"I know I don't have to leave, Mom, but I can't stay here anymore. I appreciate everything you and Dad have done for me, but I have to live my life the way I want to live it," I said boldly.

She shook her head in disbelief. "But that's just it, Kori. You're not living it! You're twenty-eight years old and have so much to live for. It's been six months since Carson died." At the mention of Carson, I knew my mother could see the hurt that passed over my face. Her voice turned soft and concerned. "You need to move on and get your life back on track."

I had heard those words from her over and over, and every time it took more and more control to keep my calm. I didn't think she would have said that to me if she knew what it felt like to lose the man you loved. I gritted my teeth and put on a fake smile like I always did in this situation. My mother knew it was forced, but she went along with it anyway.

"I'm trying, Mom. That's why I'm moving back to Charlotte, so I can start over. I'm going to start working again and go from there," I informed her, anything to appease her so I could leave. What I hadn't told her was that I was moving back, but I wasn't going back to mine and Carson's home. I rented a condo and planned to stay there until I got the strength to go back home. I knew my parents would find out eventually, but for now I didn't plan on telling them. My mother sighed and pulled me in for a tight embrace. Hugging her with all I had, I breathed in her motherly scent, the aroma that had been my comfort growing up. Other than my grandmother, my mother had always been my biggest supporter.

"That sounds great, sweetheart. You're always welcome to come back any time you want." Releasing her hold, she looked me in the eyes. "I love you, care bear. You *will* get through this. You're strong and I have complete and utter faith in you."

I nodded, quickly averting my eyes so she couldn't see the tears building up, about to fall. "I love you, Mom," I said as I opened the car door. "I'll call Dad when I get on the road to tell him good-bye."

"He'd appreciate that," she agreed.

I hated that I'd missed him, but his job had called him away on business. He spent most of my childhood years on the road, so I figured that's why my mom and I were really close. She was all I had growing up. My father was a hard man to get along with, always so stern and overprotective. However, after being here and spending time with him, it made me realize that all he ever wanted in life was to make me happy and to make sure my mother and I had everything we needed. My mother began waving at me before I started to back out of the driveway. When I sidled down the road, I took one last look in the rearview mirror. She was still waving, and as she slowly disappeared out of view, that's when the tears began to fall.